WHITE PEOPLE ON VACATION joins binge drinking and anti-capitalism, sex and environmental wreckage, coming of age and apocalyptic doom. It's a hilarious novel about despair, a satire of American ugliness that achieves moments of great beauty. Most of all, it's a hell of a book.

— JENNIFER WORTMAN,
author of *This. This. This. Is. Love. Love. Love.*

WHITE PEOPLE ON VACATION

WHITE
Alex Miller

PEOPLE

ON VACATION

MALARKEY  BOOKS

Published by Malarkey Books.

Cover & book design by Alex Miller
Typeset in Freight, a very cool typeface.

Cover photograph by Angelo Pantazis via Unsplash.
Author photograph by Shelly Bradbury.

Interior photos by //Roman (title page), Kvnga (pages 2-3), Rhiannon Elliott (pages 76-77), Samantha Sophia (pages 114-115), Benjamin Sow (pages 230-231), and Stephen Leonardi (pages 296-297), via Unsplash. All of these photographers are phenomenal and you should love them.

All power to the people. A better world is possible.

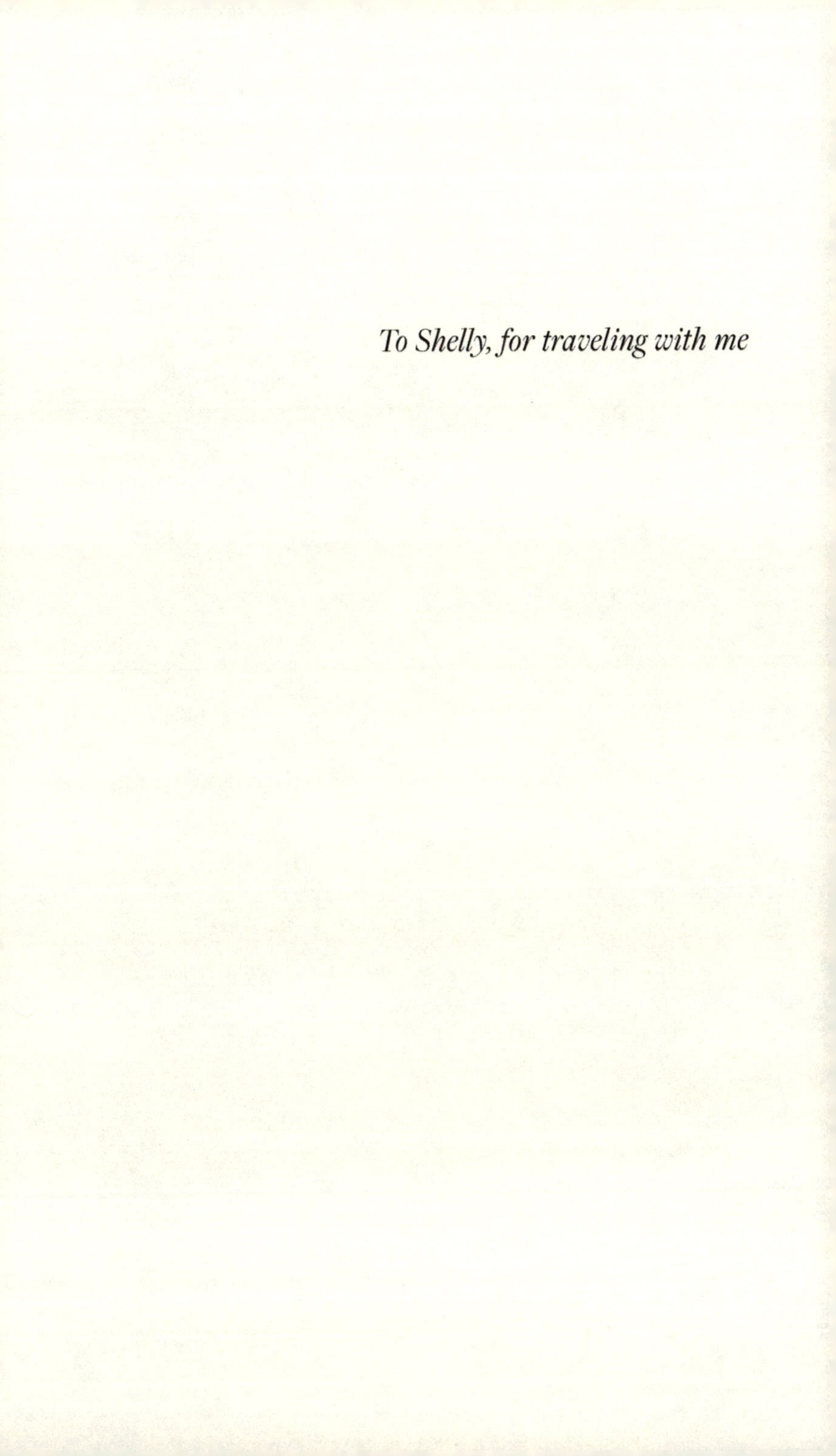

To Shelly, for traveling with me

PART
ONE

MY LIFE TO LIVE

ONE

I USED TO SPEND A LOT OF TIME thinking about the end of the world. Not the rapture or any of that *Left Behind* conspiracy theory stuff that gets evangelicals so horny, but all the ordinary things you see every day in the news— global warming, planet-killing asteroids, strategic nuclear weapons. I enjoy reading the news, but it can be depressing. After a while, all the garbage piles up in your head. It's important to take your mind off it. You can't spend your life dwelling on all the world's tragedies and injustices. Think about something else. Something happy.

My apocalypse fantasies peaked when I was a senior in college. I remember one afternoon at the end of fall semester, when I looked outside the window of my dorm room and imagined a ten-kiloton warhead detonating above the center of campus. An intense flash of light—silent and blinding. Followed roughly a millisecond later by the noise of the shock wave, a roar like thunder from the heart of a storm.

"You left out a comma," Natalie said. She pointed to a line I'd typed on my laptop screen, which cast a pale glow across my dorm room. I'd been filling out an application for a summer internship at the Internal Revenue Service. I'd typed a paragraph in a field labeled, *Why do you want to work for the IRS?*

"That's an Oxford comma," I said. "I don't use those."

"The IRS loves the Oxford comma." Natalie had a talent for sounding incredibly authoritative even when she had no idea what she was talking about. She'd been my girlfriend for a long time. We started dating in the eighth grade and somehow never stopped. You spend that many years with someone, you get to know them. Something else I knew about Natalie was not to trust her judgment on comma placement. Regardless, I added the comma. You spend that many years with someone, you learn to compromise.

"Why *do* you want to work for the IRS?" Natalie was blond and pretty. Too pretty to date an IRS intern.

"To steal my supervisor's password and leak Donald Trump's tax returns to *The Washington Post*."

"That's not funny," she said, squinting at me the way she would when I wasn't funny.

"I'm joking."

"The IRS hates jokes."

I looked out the window again, imagined the shock wave moving toward me in slow motion, shattering the windows of the student center, reducing the science building to dust and ash. Then it was on me, pounding like a sledgehammer against my chest. And then I had no chest. I was nothing. Gone in an instant.

"Focus," she said. "Don't fuck this up."

What can I say about Natalie? She was a good student. A good daughter, too. Her parents loved her. Everybody loved her. She would make a fine intern at the IRS. Maybe the greatest intern in the history of the agency. Natalie was the kind of person who never thought about the end of the world.

TWO

Natalie took me out to lunch at O'Charley's.

Sometimes in life, you find yourself somewhere amazing. Maybe you're hiking in the deep woods and suddenly face to face with a waterfall sparkling silver in the morning light. Or you're driving on a highway in the mountains, and you round a curve to see a gorgeous valley open up below you, with sunbeams gently brushing the treetops like fingertips of the hand of God. Life occasionally presents us with moments like these. Moments of transcendence. Most of the time, however, life is boring. Sometimes you find yourself eating lunch at O'Charley's.

Natalie and I shared a table and ordered hamburgers. Chain restaurants like O'Charley's don't hire the best cooks, so it's important to keep your order simple. Avoid shellfish. Don't order anything that claims to contain chorizo.

I listened to Natalie chew a big mouthful of meat, and I thought about the end of the world. I kept it to myself. When you've been dating for so many years, you learn to carve out your own private space. You keep secrets. Anyway I knew Natalie didn't want to hear about nuclear winter or killer viruses. She had very little tolerance for weird behavior. It's a miracle we stayed together for as long as we did. Back then, weird behaviors were all I had going for me.

"The IRS is a good fit for us," Natalie said after swallowing. "We'll be in Washington. Center of the universe."

Natalie had a dream, and the dream began with both of us landing internships at the IRS. Once we were in D.C., we'd look for better jobs. D.C. has lots of jobs. Government jobs. Contractors. Think tanks. Media. Natalie liked to say D.C. was our chance to have a real life. That's what she wanted. A real life.

"Have you even been to D.C.?" I asked. "Have you seen the traffic? If I had to commute to work on I-95 every day, I'd kill myself. I don't understand how everyone in D.C. hasn't killed themselves already."

"Nobody is forcing you to go," Natalie said. She ripped off the end of a buttered roll and stuffed it in her mouth. At O'Charley's, bread is complimentary.

"Listen, I really do want to work at the IRS," I said, even though I did not, in fact, want to work at the IRS. The truth is, I didn't want to do anything. I'd spent nearly four years in college and still didn't know what to do with my life. This was a problem. I would graduate in just a few months. Graduation cast a cold shadow over my every waking hour. The idea about college is you prepare to do some job for the rest of your life. I majored in English with a minor in art. All I'd prepared for was to become the most useless person of all time.

"I'm tired of talking about the IRS," she said.

"So am I."

I reached across the table and took the last roll from the basket before Natalie could eat it. Natalie possessed a very fast metabolism. She could eat anything and not gain weight. This was useful for her but dangerous for me. Sometimes she hogged all the bread.

"Let's talk about Hawaii," she said.

THREE

Aside from the IRS, the most important thing in our lives was Hawaii.

Natalie had talked her parents into paying for the two of us to take an expensive vacation over Christmas break, sort of an early graduation present. They'd agreed to pay my way because my parents were broke. My parents didn't even have money to send me to college. I'd paid for the whole shebang with student loans. Some of the loans were good ones subsidized by the federal government, but others were from loan-shark banks that charged usurious interest. I only had a few months before I had to start repaying the loans. I didn't want to think about it. Easier by far to think about Hawaii. Avril and Roger were going with us. Avril and Roger also had rich parents.

Natalie finished her hamburger and told me all about Hawaii. Her rich parents had taken her there on vacation when she was a kid.

"You haven't *lived* until you've seen Kealakekua Bay," she said. "Nate, you haven't *lived*."

I guess it's hard not to brag about your vacation to some tropical wonderland, especially while describing it to some poor loser who's never been west of the Mississippi River. Anyway it annoyed me.

"Sounds great," I said, reaching across the table to hold her hand. She pulled away, dropping her palms into her lap under the table. She went on talking and smiling like nothing happened. She told some story about her family's vacation to Hawaii. This happened before her parents split up. Natalie's story wasn't terribly interesting—something about a Filipino selling coconuts at the mall—but I nodded along and pretended to care, like always.

She kept talking and talking. She told me Hawaii was just what I needed to get over my depression. She told me some random facts she'd memorized. Did you know Hawaii has its own time zone? Or that there are only twelve letters in the Hawaiian alphabet? Natalie knew a lot about Hawaii. She knew Kilauea was the world's most active volcano and Mauna Kea was the tallest mountain in the Pacific. She said some other things, but I stopped listening. I thought about the end of the world. I looked at Natalie's blue eyes and blond hair, her face eerily devoid of blemishes. She said *surfboard*. She said *pineapple*. I imagined a great volcano erupting from the ground between us. Diners fled the restaurant or hid, terrified, beneath tables. The ground shook, the roof and walls of O'Charley's crumbled and collapsed. I alone stood amid the wreckage and debris, marveling at the swift totality of destruction. The volcano roared beneath a sky lit red by the fires raining down upon the doomed people of Earth. I considered trying to hold Natalie's hand again but didn't.

FOUR

The waiter brought the check. After putting it on the table, he broke waiter protocol by speaking to Natalie instead of me. He smiled his seductive waiter smile and thanked her for dining at O'Charley's. He looked deep into her eyes. He introduced himself as Andy and said he hoped she'd enjoyed her meal. He told her to ask for him by name the next time she dined at O'Charley's.

Guys acted like that around Natalie all the time. Something about her made every guy act like a creep. Something made every guy think he was Bradley Cooper. The waiter, really, was very average. Only about as good-looking as me, which is to say *extremely* average. He was just some white guy. Murfreesboro was full of identical white guys. I felt bad for him because he wasn't lucky enough to go to Hawaii. There in the restaurant, I put a curse on the waiter: *may you live your entire life among white people and never see any adventure or excitement.* It was a good curse. The curse of white people.

These encounters with random horny guys were just one of the drawbacks of being Natalie's boyfriend. To tell you the truth, dating her could be a real drag. All our friends acted like we were the perfect couple. Nate and Natalie. Natalie and Nate. People treated our relationship like a universal constant, as if we were destined to be together for eternity. And sometimes I felt the same way. Like there was no way out.

Once the waiter left, Natalie asked if I would pick up the check. She asked in a very annoying way, more like a suggestion. I basically had zero money in my bank account. Natalie, on the other hand, was flush with cash. She didn't have a job and didn't need one. She had a rich father. He let her charge as much as she wanted on a credit card, and at the end of the month he paid it off.

I stared at the check.

I thought about the volcano.

FIVE

After lunch I drove Natalie back to the campus of Middle Tennessee State University. I don't know who named the college, but I assume they were trying to make it sound like the most boring place in the world. MTSU was situated in the town of Murfreesboro—also boring. How boring? In a town like Murfreesboro, going out to eat at O'Charley's is a big deal.

I drove Natalie's car. I didn't have a car of my own or even a job to pay for one. Natalie didn't work either, but her parents gave her a car for her sixteenth birthday. This was the difference between me and Natalie. Her parents were rich and gave her stuff. My parents were not, and did not. And I didn't blame them or hate them for it. It's not like they set out to deprive me. They just didn't have any money. If you don't have money, you can't give stuff to your kids. That's everything I know about economics.

I turned the heater on full blast. Cold air blew out of the vents. Natalie squirmed and took her iPhone out of her blue jeans. She pressed a button to make the screen light up. She tapped the screen a few times. She made a move in *Words with Friends*.

"Who are you playing?" I asked.

"Roger."

In the dimness of the December afternoon, the screen cast a pale light on her face. She looked like a zombie from a horror movie.

"Since when does Roger play word games? I thought you played with Avril."

"Avril's smart," she said. "I always beat Roger."

Whenever anyone asked me how I felt about Natalie, I always gave the same canned response—*she's amazing*. That's a good and correct thing for a boyfriend to say, but if I'd ever bothered to answer the question honestly—and I never did—I'd have said Natalie was completely ordinary. The most normal human I'd ever met. Natalie was the type of person who just lives a life and doesn't give a fuck about too much else. The type who buys iPhones and hundred-dollar jeans, who is going to grow up and make lease payments on a brand new SUV, who buys a big house in a nice neighborhood before popping out a few kids. The kind who is sad, sometimes, when she stands in her closet among the things she owns, because she knows that although she can, on occasion, drop a thousand dollars on a handbag, she will never be able, like Oprah, to drop thirty-eight thousand on a handbag. That's Natalie. She was like exactly everybody else.

I turned onto the highway and took it through town. Traffic moved slowly. I sat up in my seat to see if there had been a wreck up ahead. I didn't see a wreck, just more traffic. I worried that I'd be late for class. Above all the traffic, the sky looked heavy with gray clouds. They seemed like the kind of clouds that could make snow, but there would be no snow. It gets cold in Murfreesboro but hardly ever snows.

"Tomorrow we go to Hawaii," I said.

Natalie ignored me, which was just as well.

The idea of Hawaii made me feel a certain way. I liked to believe there were still good places in the world where people were basically happy. All around me on the highway, drivers cursed under their breath and honked horns. Clouds of exhaust spewed

from tailpipes. I imagined that instead of bumper-to-bumper au-
tomobiles, I gazed at a long line of swaying palm trees.

The setting sun cast its golden beams over the Pacific Ocean.

A salt breeze blew in from the water.

Maybe in a place like that, I could be happy.

Maybe I'd love Hawaii and never come home or be miserable
ever again.

SIX

I dropped off Natalie at her dorm so she could pack for Hawaii. Then I grabbed my bookbag out of the back seat and walked to Peck Hall. I had to turn in an essay that would serve as the final exam for a film studies class. The essay was no big deal, just the usual stuff about how Godard was a communist.

Back at the beginning of the semester, Roger gave me a hard time when I told him I'd enrolled in Ms. Hill's film class. He told me she'd make us watch *Roots* and *Malcom X* and *The Color Purple*. He told me I was fucked. He told me I should drop the class, because she only gave A's to Black people. Well, her class that semester was on the French New Wave, and I was her best student, so that should tell you everything you need to know about Roger. The class watched *Jules and Jim* and *Breathless*. We watched Truffaut's films about Antoine Doinel. We watched *Claire's Knee* by Rohmer and *Happiness* by Agnès Varda. As the final approached, we went hard on Godard: *A Woman is a Woman*, *Tout Va Bien*, and *Week End*.

I took a seat next to my friend Damon. I met him sophomore year. He was an English major, like me, and we lived in the same dorm. Unlike the rest of my friends, he knew a lot about the French New Wave.

After everyone in class turned in their papers, Ms. Hill told us we were free to go—but if we wanted, we could stick around and watch one more movie, just for fun. Another Godard film, *La Chinoise*. Half the students immediately left the classroom.

Ms. Hill explained that the movie was released in 1967, the year before student protests sparked uprisings all over France. She turned off the lights and played the movie. A group of French university students lived together and plotted a violent communist revolution. Jean-Pierre Léaud played one of the students. You can't get any more French New Wave than that. Jean-Pierre Léaud had become my personal hero. In his movies, he spoke passionately about radical politics, and all the French girls loved him. I wanted to speak passionately about radical politics. I wanted French girls to love me.

Much of the movie came in the form of long monologues by the students, in which they explain the particularities of their radical beliefs. Jean-Pierre Léaud stood at a blackboard covered with the names of history's greatest writers—Sartre, Goethe, Sophocles, Chekhov, Shakespeare. He erased the names until only one remained. Brecht. I had no idea who Brecht was. I wasn't actually intelligent enough for French movies. But watching them did make me feel smart and cultured, in a snobby way, and maybe that was the point.

"I can't take this shit," whispered the girl beside me. I didn't know her name. We'd been in class together for months, but I never learned it. I only knew her as *the hot girl in film class*. She always wore a nice Burberry jacket.

The hot girl in film class stood up, slung her backpack over her shoulder, and left the room. She reminded me of Natalie. There's no way Natalie would sit through a Godard movie. And she would have loved that Burberry jacket.

Toward the end of the film, the character Veronique makes up her mind to commit a violent act in the name of revolution. She takes a train to Paris, intent on murdering the visiting minister of culture of the Soviet Union. The scene on the train is amazing. By chance, Veronique meets Francis Jeanson, a real-life political philosopher who played himself in the film. Jeanson was tried in absentia for treason against France for creating a network to funnel money to the National Liberation Front of Algeria, which was fighting a war for independence in the French colony. Jeanson talks to Veronique and senses she is planning revolutionary violence. He tries to dissuade her, but she is resolute. She departs the train and enters the hotel where the Soviet culture minister is staying. Then she fucks everything up. She goes to the wrong room, kills the wrong guy.

Ms. Hill led a discussion with the few of us who had stayed to finish the film. I did my best not to participate. I never spoke in class. Some students are really good at speaking out and answering questions. Not me. I was good at shutting the hell up.

Ms. Hill asked us about the ending. Damon raised his hand and said something intelligent about the rationales for political violence. I tuned out the classroom discussion and thought about *La Chinoise*. If I had directed the film, I would have ended it differently. My ending is not original: I stole it from *The 400 Blows* and *Week End*.

In my ending, Veronique successfully assassinates the Soviet culture minister. Then, as police descend on the hotel with blaring sirens, she steals a car and drives south on the highway, drives until she runs out of road. She gets out of the car and runs toward the ocean. A series of long shots capture Veronique running across the sand toward the sea. She stands in the water, with waves crashing against her legs and skirt. She holds a fist high and triumphant. "Hail, ancient ocean," she says, the camera zooming tight on her face. "Hail, ancient ocean."

SEVEN

Me and Damon walked out of the classroom and through the building's long yellow hallways. By now, finals had wrapped up for most classes, and the buildings were deserted. Our footsteps resounded sharply in the wide concrete passageway.

"I'm gonna marry Ms. Hill," Damon said.

"That's weird," I said. "She'd make a weird wife."

"She'd be great," Damon said as we walked. "I'd come home to our apartment in the city, and she'd be there listening to music—Thelonious Monk or Billie Holiday. And not on Spotify or Amazon. Ms. Hill is all about that vinyl. She'd hand me a glass of wine, and we'd sit by the window and look over the city at sunset and talk about French films and socialism."

We turned at a stairway and started down the steps.

"Well, now I want to marry Ms. Hill too," I said.

Damon asked if I was going home to Nashville for Christmas break. I cringed. I didn't want to tell him about Hawaii. Didn't want to tell him he wasn't invited. I'm not sure why we didn't invite him. Everybody liked Damon. Still, this wasn't the first time me and my friends had forgotten to invite him to something. Somehow we always forgot to invite Damon.

"Yep," I said, my pulse suddenly racing. "Just going up to Nashville."

We approached a pair of heavy metal doors that would take us out of the building. On the wall beside them hung a plastic sign that informed us—in bold red letters—that in the event of a nuclear strike the building would serve as a bomb shelter. The sign made me think about the end of the world, warheads detonating and leveling all of campus and the city, a bright-hot light enveloping me, heat boiling the skin off my bones, my skeleton burning black, crumbling to dust, scattering on atomic winds.

I pointed to the sign.

"Do you ever worry about that stuff?"

Damon shrugged.

"Once the nukes start dropping, nothing left to worry about."

EIGHT

Outside, Damon told me to have fun over the break and wished me a Merry Christmas. Then he left to get dinner at the cafeteria in the James Union Building. I considered going back to my dorm, but I knew Natalie would be there. We each had our own dorm rooms but practically lived together in mine. I sat on a bench outside Peck Hall. Pulled out my phone. Checked messages. Turns out, I didn't have any messages. I looked around at the campus and all the students. I kept my phone out so I'd look like a busy person preoccupied by his active social life. The mid-December weather felt depressingly bleak. The limbs of bare trees scratched like bony hands against gray clouds. Winter had barely begun, and already I couldn't take it. Hawaii would be better. Warm and sunny. Hawaii would be a verdant paradise, and I'd be happy there and find peace.

A lot of students hung out on the quad. They all looked alike. Slightly different versions of the same person. All the guys that semester had been growing beards. Everybody wore North Face or Marmot jackets over flannel shirts, and the girls wore cute scarves and leggings and boots. It was like the student body had agreed to abide by a dress code, only it was some secret nobody ever talked about, something hashed out on an underground Reddit forum.

Everybody looked so nice.

I hated to think of graduating and leaving all those nice people behind.

Hated to think of their nice bodies burning in the nuclear fires.

NINE

I opened Twitter on my phone. I read a tweet from the president.

Despite a persistent and vile bias from the dishonest mainstream media, the Trump Administration has risen to greater heights than any other Administration.

Donald Trump was the dumbest president in the history of the United States of America. I looked around again at all the well-dressed students. I wondered how many voted for Trump. I wondered why so many people had believed that a skeezy New York real estate con man would restore America's greatness. The only rational explanation I could think of was that a lot of Americans were really stupid. Of course, I knew plenty of students who hated Trump. They gave me hope. But they could be ridiculous, too. They would moan and complain about living in the worst period in American history. Except it wasn't the worst. Bad but not worst. The Civil War was worse. So was World War II. Trump's presidency wasn't the worst time in the nation's history—it was the dumbest.

Twitter began to irritate me, so I opened Facebook. Facebook was terrible. It hoovered up everybody's private information and vacation photos with their grandparents in Orlando and sold it all to hackers in Vladivostok and Azerbaijan. Everybody knew it. Everybody knew Facebook was terrible. Still, I kept using Facebook. Most people kept using Facebook.

I scrolled past news articles and some angry political posts from people I'd known in high school but never really talked to anymore. I had a plan to deal with those jerks—lay low for a few years until they forgot about me, then quietly unfriend them. I read posts by some guys a few years older than me. Judging by their Facebook activity, they all lived some version of the same life. They worked entry-level jobs at insurance and health care companies. They'd gotten married and taken out mortgages on houses, and now their wives were pregnant. My feed had been hijacked by posts about weddings and babies and pets. I wished I had cooler friends who did interesting things with their lives. I wanted a friend list full of poets and travelers. Instead all I ever saw were photos of little baby Piper in her zebra onesie.

Sitting there on campus in the cold, it was easy to imagine the entire arc of my life. I'd graduate from college in the spring, and from there the dominoes would keep falling. I'd intern with the IRS before finding a real job—probably at the IRS. Marry Natalie. Purchase a house in the D.C. suburbs. Produce a few kids. Commute to work. Come home and watch TV. Sit on the couch. Get fat. Look out the window sometimes and wonder if there's more to life, wonder where my youth went, why nothing brings me joy anymore. Wonder when me and Natalie stopped loving each other or if we'd ever been in love. Wondering why there's so much to wonder about, so many questions left unanswered. Wondering, in my final hours, what even was the point?

TEN

Later I went to the coffee shop at the university center. I stood in a long line. A douchebag at the front ordered something ridiculous. The douchebag said *almond milk*. He said *Chemex*. Part of me felt relieved the douchebag took so long to order, because it gave me time to figure out what I wanted. I had some anxiety. Ordering at coffee shops can be stressful. Everybody else knew exactly what they wanted. What if I ordered something stupid? That would be terrible, all the snobs in line snickering behind my back. When the time came, I asked for a regular cappuccino. A safe order. No shame in a cappuccino.

I sat at a table with my drink. I stirred the top layer of milk broth into the rest of the coffee. I took a sip and immediately regretted ordering a cappuccino. Whenever I ordered a drink at Starbucks, it would taste like something wonderful—caramel or chocolate or the cinnamon-laced soul of a pumpkin—but the cappuccino from the fancy coffee shop on campus tasted like plain coffee and milk. I sipped it with a straight face, so everybody would think I'd ordered it on purpose.

Avril stood at the counter, paying for her coffee with cash. The student cashier stared at the bills, dumbfounded, as if he'd never seen dollar bills before. He slowly rang up her order and made change. When Avril left the counter, I waved her over to my table. I asked her if she'd finished her exams.

"Just now," she said. She sipped a plain black coffee.

"Think you passed?"

"I always make A's," she said, as if it were the most obvious fact in the world.

"I wish I could stay in college forever," I said. I told her about me and Natalie applying for internships at the IRS, and how I didn't want to do it, didn't want anything. I had no dreams or aspirations.

"If all I had to look forward to after graduation was an internship at the IRS," Avril said, "I would probably kill myself."

I asked about her plans. She smiled. Sipped her coffee.

"Go to the mountains and make class war," she said.

Predictable. Avril always said stuff like that. *Class war* and *bourgeoisie* and *proletariat*. More than anyone else in my life, she resembled a character from a Godard movie. Nobody took her seriously, though. She wasn't a communist. She just liked how it felt to pretend.

"But really," I said. "Do you have a job lined up? An internship?"

She took a long sip.

"Mountains," she said. "Class war."

I changed the subject. I asked if she was excited about Hawaii. The question seemed to bore her. She told me she expected it to be fine. Except for Roger. She said we never should have invited Roger.

"Roger's okay," I said.

"The thing I'm looking forward to most about graduating is never seeing Roger again."

I didn't ask her to elaborate. No need. I knew all about Avril and Roger.

Avril ran a hand through her hair—fake red like a cherry Blow Pop. She smoothed a few strands out of her face. She looked at me like a visitor at the MoMA trying to make sense of a Jackson Pollock.

"If you change your mind about the IRS, you can always come to the mountains with me and make class war."

I laughed nervously, told her I wouldn't be any good at it.

She asked why I wanted to work at the IRS.

I told her it was my dream job.

She smiled.

She asked if I'd ever fired a gun.

ELEVEN

I met Avril freshman year.

This was long before she became friends with Natalie or developed an interest in class war. Avril didn't like me much at first, and I don't blame her. Back then, I was plenty unlikable. We didn't know it on the night we met—wouldn't even have guessed it, really—but someday we would become close friends. Sometimes I think ours was as close as any other friendship in my life. But if you'd asked me after that first night if I thought me and Avril would hit it off—I don't know—I probably wouldn't have said anything, but secretly I'd have slid into a major depressive episode, because the truth is that I liked her a lot, but she didn't feel the same about me. She wanted me to buzz off. Wanted me to wander somewhere far away from her and die.

It was maybe February or early March and a cold night, cold enough to snow. I was at a party at some douchebag's house. I rooted around his fridge for beer. There was plenty of beer, but it was all Natural Light, in bottles and cans. I searched for the good stuff, but there was no good stuff. I took a can. If I had to drink pathetic beer, I wanted to drink in the most pathetic way possible.

A girl behind me asked for a bottle. She had fake-red hair cut short, so it didn't fall past her neck. I noticed she wore too much eye makeup, and a black miniskirt and fishnet stockings. After I handed her the beer, I expected her to ignore me. Usually girls only paid attention to me if they wanted something.

"I like your shirt," she said.

I looked down. I wore an Atari shirt.

"It's a nerd shirt," I said.

"I like nerds," she said.

I wanted to stay and talk, but suddenly all I could think to talk about was Natalie. There's nothing lamer than talking about your girlfriend to the new girl who's hitting on you.

So I ran away.

"Well," I said, nodding to her and holding up my beer can in salute. I went to the living room and sat down on a couch. *YouTube* videos played on a big TV mounted to the wall. Damon told C.J. about global warming. C.J. ignored him. It was C.J's house and C.J's party. He was a junior, and he acted a lot older than me. I mean, he was only two years older, but it felt like much more than that. Like he was a lot more mature. Anyway he fucked a lot of girls.

"We're killing ourselves," Damon said. "Everybody wants to drive a car and have air conditioning. Everybody wants an easy life. But they don't understand the consequences."

"I want a car," I said.

"Do you want drought? Do you want extinction events?"

"No," I said. "I just want a car."

"You're part of the problem," Damon said. "You know how hard we're fucking the planet, but you won't do anything to stop it. You just sit back and watch. You're just like everybody else."

C.J. leaned over Damon to talk to me. His breath smelled like bourbon, like his mouth was the waste pipe at a Kentucky distillery, like he hadn't done anything all day but suck down bourbon.

"I see you met Avril," C.J. said.

"Who? Oh yeah, Avril."

"I'm gonna bang that skank," he said.

I took a sip from my can.

"Nice," I said. I tried hard to say it in an energetic way, like a football fan after his team scores a touchdown at the Super Bowl. I took another sip.

"She's stalking me. Or something," C.J. said, slurring his speech so *something* sounded like *shomething*.

Just then the front door opened, and Roger came in from outside. He wore a big coat and a scarf wrapped around his neck. Snow had piled on his stocking cap and shoulders, and wind blew in behind him like ice.

"Avril's in the kitchen," C.J. said.

"Good," Roger said. He took off his coat and hat. "Bang that skank."

"That's what I do," C.J. said. "I'm the skank banger. The only problem with banging skanks is afterward they get more obsessed with you."

"She won't," Roger said. "Not once she sees your tiny dick."

"You should fuck her too," C.J. said.

Roger burped. The cloud of gas he emitted smelled like beer.

Around that time, Avril came into the room. She stumbled, a little, as she walked, and kind of collapsed in a chair near the couch. She burped. She laughed about the burp. A Drake video played on *YouTube*, and Avril mouthed the lyrics. She had finished the beer and now drank from a cup that smelled like Mountain Dew and vodka.

"Hey Atari," she said, "did you ever play *Joust*?" She slurred her words, so *Joust* sounded like *Jous*.

"It's a great game," I said. "Classic."

"Love that shit," Avril said, waving her drink so it almost spilled.

"Did you ever kill the pterodactyl?"

"Only once," she said. "Goddamn pterodactyl. Just once I got lucky. Lined up everything perfect."

I had more questions for Avril, like if she'd played the Atari 2600 or 7800, and if she'd ever played *Combat* or *Star Raiders*, but just then C.J. crouched beside her and whispered in her ear.

She looked at C.J.

She looked at Roger.

"Seriously?" She held her hand over her mouth and giggled.

C.J. turned to Roger.

C.J. nodded his head toward the stairs.

"Game time," C.J. said.

Avril finished her vodka-Mountain Dew in one big chug and stood up and fell down. She laughed. C.J. and Roger helped her to her feet. C.J. hefted her and slung her over his shoulder. The three of them went upstairs. Roger was drunk and tripped on the stairs. Avril laughed and laughed.

Me and Damon sat on the couch and watched videos. We watched Jordin Sparks sing "No Air."

"I hate this song," Damon said. He reached into an inside pocket of his jacket and pulled out a joint. He lit it with a Bic lighter. He took a hit and passed it to me. I took a hit. Smoke rose off the tip.

"One way to stop global warming is to spray sulfur dioxide into the atmosphere. Spray a lot of it," Damon said. "It'll block sunlight. Cool off the planet."

"Don't we need sunlight?"

Damon shrugged.

I told him I had to piss. I went upstairs and found a bathroom and pissed. On the sink I saw three different varieties of Axe body spray. I left the bathroom and noticed a doorway partially open down the hall. Noises emanated from the room. I thought about what I should do. I walked to the door and peeked inside.

C.J., Avril, and Roger were mostly naked on the bed. C.J. and Roger faced each other with Avril on her hands and knees between them. Roger fucked her from behind while Avril sucked C.J.'s cock. He pressed his hand on the back of her skull to push her face farther down on his penis.

I must have made a noise because C.J. noticed me.

C.J. grinned.

C.J. nodded.

C.J. winked.

Avril gagged and took his penis out of her mouth and retched some fluid onto the bed. That's when she saw me. She stared through glazed eyes, and her mouth—moist and sticky—hung open. Her face didn't look like it belonged to a real person anymore. It looked like the face of one of those mannequins in a department store. Anyway I didn't have much time to think about her face, because C.J. stuffed his dick back in her mouth and resumed humping.

When I got back to the living room, Damon was finishing off the joint and watching a Katy Perry video. Katy Perry sang "Teenage Dream."

"Let's go," I said.

On the way out, I stopped in the kitchen for more beer. I stuffed cans in every pocket of my coat. I stole like five cans. Then I took another and opened it. Me and Damon set off through the snow toward our dorm. It fell heavily from the dark sky, and the wind gusted like a succession of icy fists. I drank from the can as we walked. My lips went numb.

"I know another way to stop global warming," Damon said. "Build a fleet of boats—I mean massive, hundreds of them—and have them evaporate ocean water and send the water vapor into the atmosphere to make clouds. All those new clouds will blot out the sun."

"I don't know if that'll work," I said. I gripped a can so tightly it crunched inward. I took another drink and coughed. "I don't know if anything will work. I think we're fucked. Sometimes bad things happen. Sometimes there's nothing we can do."

After I got back to the dorm, my head felt full of snot. I fell asleep, and when I awoke I had a terrible cold. I stayed sick for a week and missed all my classes. During the time I was sick, the weather changed for the better.

I remember a day—three weeks, maybe four weeks after the party—when the air felt warm like spring had come early. Campus looked new and green. Fledgling blades of grass swished softly beneath my sneakers. It was the kind of day that made me feel like a kid again, the kind that reminded me of hours spent in playgrounds, on swing sets and slides.

Pretty soon I noticed a girl leaving a dining hall. Avril. I recognized her fake-red hair. I hurried to catch up with her. I felt dizzy as I approached. My body dumped adrenaline hormones into my bloodstream. I wanted to say something important. I wanted to announce that even though we'd only recently met, I knew I loved her.

"Hey," I said.

She turned. Scrunched her eyebrows. She didn't wear so much black eye makeup as before.

"It's me," I said. "Nate. From the party."

"Nate," she said, no longer looking at me. "Nate from the party."

"The party at C.J.'s house," I said.

Avril smiled a little, then frowned. She looked at me again. She shook her head, and a lock of fake-red hair slipped over her eyes, casting a shadow.

"Don't remember you," she said.

"I wore the Atari shirt."

She shrugged.

"We talked about games," I said. "We talked about *Joust*."

"Just stop," she said.

"Pterodactyls."

"I said stop," she said, and I detected a tone in her voice that I hadn't heard before—I mean from anybody, ever. She sounded angry and sad all at once, like she didn't know whether to punch me or just shatter into a million pieces.

"Go away," she said. "I don't care anymore. I don't care about *Joust*. It's a dumb game for kids."

"I'm sorry," I said.

"You're not sorry," she said.

"But I am, really."

"No," she said. "You're not. Anyway I don't care if you're sorry. It doesn't matter if you're sorry. You're just like everybody else."

TWELVE

I finished up at the coffee shop and went back to my dorm. I thought about what Avril had said about class war. I didn't take it seriously. Avril was always saying something crazy. She was the only person I knew who was crazier than me.

When I got back to my dorm room, Natalie was sitting on the bed and watching TV. She ignored my entrance, so I started packing for Hawaii. The flight would leave in the morning. I already should have packed. I hadn't been taking the Hawaii vacation seriously. It had come as a surprise. Nothing in my horrible life had prepared me for Hawaii.

"Don't forget your bathing suit," Natalie said, her eyes focused on the television screen.

I rummaged through a pile of clothing on the closet floor. From beneath some fossilized socks and undershirts I unearthed my bathing suit. Canary yellow. Breathtakingly ugly. I didn't understand why I still owned it. My mom bought it for me in high school, in preparation for an overnight camping trip with my church youth group. I hadn't ever worn it in college. I hadn't gone swimming in college.

The yellow swim trunks made me remember the youth group trip for the first time in years. Natalie had gone with me. The church leaders took all of us canoeing ten miles down the Buffalo River. I remembered Natalie's black bikini and cutoff jean shorts. Everyone in my youth group got sunburned on the river. Natalie got sunburned worst of all because of the bikini.

"Does this look okay?" I asked, showing her my yellow trunks.

"Don't bring that," she said.

"I think it's okay," I said.

"Instead of bringing it," she said, "you could just kill yourself."

THIRTEEN

While I finished packing, Natalie watched *The Real Housewives of Dallas*. It was currently her favorite show. Her favorite shows depended on the season and network lineup. Her true favorite show was *The Bachelor*, but it had wrapped up for the season. Until new episodes aired, her temporary favorite was *Real Housewives*.

Natalie sat on my bed and texted with someone while she watched the show. Every once in a while she would laugh out loud. I didn't know if she was laughing at the show or what was being texted. I wondered who she texted. Some hot guy? Someone down to fuck? I wanted to know but didn't ask. It's stupid to ask your girlfriend who she's texting. It's none of your business.

"Do you want to get dinner with Roger tonight?" she asked.

"I don't know."

"Avril is going."

"Can we eat Roger?" I grinned big like I'd made a hilarious joke. Natalie ignored me.

I sat beside her and watched *Real Housewives*. The housewives got their nails done at a salon. All the housewives looked taller than me and had fake boobs. They wore a lot of makeup and talked loud. Even their normal voices sounded like yelling.

"If I ever catch my man cheating on me, I'll cut him," shout-talked one of the housewives while an Asian woman painted her toenails. The housewife made a face when she said *cut him*. A serious face. The kind murderers make before butchering their victims.

"That's right," Natalie yelled at the TV. She laughed really loud. She jabbed her hand into my ribs. "Go on and cheat and see if I don't cut you." Natalie laughed and laughed.

I pulled out my phone and swiped a finger across the screen. I checked Twitter and read a good tweet.

Slept on a damp towel last night and that's my whole life

I tapped the screen to like and retweet it. I hoped Natalie would think I was texting someone. Some hot girl down to fuck. I closed Twitter and opened *The Washington Post*. I didn't know any hot girls down to fuck. All I ever did on my phone was tweet and read news and check Facebook. I never actually called anybody. I didn't need a phone. I needed some sad device for lonely people.

I read a story about the loss of sea ice in the arctic. It had been a bad year for sea ice. The story said the Arctic had seen the steepest plunge in sea ice in 1,500 years. Scientists saw no indication that the Arctic would ever return to its reliably frozen state. The melting was unprecedented in human history. The story was full of science words like *feedback loops* and *permafrost* and *calving events*. I closed my eyes and imagined the Arctic in winter. A sheet of white ice stretched as far as the eye could see. I imagined standing on the ice and feeling cold air against my face. A sunset painted the sky red and orange. Even from deep within my fugue state, I heard the women from *Real Housewives*. One housewife gave relationship advice to another.

"If a woman tries to steal your man, fuck that bitch up," said the first housewife.

"Mmm-hmm," said the other housewife.

I opened my eyes and put away the phone. I held Natalie's hand. We watched *The Real Housewives of Dallas* together. It would always be like this. We would come home from our pathetic jobs at the IRS and sit on our couch and hold hands and watch TV. We would do it for a hundred days. A thousand. This was my life. Sitting on a couch with Natalie watching TV.

FOURTEEN

Here's something I remember about Natalie.

When we hooked up back in junior high, I felt very excited to have a girlfriend. I guess if I'd known she'd be my only girlfriend for the next decade, I wouldn't have been quite so excited. I'd still have felt a little excited, because—hey—first girlfriend. But my excitement would have been tempered with regret.

Anyway I'd been crushing on her since third grade. She looked like all the most desirable girls on the Disney Channel—tall (but not taller than me), skinny (but not skeletal). She wore T-shirts with colorful Japanese *Pokémon* characters and short Jordache shorts revealing miles and miles of skinny legs.

I didn't make much progress toward hooking up with her until junior high. Our school held a dance at the beginning of eighth grade. It took place in a gymnasium. The room was dark and smelled subtly of hormones. Crepe-paper streamers hung from doorways. A disco ball painted the ceiling in trippy reds and blues. Most of the guys my age hung out on the visitors' side, leaning against the wall in a long line as if awaiting execution. Some of us talked about video games or Iron Man movies. Others stood silent, arms crossed, sneaking glances and thinking grownup thoughts about the girls across the basketball court.

I remember Natalie wore a shimmering green dress. She came over to our side of the gym and walked along the line of boys, examining each of us like a USDA inspector at a slaughterhouse. Alicia Keys sang a soft ballad through the DJ's speakers. Natalie stopped in front of me, looked me up and down. Her dress shimmered with new ferocity. She asked me to dance. Next thing I remember is standing with her in the center of the court, my hands at her thin waist. We shuffled awkwardly, almost to the beat. At that moment she owned me. I summoned the courage to look into her eyes. She smiled shyly and glanced away. Her dress shimmered again, this time softly, gentle like rain. I hoped Natalie would go on owning me forever.

FIFTEEN

Something else I remember about Natalie.

She invited me to her house the weekend after the dance. The size of the house impressed me—much bigger than anywhere I'd lived. It stood in a well-manicured neighborhood of similarly impressive McMansions.

We spent the afternoon watching Nickelodeon and Disney in the basement. We watched *Spongebob* and *Phineas & Ferb*. This was a chaperoned date, so her stepmother kept tabs on us. We sat on opposite ends of a plaid couch. Twice when the stepmother left to go to the kitchen, I scooted over to kiss Natalie. These were exploratory kisses, nervous and hopeful.

Later she took me upstairs to her older brother's room. He was only older by a year, but that put him in high school and a more refined social order. I felt nervous around him, unsure what to say. Natalie showed me a hamster in a cage on her brother's desk. The hamster sat on a bed of sawdust. He didn't eat or run around or play on his wheel. He was a depressed hamster.

"He's mine," Natalie said. "I named him Pikachu."

Her brother, sitting on the bed and with one hand in a base-ball glove, corrected her. He said the hamster belonged to both of them, that their grandparents gave it to them to share.

"It's mine," Natalie said. "It's not your hamster. It's mine."

"It's mine too," her brother said.

They went back and forth like that for a long time, growing louder and angrier until their father and stepmother came upstairs. Only, even in front of the grownups, Natalie wouldn't stop.

"It's mine! It's mine! It's mine!" she yelled, red-faced and crying.

"Grow up," her brother said.

Natalie snatched a book off his desk—a thick one, his algebra textbook from school. She hurled it across the room where it thumped against the wall, leaving a mark.

"It's mine!" she screamed. "Motherfucker I'll kill you! The fucking hamster is mine!"

SIXTEEN

I got bored watching *The Real Housewives of Dallas* and went to my closet to look at shirts. I wore a plaid shirt and liked it but wondered if a different plaid shirt would be better. I owned a lot of plaid shirts. You can tell what stage of life a person is in by their clothing. People wear plaid shirts when they're young and have no authority or responsibility.

I liked to imagine a future in which I'd wear better clothing. I'd work some important job in a skyscraper in a big city, and I'd own fancy dress shirts and suit jackets and blazers and cardigans. In this future, I would be an evil corporate lawyer, and I'd wear my snazzy outfits in the courtrooms where I'd successfully argue that it wouldn't be cost-effective for my client to clean up all the benzene it dumped into the drinking water at the children's home.

I changed out of my plaid shirt and into a slightly different plaid shirt. I felt good about my decision. I checked myself in the mirror. I felt bad about my decision.

I paced around the room. Natalie told me to stop pacing. I sat on my bed and opened my laptop. I read a Wikipedia article about the global food supply. I clicked a link and read a super-nerdy article about crop and livestock production. I leaned back against the headboard, drummed my fingers softly on my legs. I thought about meat. I thought about vegetables and how I always tried to avoid eating them because they taste bad. I thought about factory farms. Fecal lagoons in Arkansas.

"Pig fuckers," I said.

I closed the laptop. I walked into the bathroom. Natalie applied makeup in front of the mirror. The bathroom smelled like old urine. I stood behind her and tried to see myself in a small corner of the mirror over her shoulder. I picked up a brush and ran it through my hair, even though my hair looked fine. I looked at Natalie. She was much prettier than I deserved. We didn't belong together. Any day now she'd dump me for a guy with big muscles and a lot of money.

"Your bathroom is so fucking small," she said.

"Someday when I'm rich I'll buy you a big house where the bathrooms never end."

"You will never be rich."

"All our neighbors will hate us. They'll be jealous of our monster house."

"No. You'll be poor," she said. "You'll keep me prisoner in a rusty trailer by the train tracks."

I thought up something funny to say.

Our monster house will kill and eat the other houses in our neighborhood. It possesses a mighty hunger. Our monster house will go on a rampage through the suburbs, feasting on the next neighborhood and the next. Its appetite will never be sated.

I chuckled but didn't actually say anything out loud.

It was important for Natalie to go on believing I was okay.

SEVENTEEN

Roger texted around seven. He was in the parking lot downstairs with Avril. We got our coats and went downstairs. As we approached his car, he honked the horn and rolled down his window. "Hurry up," he said. He honked the horn again. He laughed like he'd done something funny. To Roger, nothing in life was funnier than honking a car horn.

Me and Natalie got in the back of the car. Avril told Roger to stop being a dick. Avril and Roger weren't dating. They'd only had sex that one time freshman year. Bad sex. Weird sex. Problematic sex. Now they were friends. Friends who'd had sex. Bad friends. Weird friends. Problematic friends.

Roger started the car and drove through the quiet university streets. As soon as he left campus he merged into gridlock on Greenland Drive. After five minutes of stop-and-go traffic, he diverted onto a side street that took us through one of those depressing neighborhoods where no one ever mows their lawns. The houses looked small, like they'd been built fifty years ago. As the evening sky darkened, the blue glow of televisions illuminated every window. It was the kind of neighborhood where everybody works all day and comes home at night and watches TV.

Roger pulled onto the main highway through town. Streetlights and neon signs lit up the road in an artificial way that made me feel safe.

Natalie leaned against me. I felt the curves of her body through her clothing. I remembered back to high school, when touching her—even just the thought of it—charged my body with hormones and electricity. But lately, touching her just made me think about how she always left her dirty dishes in the bathroom sink for me to wash or all the times she'd nagged me to apply for an internship at the IRS.

Roger navigated the traffic-choked streets for a half hour before we pulled up to the Outback Steakhouse near the mall. Approximately 10,000 miles of parking lot surrounded the restaurant. We got out of the car and walked toward the entrance. I looked around at all the other cars. I thought about how much gasoline they used. I thought about how much metal and plastic and glass went into producing them. It didn't seem possible that human civilization could produce all the gasoline, metal, and plastic required to sustain itself. I felt like I didn't understand anything about the world.

In the foyer of the restaurant, a hostess who looked like a student at the university smiled all big and fake, like she was in a shitty mood but couldn't show it directly because her boss required her to always act joyful and positive. She was skinny and wore a black dress. Her earrings glowed golden in the dim light.

The four of us sat at a booth and pored over the menus. I looked around at the other tables. A lot of families ate at Outback Steakhouse. Gray-headed husbands and wives ignored each other while their bored kids played on phones and iPads. For me, the experience was like traveling forward in a time machine to see my future. Someday, I would be the overweight father with nothing interesting to say. I would sip overpriced beer while my equally overweight wife complained about the service.

Our waiter showed up looking bored. He had longish hair and a stubbly beard like Kurt Cobain. He looked much cooler than me or any of my friends. Roger ordered a steak. Me and Natalie ordered chicken. Avril ordered a big salad.

"Are you on a diet?" Natalie asked.

"She's always on a diet," Roger said.

"No," Avril said. "I just stopped eating meat."

"That's a diet," Roger said. "That's what a diet is."

"Are you going vegan?" Natalie said, her eyes lighting up. "My cousin is vegan. She's super skinny."

"I just don't want to eat animals anymore," Avril said.

"That's stupid," Roger said. "That's a stupid diet."

"Animals are sentient beings that can think and experience emotions," Avril said. "They feel pain, fear, and love."

"Animals are dumb," Roger said. "I grew up around cows—out in the country, where everybody makes their money in ranching. Cows are extremely stupid. They'd be extinct by now if we didn't keep them around for eating."

"Meat causes cancer," Avril said. "Scientists know this. The World Health Organization says eating processed meat gives you cancer."

"So dumb," Roger said. "Can't you do math? Millions of people eat meat. So why aren't they getting cancer?"

"Millions of people get cancer," Avril said.

Everybody in the restaurant had big cuts of meat on their plates. They tore into them with forks and knives, grinning and laughing with mouths full of seared flesh, their lips glistening with grease. Blood pooled on white china.

"Do you ever think about the cows and pigs at the slaughterhouse?" Avril asked. "The slaughterhouse makes a big pile out of all the dead animals. It dumps the carcasses on a conveyor belt and cuts them open with saws. It's disgusting. I don't want to think about it because it's so disgusting."

"So don't think about it," Roger said.

"Meat holocaust," I said. Everybody ignored me.

"Just admit you're on a diet." Roger smirked and stared at Avril's breasts. "You felt fat this week, so you stopped eating meat."

Avril put her hand on Natalie's arm and told her she hated him.

I looked down at the table and whispered, "Meat holocaust."

Natalie complained that the drinks were taking forever. It was Friday night, and the restaurant was packed. The dining room was loud and smelled of blood. Eventually the drinks arrived, then the food. Natalie said her chicken was cold, and she sent it back. We ordered more drinks.

EIGHTEEN

Natalie talked about Hawaii. This was a relief. Sometimes, to survive dinner, you must ignore the meat holocaust and talk about something pleasant. Something like Hawaii. Natalie told us we should take a helicopter tour of the island.

"What island are we even going to?" Roger asked.

"Hawaii Island," Avril said. "The Big Island."

"With Honolulu and Pearl Harbor?" Roger asked.

"No," Avril said. "That's the wrong island."

"What's the point of Hawaii if you can't see Honolulu or Pearl Harbor?" Roger asked, scowling.

I noticed C.J. at a table across the dining room. He was a senior and had been one for at least three years. Roger waved at him and motioned for him to come over. Roger stood and shook C.J.'s hand. C.J. winked at Avril. She picked up her wineglass and drank and acted like she hadn't noticed.

"This place is great," C.J. said. He dressed nicely in a blazer and gray vest. He wore a tie loose around his neck, and his breath smelled like bourbon. "The steak here is great. I'm done eating anything else. From now on, all I'm eating is steak."

Roger motioned around the table. "None of these dweebs ordered steak."

C.J. pointed at me. "Jesus, this is a steakhouse. Don't be a pussy, Nate. Eat some steak. You're embarrassing me. I feel embarrassed for you. Chicken is for girls who don't want to feel fat when you fuck them." C.J. winked at Avril again.

"Give me steak," I said, raising my fork and knife like weapons.

"Give the man some steak!" Roger said.

Natalie cut off a bite from Roger's plate and fed it to me from his fork. I chewed the steak, tasted its juices. The steak really was amazing. I felt bad for the cow. I felt bad because it lived its entire life in some tiny, manure-soaked cell. I felt bad because it died in a filthy slaughterhouse, executed by a shot in the head from a bolt gun. The steak tasted delicious.

Roger asked C.J. what he would do after graduation. C.J. said he'd been hired as a legislative aide to Marsha Blackburn, a terrible Republican senator who had been a politician in Tennessee pretty much since the beginning of time.

"Marsha's gonna help Trump build the wall," C.J. said, grinning like a high school sophomore about to get laid for the first time. "Marsha's gonna keep the Mexicans out."

"Lock 'em up," Roger said. "Don't they know what *illegal* means?"

"Keep Mexicans in cages," C.J. said, slapping Roger on the back. "That's the campaign slogan, right there. That's a winner."

Avril wasn't having it.

"Why don't you guys just admit that you're Nazis?" she asked. "Building your Nazi-ass wall because you're so fucking terrified of brown people. Why don't you just admit who you are?"

"Eat your salad," C.J. said.

"Meat holocaust," I said.

"What?" C.J. asked.

"Nothing matters," I said.

"Jesus, Nate. When did you become such a cuck?" C.J. asked. Roger snorted.

"Yeah Nate, don't be such a cuck," Roger said. He laughed and pounded his fist on the table. He looked at C.J. with a particular gleam in his eye. This wasn't the first time I'd seen him look at C.J. this way. I'd come to recognize that gleam as love. Roger loved C.J. and wanted to be just like him. In many ways, Roger and C.J.'s love was very dumb, but in other ways it was beautiful. Sometimes I'd imagine writing a Broadway musical about them. I would call it *Dumb Racists in Love*.

C.J. talked to Roger some more before leaving. A song by Lana Del Ray played over the speakers. Natalie and Avril mouthed the words. They didn't sing very loudly because neither of them were any good at singing. The song was about money and love.

I went back to eating my chicken. I regretted ordering it. I wanted a steak of my own, a big one cooked rare. My chicken looked pathetic, all limp and weak. I cut a bite-sized portion with my fork, then speared it and held it up to the light. I sighed in quiet resignation.

"Meat holocaust," I said.

"Let's go to Main Street Live," Natalie said after her third glass of wine. "It's too hot here. Everything smells like meat."

NINETEEN

I used Natalie's credit card to pay our tab. She picked up her purse from where it hung from its strap around the back of her chair. She smiled at Roger and Avril who waited by the door. Streetlights illuminated the parking lot outside. The world beyond Outback Steakhouse looked like one big parking lot. The ultimate parking lot. A parking lot extending to the far end of the universe.

"The waiter sucked," Natalie said. "Everything came late and the chicken was cold." She raised her top lip and crinkled her nose, almost sneering. "Don't leave a tip."

"Okay," I said.

Natalie walked over to her friends. I left the waiter a big tip.

"The revolution will be followed by summary executions," I said when I joined them at the door.

"What?" Natalie said.

"It doesn't matter," I said.

TWENTY

We saw a car crash in the parking lot. We were standing right outside Outback Steakhouse when two vehicles smashed into each other. A small Honda hatchback had been trying to pull out of a parking space when a big SUV came along. The Honda got pounded. I guess the SUV driver didn't see the hatchback. Maybe the driver was distracted by his phone or messing with his radio. Maybe the driver was just a bad driver. It's hard to say why these things happen. The SUV never hit the brakes or slowed down. It just kept coming and plowed into the hatchback. The impact of the crash bumped the hatchback forward by several feet. Shattered the back window. The crash mesmerized me. I couldn't believe it was real. I'd watched thousands of crashes in movies and TV but never in real life. The crash didn't sound like I expected. It wasn't very loud. It sounded like a gigantic sheet of aluminum foil crumpling into a ball.

The four of us stood in the cold and watched the aftermath. A bunch of people came out of the restaurant. Everybody stood around and gawked. The airbags in both vehicles had deployed. More people crowded around to watch. A few people went over to the vehicles and asked the drivers if they were hurt. The guy in the SUV said he was okay, and he tried to get out, but a man and a woman told him not to move, to wait for paramedics. The woman in the Honda moaned and moaned. People went to her window and asked if she was okay. She wouldn't answer. She kept on moaning.

"What a mess," Natalie said.

"Holy goddamned shit," Roger said. "Best thing I've seen in my life."

I wasn't listening. I thought about the end of the world. The crash scene looked almost supernatural. Streetlights bathed it yellow. Everybody stood around listening as the Honda driver moaned. I felt my mouth curling into a big, creepy grin. I struggled to regain composure. I didn't want anyone in the crowd to think I was crazy. I didn't want them to know.

"The Permian-Triassic extinction event eradicated more than ninety percent of animal life on Earth," I said to Natalie. "That was 250 million years ago."

"How does anybody even know that?" Natalie asked.

"Fossils or something," I said. "Ice core samples."

"What are you talking about?" Natalie asked.

The police showed up and then the ambulances. The lights of the rescue vehicles illuminated the parking lot in blues and reds, beautiful like Christmas. The paramedics pulled the woman out of her smashed car. She wasn't bleeding, and none of her bones appeared broken, but regardless she kept on moaning. The cops ticketed the SUV driver. By then, most of the crowd had dispersed. I didn't want to leave. I didn't want it to end.

"This is boring," Natalie said. "Let's go to the club."

"Ice core samples," I said.

A cop in an orange safety vest took photos of the wreck. He crouched by the crumpled rear of the hatchback. The flash of his camera split the night like lightning.

"It's like watching TV," Natalie said.

"A police show," I said. "A murder show."

A narrow strip of lawn separated the restaurant from the parking lot. The grass there had turned brown and died. I stared at the patches of dirt where grass used to be, and it reminded me of my whole life. I closed my eyes and imagined Hawaii. A verdant land of forests and tropical flowers. Fire and smoke erupted from a volcano. I imagined watching it all from a distance, standing on a hilltop with birds.

"Should we go to the club?" Avril said. "I feel sick."

"Fuck yeah the club," Roger said. "Tonight's our last night in town. Let's go to the club."

TWENTY-ONE

Roger fumbled with the key fob while trying to unlock the car doors. Wind gusted in the parking lot. My nose went numb and started running, but overall I didn't feel very cold because of all my drinking. Natalie asked Roger if he was okay to drive. He grumbled something indecipherable. He unlocked the doors, and we all piled in, and he started the engine. Natalie took the passenger seat, and Avril and I sat in the back. Roger pulled the car onto the highway. He merged into the wrong lane but quickly saw his mistake and swerved across the center line. Natalie said "fuck." Roger grumbled something indecipherable. He took a hard turn on Broad Street. Avril's body slid into mine. Her hair brushed my neck, and I smelled perfume, something expensive from a department store at the mall, the kind of place I avoid because I'm broke and don't deserve to be there. Roger leaned forward to adjust the defrost. He grumbled something indecipherable. Natalie played *Candy Crush* on her iPhone. Light from the phone made her look like a corpse. I smelled Avril's perfume again. I whispered to her.

"We'll go to Hawaii and run away. Roger and Natalie will never find us." My lips were millimeters from her ear. "Run away to a house in the jungle. We'll live together in the jungle and never eat meat."

"I'm already in love with our jungle house," Avril said.

She held my hand in the back seat.

I worried at first that Natalie or Roger would look back and see us. I closed my eyes and imagined Hawaii. Sand and palms. Flower petals glistened, wet from dew and their own sap. Birds sang in the treetops. Sunbeams pierced the canopy to dance on the rainforest floor. I envisioned Avril's sun-drenched face. She smiled. Danced. Beckoned to me. The ocean rumbled, distantly, as waves crashed against the land. I moved toward her. Touched her. The crashing surf created a sound like thunder, like all of nature roaring my name.

TWENTY-TWO

Roger pulled up to a wooden building that looked like a shack out of the 1940s. Neon lights glowed through a downstairs window. One small pipe on the roof vented smoke, white against the sky. The building looked like it could collapse at any moment.

"Is this it?" Natalie asked. "This looks like a place where people get stabbed. I think I saw this place on the news."

"Jesus," Roger said. "It's fine."

"Those people in the alley are smoking meth," Avril said.

"What the hell do you know about meth?" Roger asked. "Just get out of the car."

"We should have gone to Nashville," Natalie said. "Murfreesboro is a dump."

The inside of the club looked better than the outside. Purple and blue lights reflected off glass. The inside of the club looked like a video game. We took off our winter coats and found a table in the back. Natalie sat in my lap while Roger went to the bar to get drinks.

"This club is full of sluts," Natalie said.

"At least one who I can think of," Avril said.

"This place is full of whores," Natalie said.

Roger came back with drinks. He'd ordered Bud Light for everyone.

"I hate beer," Natalie said. She drank from her bottle of Bud Light.

We sat and drank. The room was long and not very wide, with tables and a bar on our end, and a DJ and lasers toward the back. About a dozen people danced in front of the stage. I didn't recognize any of them from campus. The DJ played something by Daft Punk. Bodies swayed under colored lights. Boys and girls leaned on each other. Everybody looked horny.

"I want to dance," Natalie said.

She took Avril's hand, and Roger trailed after them, and pretty soon they blended into the crowd on the dance floor. I kept sitting and drinking. A while back, I'd made an important decision to stop dancing. Me and Natalie used to go out dancing all the time. I was bad at it. That's what Natalie told me. A bad dancer. So I tried harder. I studied, watched *YouTube* videos of people dancing. Nothing helped. Natalie always made fun of my dancing. She told me I looked like I was having a seizure. So I stopped. I hadn't danced since the summer before junior year. Mostly, people didn't notice. I would just sit at a table and drink. It was more fun that way. More fun than dancing. Whenever I thought about dancing, I had the urge to jump off a tall building.

After I finished my beer I drank Natalie's because I knew she wouldn't miss it. I watched Natalie and Avril grind on the dance floor. Avril looked excited, like she wanted to fuck Natalie. Then Roger danced with Natalie. Roger looked excited, like he wanted to fuck Natalie. It bothered me a little to watch them, but they always danced together and nothing had happened. When I finished Natalie's beer, I went to the bar and ordered two hurricanes. The bartender had brown eyes and Japanese Gundam tattoos on her arms.

"You must really like hurricanes," she said.

Roger was drinking beer at the table when I got back from the bar. The girls still danced. I sipped one of the hurricanes. Roger burped.

"You should dance with Natalie," he said.

"You've seen me dance."

"Everybody's drunk. Nobody cares. Christ. Get over yourself and dance with your girlfriend."

I shrugged. I looked at my drink.

Avril came back with a vodka cranberry for herself and another hurricane for me.

"I'm trying to get you drunk," she said.

On the dance floor, Natalie rubbed herself on some random guy. The guy wasn't even hot. He looked like some dumb townie. Just another boring white guy. She touched his arm and banged her pelvis against him.

"What do you think about when you sit here not dancing?" Roger said.

"Fuck off," I said.

We drank and I felt the bass vibrating my body. I wanted to be like Roger and not worry about anything. People who could dance and never worry were much happier than me. Natalie showed up with some vodka drink. She sweated and smiled and looked radiant.

"I got you a hurricane," I said.

There were a lot of drinks on the table. Natalie leaned against me and felt warm and seemed happy for the first time in a long time.

"Nate wants to dance with you," Roger said. "Told me so. Just now."

Natalie rolled her eyes and sipped her vodka drink.

I held her hand. "Let's never dance again."

"Good plan," Roger said, raising his beer thoughtfully. "I'll give up dancing too."

"Just what I need," Natalie said, "another man in my life who won't dance."

My phone vibrated in my pocket. I checked it and saw that Damon had sent me a message. He wanted to know what everybody was up to. He wanted to know if me and Natalie and Roger and Avril were out somewhere.

"It's Damon," I said. "He wants to hang out."

"Oh God," Natalie said. "We just can't. I don't want to be the one to tell him about Hawaii."

Roger laughed. "Poor Damon." Roger laughed again.

I didn't know what to tell him. I slid my phone back into the pocket of my jeans. Sometimes the kindest thing you can do is nothing at all.

Natalie finished her vodka drink. She, Roger, and Avril got up to dance. I stayed put and finished my hurricane. I put my feet on a chair and leaned back and enjoyed the music and my friends dancing.

"Everything is going according to plan," I said out loud, because with all the music nobody would hear me or even care.

TWENTY-THREE

The DJ played "Monster" by Eminem and "Timber" by Pitbull and "My House" by Flo Rida. Everybody in the club loved the DJ. Everybody cheered and asked for more. He played "Starships" by Nicki Minaj.

I hated the club. I asked myself what Jean-Pierre Léaud would do if he were there with me. Probably he'd make some biting comment about capitalism and fall in love with Brigitte Bardot. That was fine for Jean-Pierre but wouldn't help me at all. I loved French New Wave movies, but they didn't provide much in the way of practical knowledge to apply to my life.

I pulled my phone out of my pocket. I opened a browser. I typed Norway into the search bar and read an article on Wikipedia. According to something called the United Nations Human Development Index, Norway is the best country in the world. Unemployment basically doesn't exist. The unions are strong and make sure everybody gets paid. The workers have short workdays and long vacations. College is free. Healthcare is free. Childcare is heavily subsidized. I read further. I read about fjords. I closed my eyes. I imagined climbing mountains and seeing birds.

The DJ played "This is America" by Childish Gambino. I closed my eyes. I thought about Norway.

"Fjords." Nobody could hear me. "Svalbard."

TWENTY-FOUR

I stood up and felt drunk. I walked to the bouncer by the door and asked if I could come back in if I left for a few minutes. The bouncer had big biceps and a meaty face. He'd recently begun growing a mustache, but it hadn't come in all the way. He probably lived in a cramped apartment where he listened to the Scorpions and White Snake. The bouncer looked at me and frowned. He acted like I was giving him a hard time. Eventually he shrugged and told me it was cool.

I walked through the parking lot. The pavement was cracked, and in some places chunks had busted out of it. Thin blades of yellow grass grew in these places. I walked on the sidewalk in front of a tattoo parlor. I don't have any tattoos, but if I ever wanted one, I wouldn't have gone to that place. It was the kind of place where your tattoo comes with a free case of hepatitis.

The air outside felt cold and stung my nose and throat. Streetlights splashed on the asphalt and sides of buildings. I felt strange, like I was no longer in Tennessee. Like I'd left the Earth to explore one of Jupiter's moons. I came to the edge of the parking lot and a chain-link fence. Here the road ran across a bridge spanning a river. On the other side of the fence, the hill sloped down to the riverbank through a thick grove of trees. I walked along the sidewalk until I found a break in the fence, then tramped downhill to the river. Shadows loomed dark beneath the trees. I kept alert for crackheads. I didn't want some crackhead to stab me. Brown grass crunched under my shoes at first, but nearer to the river the ground turned muddy. My sneakers sunk into the muck. I stopped and listened as the river gurgled. Light from the sky and city rippled along its surface.

The river stunk. It smelled like dead animals and rotting meat. Smoke rose from chimneys in the distance. I shivered and crossed my arms. I saw the city lights and thought about how the land probably used to be a forest, but people cut it down to build a lot of ugly buildings and highways and parking lots. The river used to be clear and full of trout, but now it crept along like slime from a toilet.

"Five dollars for a blowjob," said a voice behind me.

I screamed. The voice behind me sounded like a crackhead—a crackhead who would stab me for my wallet to buy more crack. I cowered from the imagined stabbing. But it was only Avril. She asked if I was okay. She stood beside me and watched the river. I felt her shoulder against mine, even through our winter coats.

"Does it piss you off when Roger and Natalie dance?" she asked.

"No," I said.

"Are you lying?"

"I don't know," I said. "Probably."

Avril asked why I came down to the river. I told her I was thinking about the end of the world. Someday some shitty country would launch some nukes, and some other country would retaliate. Then everybody is fucked. There are a lot of nuclear missiles. We could launch enough missiles to wipe out all life on the planet.

"This is why people say you're weird," Avril said.

"People pretend everything is fine, but it's not," I said. I waved my hand at the garbage and polluted river and smokestacks in the distance. "Everything is fucked."

"Everything is fucked," Avril said.

I liked Avril's fake-red hair. I liked the black leather dog collar she wore as a choker. The wind scattered her hair across her forehead, and she blinked back tears—not because she was sad but because the wind stung her eyes—and before I thought much about it I moved close and kissed her, and I liked the way her lips and breath felt warm against my skin, and we kept at it for a while, and afterward we stood together, my arm around her, and watched the river glistening under the moonlight. Nothing seemed as bad as it had before. The river wasn't such a bad river after all.

TWENTY-FIVE

Me and Avril sat close together in a dark corner of the club. We watched Roger and Natalie sway on the dance floor. Avril laid her head on my shoulder and squeezed my leg beneath the table. We talked about finding time to be alone together. We talked about Hawaii. After the next song, Natalie and Roger stopped dancing and went to the bar. Roger got another beer, and Natalie got a big blue margarita. We drank and listened to music but didn't talk much. Avril said she was tired. Natalie said she was tired. We paid our tabs. I paid with Natalie's credit card. I didn't like a lot of things about Natalie, but I was deeply in love with her credit card. We went out to the parking lot and got in Roger's car. He fumbled the key when he tried to put it into the ignition. After a few tries, the car started.

"Are you okay to drive?" Avril asked.

She sat in the front beside him, with me and Natalie in the back.

Roger answered by muttering something incomprehensible. He switched on the lights and started driving. I put my arm around Natalie, with my palm on her silver dress and my fingers brushing her fake-tan skin. I ran my hand along her arm. She felt familiar. Normal and boring. I closed my eyes and imagined holding Avril. Her body would radiate warmth and joy. Her body would feel like a whole new world of sunlight.

"Who's hungry?" Roger said.

Nobody answered.

"I'm going to Waffle House," he said.

TWENTY-SIX

We pulled up to the Waffle House off Highway 96 sometime after midnight. The parking lot was mostly empty, but a lot of people crowded inside. About half were college age, and the rest were those older, weirder people who only come out at night, people with facial tattoos, dreadlocks, and missing teeth. Roger ushered us toward an empty booth by the window. We passed a table where a guy I knew named Josh was sitting. Josh had been one of my good friends freshman year, when we had a lot of classes together. I hadn't seen him much since then, because he'd gone on to major in something productive, like engineering or computer science. At Waffle House he sat with two girls who I also recognized, vaguely, from campus. They had that STEM look about them. The three of them probably could have pooled their talents and founded a tech company, or hacked the Pentagon and shut down all the nukes, if they'd wanted. But that's not what they wanted. They wanted to eat hash browns at Waffle House, like everybody else.

Josh's face lit up when he saw Roger. Josh formed his hands into gun shapes.

"Roger!" Josh said, firing his gun hands.

"Josh!" Roger said.

"Rog!"

"How you been, man?"

"The Roginator!"

Me, Natalie, and Avril got into our booth while Roger stayed behind with Josh. I overheard Josh say, *So you and Avril?* Roger laughed and said, *That slut is one hundred percent dyke.* Josh and Roger laughed. I stole a glance at Avril. Her face stiffened. She acted like she hadn't heard, but she definitely heard. She pulled out her phone and swiped across the screen.

Roger came over. Me and Natalie had taken up one side of the booth, so he had to sit beside Avril. This was unfortunate because of their mutual hatred. They'd hated each other since that party freshman year. They were both friends with me and Natalie but hated each other. Avril ignored him and stared at her phone.

Roger had short-cropped hair and a big jaw and muscles. He looked like any other frat guy, except his grade point average was too low to join a frat. He didn't look like the kind of guy you'd expect to see sharing a booth at Waffle House with Avril, with her fake-red hair and pale skin, her black Pixies T-shirt and leather dog collar.

Natalie took a menu from a rack at the end of the table. The menus were single sheets of paper laminated in plastic. Two menus were stuck together with grease, and when she pulled them apart they made a slurping noise. The menus were colorful with large photographs of food. They didn't look like real menus. They looked like pretend menus for kids playing a game.

"Everything is gross," Natalie said. "What's a patty melt?"

"Patty melts are good," Roger said. "Patty melts are sexual."

"Nothing about Waffle House is sexual," Natalie said.

"Patty melts are a thousand calories," Avril said. A lock of hair fell over her face. "Patty melts are a heart attack."

"I don't know what I want," Natalie said, turning to me and scrunching up her face.

"Patty melts are okay," I said. "They're greasy."

"Everything here is greasy," Natalie said. "The people are greasy."

A waitress walked up to our booth, and she was polite enough to pretend Natalie hadn't insulted her. The waitress was obese with small breasts. Natalie ordered a patty melt and a Diet Coke. After the waitress walked away, Natalie made fun of her obesity and small breasts. Roger laughed. He called the waitress a dyke. In Roger's imagination, any woman he didn't want to have sex with—or vice versa—was a dyke.

Avril ignored everybody and messed with her phone. I asked what she was reading. I expected her to say Twitter. Whenever I want to ignore people, I scroll Twitter. Avril looked up and said she was reading about the Great Pacific Garbage Patch.

"Great Pacific Bullshit Patch," Roger said.

Avril told us about an enormous field of plastic garbage floating in the ocean, somewhere in the vicinity of Hawaii Island. A powerful oceanic gyre gathered plastics from all over the ocean and whirled them into a vortex of garbage stretching for miles.

"The ocean is a big place," Roger said. "There's plenty of room. Stop crying about it."

"I'm just reading," Avril said. "It's just interesting."

"I'm so tired of all the environmental bullshit," Roger said. "Listen, you've got to get ready for what's coming. Trump is making all of us rich. It's a different world now. Trump is cutting regulations. Trump is murdering the EPA. Trump doesn't get misty-eyed over some baby penguins. He doesn't give a fuck. When Trump is through, there will be *more* plastic garbage in the ocean, not *less*. And you'll love it. Because you'll be rich."

"I'll be an intern at the IRS," I said.

"The stock market has been gangbusters for three years now," Roger said. "It keeps going up. The stock market loves Trump. We're all gonna be rich."

"Trump will drown you in your own garbage," Avril said. "And I'll laugh, because that's what you and all your crypto-Trump-fascists deserve. To drown in your own garbage."

"Could we not talk about politics, please?" Natalie asked. "It doesn't matter, anyway. Talking about it won't change anything. Could we please just talk about anything else?"

We sat around the booth not saying much. Avril resumed reading on her phone. This encouraged Natalie to get on her own phone. I looked out the window. A man stood on the corner holding a cardboard sign saying he was homeless and needed money. He wore a stocking cap and a big coat that didn't fit well. A couple holding hands walked by. They looked down at his sign, then kept walking like they hadn't seen him. And I knew I would have done the same thing. It's depressing, but it's true. I never give money to anyone.

"I have an idea for an online dating site," Roger said. We all looked at him. "I'll call it *Garbage Vortex*."

All of us laughed.

"Even Avril could find a boyfriend on *Garbage Vortex*," he said.

We laughed again, but Avril more quietly than the rest.

The waitress brought our food. She accidentally gave my hamburger to Roger, and Roger's bacon to me, but we sorted it out. After she walked away, Roger said, "Her vagina is a garbage vortex," and everybody laughed again.

TWENTY-SEVEN

I kissed Natalie an hour later back at the dorm. She sucked my face hard like she wanted me. I turned off the light, and we fumbled into bed. We kissed and took off our clothes.

"It's been so long," I said.

"Wait," she said.

"What?"

"Wait, wait get off."

She hit me on the shoulder. I rolled over. She sprang out of bed, ran naked to the bathroom. She didn't turn on the light. I heard her retch into the toilet in the dark. I left her alone to puke. It's respectful. Whenever I puke, I prefer to be alone and unbothered. She puked for a long time, on and off. When she finished, I opened the bathroom door and went inside. The small room smelled like alcohol and vomit. She knelt by the toilet. I held Natalie's arm and led her to the sink. She washed the puke off her face. She gargled and spit. I handed her a clean towel. I told her I loved her. And I meant it. At that moment I loved her. And I think—briefly—she loved me too. It didn't matter, but it was nice. It's nice to have somebody to love.

PART
TWO

FLOWN HERE
NOT GROWN HERE

TWENTY-EIGHT

THE ALARM CLOCK RANG in the dark. Natalie told me we had to get to the airport early because of security. She said she still felt drunk and didn't want to get up. I trudged out of bed and gathered my bags. I wandered around the dorm in search of anything I'd forgotten to pack. I packed my toothbrush and phone charger.

The morning was cold. The windows had frosted over, and, once I got outside, the air scraped my throat raw. The drive to the airport took less than an hour. Traffic on I-24 rolled slowly as morning commuters jammed the highway. Every vehicle on the road was a big truck or SUV. They raced by us, spewing white clouds of exhaust like wagging tongues from their tailpipes. I kept checking the sky to see if it would snow. The sky looked gray and turbulent, but it didn't snow.

At the airport, I expected to speak to a person at the ticket desk like people do in movies, but everything was automated. Natalie stood in front of a touch-screen monitor. She tapped it with her fingers. Of the two of us, she was the optimal person to use the machine because she had more experience tapping out messages on her iPhone. The machine asked for our names. It prompted her to swipe a credit card. The machine requested our flight number. Natalie looked at her itinerary and typed the number. The screen turned red. The screen flashed an "X." The machine beeped.

"Fuck," Natalie said.

"Type the number again," I said.

"This machine is broken."

"Try it again."

"I feel sick," Natalie said. "I'll throw up all over the airport."

"Fuck," I said.

A long line of people stood behind us. Some of them shifted their weight nervously. Natalie ran her fingers through her hair. She typed our flight number again. The screen turned blue. The machine spit out two boarding passes. A man appeared from behind the counter. He smiled and took our luggage. He looked at a computer screen. He raised his eyebrows twice. He told us he wished he was going to Hawaii. He said we were lucky. He pronounced *lucky* in a peculiar way, like a prisoner to his cellmate who was getting out on probation.

TWENTY-NINE

Me and Natalie walked down a long and boring corridor. We took our place at the end of a line of people waiting to go through security. The line moved slowly. Someone in a uniform stood behind a lectern and asked for identification. He examined our driver's licenses. He looked at our faces. He frowned. About a thousand creases formed across his face. He returned our documents and told us to proceed. His breath smelled like old meat. We moved forward and into another line, which eventually broke into several sub-lines, each leading to conveyor belts and millimeter wave detectors.

"Do you feel any better?" I asked.

"I'm about to vomit," Natalie said. "I'm about to die."

I put my backpack into a plastic tray and placed it on a conveyor belt that would carry it through an x-ray device. I unbuckled my belt. I emptied my pockets and put a few items in another tray. I walked forward. A woman in a navy blue uniform came up behind me.

"Take off your shoes, sir," she said.

She had the straight-backed posture of the librarian at my old elementary school. She did not smile.

"What?"

"Take off your shoes, sir."

I took off my shoes and put them in a bin, and I put the bin onto the conveyor belt. I walked through a millimeter wave detector. An equally stern woman behind the detector told me to stand on a pair of yellow footprints inside the detector. She told me to hold my hands above my head. The machine came to life. Antennas spun around me. The woman motioned for me to exit the machine. Then she held up her hand to make me stop. After a few seconds she told me I could go. I walked to the end of the conveyor belt and took back my shoes.

"Why did they make us take off our shoes?" I asked.

"It's important," Natalie said. "It's for security."

"Was that machine a metal detector?" I asked.

"It's like an x-ray, only more advanced," Natalie said. "It takes pictures of people through their clothes. Naked pictures. The pictures of naked people show up on a computer in a security booth."

"There's no way," I said.

"It's important," Natalie said. "It's for security."

THIRTY

We walked down another boring corridor toward our gate. We came to a big area with restaurants and stores—a McDonald's and Chick-fil-A and a place selling expensive jewelry. Roger and Avril sat on a bench in the middle of the walkway.

"It's like someone built a mall inside a concentration camp," I said.

"Buy me a Cinnabon," Natalie said.

"I thought you felt sick," I said.

"Cinnabon," she said.

She and Avril got in line at Cinnabon. I sat down next to Roger. I rubbed my eyes and yawned. I watched Avril and Natalie.

"Remember that time you fucked Avril?" I asked.

Roger shrugged. He scratched his jaw.

"She thinks she's better than everybody else," he said.

I watched Avril order a Cinnabon. My eyes lingered on her legs and ass.

"What was it like?" I asked.

Roger scratched his jaw again. Flexed a bicep. He watched Avril buy a Cinnabon.

"Mostly she sucked my dick," he said. "I didn't fuck her long. C.J. did most of the work. C.J. wore her out."

"But what was it like?"

"Boring," he said, shrugging. "She was drunk. We were all drunk. She was limp. I might as well have been fucking a blowup doll. It was like having sex with Pinocchio."

"That's weird," I said.

"She thinks she's so fucking smart," he said.

Natalie and Avril walked over to us and ate their Cinnabons. They tore off little bits and put them in their mouths. They talked about bathing suits. They said they wouldn't look good in their bathing suits if they kept eating Cinnabon. They laughed and kept eating. Natalie asked if I wanted a bite. I opened my mouth. She tore off a small piece of the pastry and fed it to me.

The Cinnabon tasted good at first and then bland.

It tasted like my whole life.

THIRTY-ONE

All of us sat in plastic chairs by the gate. We didn't talk. We looked at our phones and swiped our fingers over the surfaces. I opened Twitter. I read a tweet by president Trump.

Airplanes have become much too complicated. Who needs pilots? You need a computer scientist from MIT. Very sad. Very sad what we've done to our products.

The tweet made me feel a lot of different things. In particular, it made me afraid to board the plane. I imagined gripping the armrests—white knuckle—as the plane fell out of the sky. I imagined an engine exploding, shrapnel tearing a hole in the cabin, passengers being sucked out into the sky, the looks on their faces, terror and disbelief. I imagined yellow-hot flames racing through the cabin. I imagined burning alive at 10,000 feet. But all the same, the president's tweet made me feel happy that I was about to fly away. Hawaii was as far from Trump as I could go and still be in America. I wanted to escape. I wanted to be free of his dangerous stupidity and all the creeps who voted for him. Soon, my old life in Tennessee would fade away, like a long and particularly weird dream. A good dream? A bad one? It wouldn't matter. No one would remember. No one would care.

THIRTY-TWO

The cabin of the plane smelled like old tweedy clothing and B.O. I took my seat and noticed how the cabin looked smaller than the ones on TV. I thought about how many people must have sat in that same seat over the years—hundreds, maybe thousands—and the gallons of sweat that had soaked into the fabric. I wondered if a colony of lice could survive in the headrest. Thinking about it made my scalp tickle. I tried to ignore it but failed. I scratched my head. I wondered if my head would go on itching for the rest of the flight.

A guy in a seat in front of me played the original Game Boy *Pokémon* in a window on his laptop. I made a mental note to search for that online when I got back. If I got back. If the plane didn't splash down somewhere in the Pacific.

"How often do planes crash?" I asked Natalie.

I sat in an aisle seat because Natalie had taken the window. She opened a book of Sudoku puzzles. She used a pen to draw numbers in little boxes in the book. The cabin was crowded and hot. There wasn't much space between my seat and the one in front of me. The plane was still parked on the runway, but already my legs felt cramped. I'd never been on a plane before. I felt some anxiety.

Natalie and her family took flights every year to places like Jackson Hole and Malibu and Vail. My family didn't take many vacations. When we did, we drove to my grandparents' place in Ohio.

"It's really unusual for a plane to crash, right?" I asked.

Natalie scrawled more numbers in her Sudoku book. Her hair hung over her face, giving her the appearance of a Muppet or an Ewok. The plane, after going nowhere for a frustratingly long time, shuddered and started moving. I closed my eyes and gripped the armrests. The plane picked up speed down the runway, and the engines roared louder than I'd expected. My hand rested only a few inches from Natalie's. It would have been nice for her to hold my hand during takeoff. She would have felt soft, warm, and reassuring. The cabin rocked violently back and forth. I felt a strange lightness inside myself as the plane lifted off the ground. I looked over Natalie's shoulder out the window and saw the city of Nashville growing smaller as the plane gained altitude. Mentally I bid the city farewell. *Goodbye Nashville. You're a good city. You would be even more fun if I wasn't broke.* I looked into the distance in a direction I thought probably was southeast. *Goodbye Murfreesboro. I hope I never see you again. I hope while I'm away you get destroyed by a meteor from space.*

THIRTY-THREE

Flying can be very boring. I slid the in-flight magazine out of a pocket on the seat in front of me, then changed my mind and put it back. Natalie played *Candy Crush* on her iPhone. The flight attendants hadn't yet given any of the passengers permission to use portable electronic devices, but Natalie didn't care. I reached into the seat pocket again for the in-flight magazine. The pages stuck together as I turned them. I wondered how long the magazine had been on the plane and how many fingers had touched it. I read an article about Barcelona. I read an article about Jay-Z, how he used to sell crack, but he escaped the ghetto to become a megastar. I read an article about how to remove wine stains from a white shirt.

"Everything is awful," I said.

"Could you not be like that, just for one day?" Natalie asked. "Just as a personal favor to me?" She tapped her phone to dismiss *Candy Crush*.

"Not be like what?"

"Pathetic and depressing."

"That's my whole life," I said.

"I don't understand you," Natalie said. "Life is good. We live in the absolute best time in human history to be alive. My life is good.

I mean it's not perfect like in the movies, but it's good. It keeps getting better. The world gets better every year."

"*Your* life is great," I said. "Everybody else is fucked. I want to go away somewhere that's not so fucked. Japan or Canada. Or Norway. Would you move with me to Norway?"

"Norway is cold," Natalie said, scrunching her face. "So is Canada."

"Vancouver is nice. I read about it online. Everybody likes Vancouver."

"I don't know," she said.

"Japan then."

"People in Japan work themselves to death," she said. "There's some weird Bushido business-cult thing. In Japan, your boss owns you. He cracks the whip. People in Japan get ulcers. They kill themselves because they're ashamed they didn't work harder."

"What about Australia? Australia might be nice. Kangaroos and wombats and universal health care."

"I just want to live in D.C.," Natalie said. She ended the conversation by pulling out her iPhone again and resuming *Candy Crush*.

I closed my eyes. Natalie came from a nice family with a big house in a swanky neighborhood, and she assumed the whole world was just like that, one big gated community of upper middle class homes where everybody owned an SUV and a big flat-screen TV. I thought about Hawaii. I hoped it would be better than Tennessee, where everybody was broke and morbidly obese and consumed by hate and misery. I imagined palm trees and beaches. White sand. An ocean of turquoise water teeming with colorful fish, turtles munching on seaweed, dolphins cruising along undersea reefs. The dolphins would see me in the water and swim close, peer knowingly into my eyes. They would squeak and click the way dolphins do, and even though I don't speak the dolphin language, somehow I would understand. The dolphins would choose me, and love me, and together we would play in the wide blue ocean.

THIRTY-FOUR

On layover in Detroit I bought a Cinnabon of my own.

The layover lasted five hours. Eating the Cinnabon made me feel greasy. Eating a Cinnabon is equivalent to spending an entire day on your couch consuming video games and Cheetos. Later we all ate lunch at Arby's. Eating is a great way to spend time when you're stuck at an airport. The line for Arby's took twenty minutes. People stood in line like someone was giving away iPhones or babies. Everybody thought Arby's was the greatest thing in the world. Arby's is okay relative to other fast food, but it's really not very good. It's barely even food.

I watched Roger chew with his enormous jaw. Whenever he bit into his roast beef sandwich, he looked like one of those guys on survival shows from the Discovery Channel, one of those guys who snares a squirrel in a makeshift trap and then cooks it and bites off the head.

Between the four of us, we ate a lot of meat. Even Avril ate meat. She shrugged and told us it's hard to be a vegetarian in an airport. Arby's was so crowded that not everybody could find a seat. People stood around that area of the airport eating meat sandwiches. So much meat. So much chewing. It's hard to believe farmers can produce enough meat to satisfy the appetite of our species. Millions and millions of pounds of meat. There are many things about the human race that I won't pretend to know or understand, but one thing I know for sure is people love meat.

THIRTY-FIVE

After lunch we bought stuff at several different shops. We had a few hours until our next flight, and there was nothing to do in the airport except wait around and shop. I appreciated the way the airport stripped away all the bullshit of life. Waiting and shopping are important. People don't realize how important those things are.

Me and Roger read magazines in a bookstore while Avril and Natalie shopped for clothing somewhere else. Roger read a car magazine. The cover had a picture of a girl sitting on a Mustang. The girl wore slutty lingerie. I read a copy of *Electronic Gaming Monthly*. There are a lot of different magazines about video games, but *Electronic Gaming Monthly* is the best. I read an article about how the new *Call of Duty* had been released. The author said the game sold a lot of units. *Call of Duty* was a series of games about shooting people. A new *Call of Duty* game was released every year, and they always sold a lot of units. Games about shooting people were very popular. Games about driving go-carts and playing sports also did well. I returned *Electronic Gaming Monthly* to the shelf and picked up an issue of *PC Gamer*.

"When are you and Natalie getting hitched?" Roger asked. He flipped pages in his car magazine. He looked at another picture of a car with a woman on top of it.

"After college," I said.

"This summer?"

"Maybe," I said.

"Don't you need to get engaged first?"

"Yeah," I said. "Natalie would like that."

"Buy her a good ring," he said. "Not some Walmart shit."

"I'll buy her the biggest, bloodiest blood diamond," I said. "I'll buy it from the torture store."

"She'll like that," he said.

I read a review of the new *Civilization* game. I wanted to play it. I would found a new civilization, and then halfway through the game I'd simply stop allowing it to advance. I'd sit back and watch as my people descended into poverty and rage.

"The new *Civilization* game will move a lot of units," I said.

"What?"

I put the magazine back on the shelf. Roger asked if I'd ever fucked anybody other than Natalie. I told him I hadn't. Anyway it was shitty for him to ask. He already knew all about it.

"If I could only have sex with one person in my entire life, I'd kill myself," he said.

"That's dramatic," I said.

"You should fuck somebody."

"I fuck Natalie."

"That's not what I heard," Roger said. He put the car magazine back on the shelf. He crossed his arms and watched people walking through the airport. "At least half these girls would fuck you, I mean under the right circumstances," he said. "Jesus. There's no good reason why you're not fucking a new girl every week. You're in college. College is where girls go to fuck guys before getting married."

"That hasn't been my experience," I said.

"I don't understand how you haven't killed yourself already."

THIRTY-SIX

Roger picked up the current issue of *Investor's Business Daily*. A headline on the cover asked, *How high can the stock market rise?*

"We're all gonna make bank," Roger said. "The stock market loves Trump. We're all gonna be rich."

In Roger's imagination, Trump was the perfect politician. Roger especially loved watching him perform at rallies. He loved how Trump would swagger across the stage and make fun of everyone who opposed him. Trump's constant lying didn't bother Roger. He liked Trump even though he knew the president was hurting people, like the Muslims who were banned from entering the country or the migrant children stolen from their parents by Border Patrol agents. Roger believed he had nothing to worry about. Trump was on his side. Roger, like Trump, was a straight white man, and he knew that Trump loved straight white men more than any other people in the world.

"Oh my god stop talking about Trump," I said.

"You love it," Roger said.

Usually when Roger started going on about Trump, I'd just ignore it. I'd pretend to pay attention but tune him out. There in the airport, I didn't feel like ignoring it anymore. Maybe it was something about traveling, being in a new place and removed from the normal rhythms of my life.

"Your hero is about to be impeached," I said. "The only reason he's not in prison right now is because he's the president. He won't be the president forever."

I picked up another video game magazine and started flipping through it, but I couldn't focus. I was tired of Roger always acting superior. Tired of him drooling over Trump.

"I don't know what your problem is," Roger said. "I don't know why you're always crying about him. Remember the inauguration? American carnage? That's right up your alley. You should love Trump. You're always saying how fucked we are."

"He's making everything worse. Rich people are getting richer and poor people are getting poorer. He's just like your god-king Ronald Reagan but dumber and meaner and somehow even less cool."

"Jeez, quit your crying," Roger said. "Cucks like you are always crying."

"Don't fucking talk to me about Trump," I said. I stuffed the magazine back into the rack. The magazine cover featured a big green alien. The alien wielded a blaster rifle. The alien licked the barrel of the blaster rifle with its long, purple tongue. "I don't want to be around to see how bad Trump fucks us over. I don't want to go out in the world and find a job and work hard to make the Trump economy a success. For what? So he can go on TV and take the credit? Some rich guy? Some shitty Manhattan con man? Some brat who pissed away all his dad's money? That's the fucker who's taking credit? He shits on the Constitution and then takes credit for all the work I do?"

"Jeez, so much crying."

"Nobody cares what you think." I looked again at the magazine cover. The alien appeared to enjoy the taste of the metal barrel. I imagined the alien firing the weapon into its mouth, swallowing, feasting on dark, cosmic energy. "Roger, you're too dumb for politics. Don't ever fucking talk to me about Trump."

THIRTY-SEVEN

Natalie and Avril arrived with shopping bags. Natalie showed off a sweatshirt she'd bought. It was blue and said *Detroit* in block letters across the chest. Then Avril showed off what she bought, some fashion shirt like you'd see in a magazine.

"I have an idea," Avril said. "For this next flight, why don't we switch partners? Like Natalie will sit with Roger, and I'll sit with Nate."

"Why would we do that?" Natalie asked.

"I'm tired of Roger," Avril said, crinkling her nose. "Roger farts."

"I smell like a man," Roger said. "You don't like it because you're a dyke."

"This is exactly what I'm talking about," Avril said. "It's not fair to make me sit with Roger."

"I'll sit by Roger," Natalie said. "I don't care."

"This one, clearly, is no lesbian," Roger said. "Natalie appreciates the odor of a real man."

"Just forget it," Avril said, crossing her arms.

"Just admit you're a lesbian," Roger said.

Throughout the discussion, I'd been careful not to say anything or take a side. Natalie could be very paranoid, and if she began to suspect anything between me and Avril, she would magically pull out a gun from somewhere and murder everybody in the airport.

We sat down in a row of plastic seats by our gate. I watched the runway and the jets flying in and out. Roger and Avril sat side by side but ignored each other. Roger stared at people walking through the airport, and Avril listened to music on her iPhone. Natalie sat beside me and played *Candy Crush* on her iPhone. If I'd had an iPhone, I would have done something cool with it. But I didn't have an iPhone. I had a dumb Android. It was embarrassing. It was old and didn't have enough memory to run many apps. Mostly it was good for making phone calls and sending texts. I preferred sending texts over actually calling and speaking to people. With a text you can get right to the point without all the bullshit of conversation.

From the window I could see part of the city. I wanted to spend a day in Detroit. I wanted to drive around and see the abandoned factories and houses. Detroit used to be an American success story, a place where all the jobs and money came from. But over time, people discovered it was cheaper to manufacture products in places like China, Sri Lanka, and Alabama—places with a lot of poor people who didn't mind working long hours for very little money. That's why Detroit was fucked. Everybody on cable news would always discuss ways to un-fuck Detroit, and before every presidential election the candidates would visit and talk about how they'd reopen the factories. It was all shit. Detroit would only get worse. Detroit's problems were the same problems of every city in the country, because every city depended on middle class people making enough money to buy things. Even post-industrial cities that create software and websites relied on people who had enough disposable income to afford their products. You'd always hear great things about the economic recovery, and how low the unemployment rate had dropped. But people didn't have good jobs with nice benefits like they'd had in the old days. People worked at Burger King. They folded sweaters at The Gap. Late-stage Capitalism sucked all of life and happiness into a final cyclone of sorrow and debt. Someday, every city in America will look like Detroit. If you don't live in Norway yet, now would be a good time to move.

THIRTY-EIGHT

Taking off from the airport in Detroit felt much less terrifying than taking off in Nashville—not because I was any braver than before but because I was bored. Air flight is a legitimate miracle but also quite tedious. All I could think about was having to do it again after we landed in Las Vegas. And that would be the big flight, the one to Hawaii. Six hours on a plane.

I was excited about swapping seats and sitting beside Avril, but as soon as we boarded, Natalie decided it was a stupid idea. She pulled me into the seat beside her. She even took the window seat again. It should have been mine, according to the tickets. Natalie took it without asking, as if her entitlement to the window seat was one of the fundamental laws of the universe.

I drummed my fingers on the armrest. I pulled the in-flight magazine out of a pouch in the back of the seat in front of me. I re-read the story about Jay-Z. I paid attention to the part about his genius for promoting his personal brand. In the article, he emphasized the importance of social-media networking to sell yourself. He said people were more likely to buy something from you if they felt like they knew you. I put the magazine away and pulled out an issue of *SkyMall*. I read an advertisement for miniature Ugg boots for dogs. I read an advertisement for a four-foot metal gong. I put *SkyMall* back in the seat pouch.

"Would it be okay if I sat by the window on the next flight?" I asked.

Natalie looked up from her Sudoku book.

"I like the window seat," she said. "I always sit in the window seat."

"Sure," I said. "But would it be okay if I sat by the window, just for one flight?"

"There's nothing to see. Just clouds." She glanced back down at her Sudoku book.

"It's pretty shitty to always take the window seat," I said.

Natalie jerked up her head like I'd slapped her, then looked down again and made a notation in her book.

"Since you're not going to do anything about it," she said, "why don't you shut the fuck up?"

I stopped trying to have a meaningful conversation. I put in headphones and searched for music in the plane's in-flight entertainment system. I listened to "Wrecking Ball" by Miley Cyrus. The song made me feel emotional. I imagined Miley sitting beside me instead of Natalie. I imagined traveling with her to Hawaii. Me and Miley would walk together in the rainforest. I would hold her hand. Miley would sing for me, something slow, a ballad, and her voice would rise to a pure note, drawing out the animals of the forest from their hiding places among the shadows of the trees. Me and the forest creatures would join together in a circle. All of us would dance to Miley's song.

THIRTY-NINE

The thing to know about the Las Vegas airport is you can gamble. You don't have to catch a cab to the casinos on the Strip or see the city or interact with people in any meaningful way. You can sit on your ass and play slots at gate 23. People seem to enjoy it.

The prospect of gambling excited Roger. The girls went shopping again while me and Roger entered a glass room full of slot machines in the middle of one of the airport's walkways. Roger exchanged a fifty-dollar bill. A lady gave him a handful of quarters. She said "good luck" and raised her eyebrows twice.

Roger sat on a stool and fed quarters into a slot machine. I stood behind him. I'd never gambled, and being around the machines made me nervous.

"The secret to winning is to play the same machine all night," Roger said.

He pulled down the arm, and it slowly raised itself back to an upright position as icons spun behind little windows. When the machine stopped spinning, the icons didn't match. Roger put another quarter into the machine and pulled the arm.

"I'm gonna make money," he said. "Gonna make bank."

"You should be a doctor," I said. "They make all the money."

"Fuck doctors," Roger said, inserting another quarter. "I'm going to Wall Street. I'm working for Goldman-Sachs. After the last time the economy crashed, everybody on Wall Street lost money. Everybody but Goldman Sachs. Goldman Sachs made bank."

"That's because they scammed people. I watched a documentary about it on Netflix. They sold phony derivatives and subprime mortgages. They used their connections to the federal government to get billions in taxpayer money, while everybody else lost their homes and went bankrupt. Goldman Sachs is basically the devil."

"You don't make money following the rules," Roger said, feeding another quarter into the machine. "Finance isn't some romantic comedy where the nice guy wins. You make money by taking it from someone else."

"I'll be sure to tell that to my future coworkers at the IRS," I said.

"The IRS sucks," he said.

"I guess," I said. "It's a job. It's money."

"There are easier ways to make money," Roger said. He put another quarter into the machine. "What do IRS workers even do?"

"I don't know. I don't care."

"I could never work at the IRS. I couldn't ever stand to be that bored."

"All jobs are boring," I said. "I don't want to work. I want to go away. Somewhere nice. Japan. I want to ride a bullet train from Tokyo to Kyoto and look out the window at Mt. Fuji."

"Japanese girls make me sick," Roger said. "Skinny. Small tits. Japanese girls are only good for blow jobs. Don't move to Japan. Just go on vacation and get a blowjob."

I thought about Japan. I imagined walking through a pine forest on a mountain path and arriving at an ancient shrine marked by torii gates. If I could step outside and see Mt. Fuji every day, I wouldn't care so much about the end of the world.

I felt my phone vibrate in my pocket. I read a text from Avril.

"Natalie's buying shit," she wrote.

"That's our Natalie," I wrote back.

"I want you," she wrote.

"Have me," I wrote.

Roger inserted another quarter into the slot machine. He pulled the handle. Lost. Inserted another quarter.

"Do you think I'll get laid in Hawaii?" he asked.

I shrugged. I didn't have strong opinions about Roger's sex life.

"I bet Hawaiian girls are easy," Roger said. "I bet they love putting out for white guys from back east. I bet Hawaiian girls are fucking sluts."

"White people stole their country," I said. "This thing about white people stealing their country might make it harder for you to get laid."

"Think about how much better off they are for being in America," Roger said. "If it wasn't for us, Hawaii would be some shitty third-world country where everybody is poor, some place nobody ever heard of outside *National Geographic*. They'd be Samoa. What the fuck good ever came from Samoa? Not a goddamned thing. I bet Hawaiian girls love white guys. I'll get tons of pussy in Hawaii."

Roger looked like all the guys in Hollywood movies and *GQ Magazine*. He was easily the best-looking guy in the airport casino. I only looked better than about twenty percent of the guys in the airport casino.

"Have you ever had trouble getting laid?" I asked.

Roger stared dumbly like he didn't understand the question.

"You'll get laid in Hawaii," I said.

Roger played slots until he ran out of quarters. We left the casino and walked to our gate, where we spotted the girls. Natalie carried a pink shopping bag. I waited for her to show me what she'd bought, but she ignored me until I specifically asked. She shrugged and rolled her eyes. She opened the bag to show me. At the bottom of the bag was a satiny-black pair of panties with the words *I got fucked in Vegas* printed across the butt.

FORTY

On the flight to Hawaii, the girls sat together in the row in front of me and Roger. Me and Roger ordered beer, and Natalie and Avril ordered wine.

"This flight is taking forever," Natalie said. "It's taking the rest of my life."

"I want to go to the beach," Avril said.

"You're so lucky to be single," Natalie said. "You'll meet some cute boy on the beach. A surfer."

Avril sipped wine, then nodded her head. "I'll fuck a surfer's dick off."

Natalie and Avril laughed and drank more wine.

"I heard you're not hurting for dick," Roger said, leaning forward to speak through the seats.

Avril gave him her *get lost, creep* look.

"Everybody says so," Roger said. "Every guy from MTSU."

"How are you always full of shit?" Avril asked. "Always."

"Own up to it," Roger said. "Nothing worse than a slut who doesn't know she's a slut."

"Jesus," Natalie said.

"Everybody should stop talking," I said.

"Don't fucking call me a slut," Avril said. She leaned over the seat, face to face with Roger. She held up her plastic cup of airline wine and waved it around, spilling a little, like one of *The Real Housewives of Dallas*.

Roger leaned away and drank from his cup of beer.

"If you don't like being called a slut, don't be a slut," Roger said. "Simple. Right Nate? Nate gets it. Nate doesn't fuck sluts."

The situation was bad. I considered what Jean-Pierre Léaud would do. Probably he would make some joyously naive statement about the brotherhood and sisterhood of all mankind, then fall in love with a redhead with beautiful green eyes. And that's all well and good for Jean-Pierre Léaud, but as usual it didn't help me with my problems. I'd already fallen for a beautiful redhead. My love for her hadn't improved my life, only complicated it. Everything became worse. My suffering had increased until I no longer cared about brotherhood or mankind. I just wanted the suffering to end.

"Everybody please stop talking," I said.

Natalie heroically changed the subject. She complained that her fingernail polish had chipped and she'd have to reapply when we landed in Hawaii. Natalie and Avril talked about nail polish for a while, and me and Roger read *SkyMall*. Later the cabin lights turned low and the flight attendants passed out blankets and pillows. Natalie rested her head on a pillow against the side of the cabin. Her hair glowed golden in the dim light. I leaned forward to talk to her.

"Feels weird to fly."

"Weird," she said.

"I've thought a lot about graduation."

Natalie didn't say anything.

"I don't think I want to work at the IRS," I said.

"That's stupid." Natalie's head came off the pillow. She craned her neck to look at me. "You have to. What else can you do? You're an English major. There's nothing you can do."

"I don't know. I think if ten years from now I still work for the IRS, maybe I'll jump in front of a bus."

"Fine," she said, anger lines forming at the corners of her mouth. "It's your life. Fuck it up all you want. Don't get a real job. Don't grow up. Just wait tables at Applebee's for the next fifteen years. Knock up a hostess. Raise an ugly baby in a trailer park. Have a great life."

I leaned forward again, farther this time, to give her a meaningful look, one that would silently communicate that I loved her and everything would be okay forever. She looked out the window. She looked at the ceiling. She looked at anything but me. She returned her head to the pillow. I kept waiting for her to say something. Turbulence ran like a tremor through the cabin. I looked at my girlfriend. I considered reaching over the seat to touch her but didn't.

FORTY-ONE

The flight to Hawaii lasted several hours. It felt like my entire life. Actually it felt like something beyond my life, like I'd fallen through some crack in spacetime and into a pocket universe outside the bounds of linear reality. I felt drowsy. I felt like nothing that happened in the airplane universe mattered to my real life.

Eventually Roger dozed off. I could tell by the snoring. I took out my phone and connected to the plane's wi-fi network. The airline charged $10 for an hour of wi-fi, and I happily accepted. Even getting fleeced by the airline was better than listening to Roger snore.

I opened Instagram and scrolled through my feed. Someone had posted a photo of their new baby. Someone had posted a video of their cat peeking out of a cardboard box. I kept scrolling. I saw a photo Natalie had posted from Thanksgiving with her family. Everybody in the picture had blond hair and attractive features. Natalie's family looked like a bunch of escaped Nazi war criminals. It wasn't their fault, but still it gave me the creeps.

I opened Facebook. Checked out Avril's profile and read a list of her favorite books. She liked *White Noise* by Don DeLillo and *The Sun Also Rises* by Ernest Hemingway and *The Dharma Bums* by Jack

Kerouac. These were some of my favorite books. It seemed significant that we liked the same writers. I looked at her photos. She'd taken a few with various boyfriends, which I rapidly clicked past. I looked at a picture of her from a hiking trip. She stood by a waterfall, and she wore a backpack and a flannel shirt with the sleeves rolled up above her elbows. She'd pulled her hair back into a ponytail, and she smiled real big and goofy and held out her hands to the waterfall like it was magic. I wanted to be in the picture with her. I wanted to walk with her through a forest of waterfalls and magic.

I looked at her pictures until I felt creepy. I closed Facebook and opened Chrome. I typed *Great Pacific Garbage Patch* into the search bar. I read a Wikipedia article. According to Wikipedia, the vortex is characterized by exceptionally high concentrations of plastic, chemical sludge, wood pulp, and other debris trapped by the currents of the North Pacific Gyre. The vortex is actually "two enormous masses of ever-growing garbage," one to the west of Hawaii and another to the east. Scientists believe the garbage patch is hundreds of miles long. Seabirds and fish and turtles sometimes mistake bits of plastic for food, and they choke to death trying to eat them. The plastics remain in the water for years as sunlight gradually breaks them down into a sludge of toxic chemicals.

I read about several garbage patches, smaller ones near Japan and Alaska. Wikipedia had a lot to say about oceanic garbage. Nobody can be quite sure how big the garbage vortexes are or even how to measure them. Some scientists say they're hundreds of miles long, others say thousands. Some say the big one is the size of Texas. Scientists don't agree on these things. I continued reading. Some scientists believe the oceans will contain more weight in plastics than fish by the year 2050. Twenty tons of plastic garbage washes up on the shores of Midway Atoll every year. All 1.5 million of the Layson albatrosses are believed to have plastic in their digestive tracts. One third of their chicks die, many because of plastic unwittingly fed to them by their parents.

"Everybody wang chung tonight," I said—quietly, whispering to my phone. "Drown in garbage tonight."

I wanted to sleep. I looked at my hands poised above the screen and noticed how the light bleached my fingers white. I stared at my zombie hands. I sat in the relative darkness and tried to envision a Texas-sized field of garbage. I imagined I was a seabird, flying over the bobbing jugs of Clorox Bleach and sandwich bags and soda bottles and little plastic toys and pellets. If I was a bird encountering a garbage vortex for the first time, I would feel proud. Proud to have discovered a terrible new world of spiritual poverty and despair.

FORTY-TWO

At some hard-to-define location above the Pacific Ocean, Roger and Natalie got up to use the restroom at the same time. Avril took advantage. She sat beside me as soon as they were gone. Something about her face looked wrong, as if she'd spent too many hours in the airplane universe, long enough for her physical body to begin fading to shadow.

"Have you thought any more about the end of the world?" she asked.

"A little. I had this dream last night where a virus wiped out the human race. Pigs spread the virus."

"Swine flu," said Shadow Avril.

"Sort of. Except the virus spread through meat. No amount of cooking could kill it."

"That's weird."

"So in the dream, everybody eats sausage and pork chops and hamburgers until it kills them. Even after they figure out something is wrong with the meat, they won't stop eating. They keep on shoveling bacon down their throats until every last human is dead."

"You're lucky I like weird people," she said. "I'm tired of Natalie, and Roger is impossible. He just farts and talks about football." She put her hand on my arm, and it felt good and I wanted to feel more of her.

Natalie returned from the restroom. Glared at us. Avril gave up the seat. Natalie glared at her some more. The expression on Natalie's face said *back off, bitch*. Natalie sat beside me. Glared.

"What was she doing here?" she asked, glaring away.

"Talking about meat."

"I'll bet," she said. "Roger warned me about her. I think Roger was right all along."

"It's scary to think about Roger being right about anything."

"Sometimes I can't stand that slut," Natalie said. Then she pulled out her phone and ignored me.

FORTY-THREE

I closed my eyes but couldn't sleep. Opened my eyes. Looked up and down the rows of people in the muted light. Everybody breathed the same air and exhaled stink breath. It seemed impossible that the cabin wouldn't fill up with stink breath. All of us should have died, suffocating on stink breath.

I closed my eyes again. Listened to the roar of engines, louder than I expected. Nobody ever told me airplanes were so loud. I thought about the engines and the long contrails of greenhouse gases streaming out of them. I thought about all the airplanes in the world, all of them trailing exhaust, and all the carbon dioxide rising from cars and chimneys and smokestacks, like pale fingers squirming toward the sky. I imagined all those gases merging into a massive cloud that descended slowly through the atmosphere, wiping out entire flocks of birds. I imagined a storm of dead and dying birds raining from the sky. Thinking about it drove me crazy. Thinking about it, it seemed impossible that all of us hadn't suffocated already.

PART THREE

THIS
PLACE WE
CALL
PARADISE

FORTY-FOUR

WE ARRIVED IN KONA in the morning. I never did fall asleep on the flight, and my eyes felt buggy the way they do when I stay up too late reading the internet. The plane shuddered slightly as it descended toward the island. Natalie snoozed in the seat beside me, and when she awoke she took a deep breath and smiled and squeezed my arm, and the light from the window lit up her face just right, and for a split second I remembered why I loved her. She had the window seat—naturally—and I leaned over her shoulder to look outside. A bright blue ocean surrounded the island, which rose up high into a mountain with a snow-capped peak.

"I love it," I said. "I already love it."

"Of course you do," Natalie said. "It's Hawaii. There's nothing to do but love it."

After we landed, the crew kept us on the plane for a long time. Nobody told us why.

"It's hot in here," Natalie said. She held her luggage and stood in the aisle among a long line of people waiting to disembark.

"Calm down," Roger said. "This will only take a minute." He flew from time to time and enjoyed pretending to be an expert.

"I'm dying here," Natalie said after another five minutes. "I'm hot. I have to piss." All of us still wore our sweaters from Murfreesboro.

After a long time and with no explanation, the crew allowed us to disembark the aircraft. We followed a sign pointing to baggage claim. We stood with several dozen people around a semi-circular conveyor belt. Pieces of luggage came down a chute, and everybody leaned in, trying to determine if it was their luggage. Natalie and I both had black luggage. All our luggage actually belonged to Natalie. Her aunt gave it to her for Christmas. None of my relatives ever gave me luggage. We weren't the kind of family that took nice vacations. I watched the conveyor belt. All the luggage was black and nearly identical.

"My head hurts," I said.

"Don't fall asleep when you get to the hotel," Roger said. "You'll sleep all day and be up all night."

A piece of black luggage made its way along the conveyor belt. I looked at it carefully. It wasn't mine.

"I feel like if I don't sleep I'll die," I said.

"If you fall asleep, you're fucked," Roger said.

"After the hotel let's find a beach," Natalie said.

"The hotel is on a beach," Avril said.

"Oh," Natalie said. "Good."

Avril grabbed a piece of black luggage as it moved along the conveyor belt.

"The beach must be awful if it's right in the middle of town," Natalie said. "We should go somewhere better. Find a real beach."

Roger pulled a piece of black luggage off the conveyor belt.

"Shit," he said. "It's not mine."

He put it back on the conveyor. It moved on for about five yards until some grandmother picked it up. She made a mean face at Roger and walked away.

"I need alcohol," Roger said, rubbing his eyes. "I can't think straight in the morning until I've had a drink."

"Here comes our luggage," Natalie said.

I stepped toward the conveyor and pulled off two pieces of luggage. Soon after, Roger's and Avril's appeared. We walked out of the building and onto a sidewalk. The light outside was blinding. All the colors of Hawaii—blue sky, green plants—appeared extremely vivid. I was unaccustomed to the vividity. The strength of the colors contributed to my feeling of dizziness and disorientation.

Palm trees lined the walkway. I stopped in front of one. The palm tree stood surprisingly tall. If a coconut had fallen off and hit me on the head, it would have killed me. My death would have been ugly and painful.

"Where are the goddamned taxis?" Roger asked. "There should be taxis."

We wandered around for a while until we found some taxis parked around the corner. The drivers looked happy to see us. A taxi took us a short distance to the Grand Lili'uokalani Hotel, by the bay and in the center of town.

The lobby wasn't what I expected. Hidden speakers piped soft music into the room. The song playing as we entered was "Jingle Bells," only instead of regular Christmas music, it was some Hawaiian version of the song. A tall Christmas tree stood in the lobby. The tree was decorated with orange and yellow tropical flowers and little figurines of Santa riding a surfboard and wearing a grass hula skirt.

"Weirdness," Avril said.

"Weirdness," I said.

We wheeled our luggage to the front desk. The clerk was a middle-aged Asian man wearing a Hawaiian shirt. He eyed us suspiciously, as if we were too young to stay at the Grand Lili'uokalani. Anyway we checked in. He handed us our keys and said *Aloha*, but even though he smiled as he said it, the word sounded fake, as if repetition had long ago beaten all wonder and magic from it.

Me and Natalie promised Roger we'd meet him in the bar after dropping off our luggage in our room. We were all staying on one of the topmost floors with views of the ocean. Not the very top but near it, high enough so we could feel like people of wealth, looking down from a safe distance on the messy world of poverty and struggle below.

Our room was small but nice. A medium-sized flat-screen TV stood on a desk. The bed felt soft and clean. The room smelled like nothing but the cool emptiness of air conditioning.

"What a nice room," I said, hefting our luggage onto a rack in the closet.

"I don't stay in bad rooms."

"It was good of your father to spring for such a nice room."

"He doesn't stay in bad rooms, either." She affected a fake British accent, waved her hand dismissively. "He taught me everything I know about avoiding bad rooms."

"How long will he keep giving you money?"

"I don't know if he'll ever stop."

She sat on the bed. I joined her, and we let our heads sink into the soft luxury of the pillows. I considered attempting to have sex with her.

"We have to meet Roger in the bar," she said.

I surveyed the room—the faded wall art, mini fridge, and balcony with a view of white sand and the ocean.

"I don't know what's real anymore," I said.

Then we fell asleep.

FORTY-FIVE

I woke up in the dark around 8 p.m. Natalie slept beside me, and in the gloom she appeared shadowy, lacking substance or detail, like a Dementor from a Harry Potter book.

"Get up," I said. "We fell asleep."

"Jesus." She lifted her head.

I heard her voice, but the room was too dark for me to see her mouth move.

"We shouldn't have fallen asleep," she said. "It's bad to fall asleep after a plane trip."

"I don't see what difference it makes."

"You'll see when you're still awake at 4 a.m."

I placed my hand on the side of her face and felt the softness of her hair and cheek. I kissed her, and she kissed me back. I moved close so our bodies pressed together. I reached for her hip and untucked her blouse and put my hand on her waist.

"Not now." She pulled away. "There's no time."

"We're on vacation," I said. "All we have is time. Hawaii is like Narnia. We'll go home in a week and find out we've only been gone for five minutes."

She got off the bed and switched on the lights. She called Roger on her iPhone. She spoke rapidly and apologized.

"We'll be right down," she said into the phone. She turned to me. "He's been at the bar all day."

"That's why he's my hero," I said.

FORTY-SIX

The hotel bar appeared dim and skeezy. Roger and Avril sat at a table in a corner. I noticed how the orange glow of overhead bulbs reflected in the contours of Roger's glass, so that when he raised it to his lips he appeared to be drinking pure light. Avril sagged against the table, her arms forming a pyramid that supported her head. Inside the pyramid stood a glass of bright greenish liquid with a slice of lime dangling from the rim. Roger nudged Avril as we took seats across the table.

"They fell asleep," he said. "Just like I told you. Jesus. You'd think they'd never flown before."

"I've never flown before," I said.

Roger didn't hear me. He shook his head and laughed and bobbed back and forth in his chair. He nudged Avril.

"They've been fucking, right?" He nudged her again and laughed with his mouth wide open. "Jesus, I bet Nate banged her ass all day."

"How many has he had?" Natalie asked.

"He was like this when I got here." Avril shrugged. "I was in my room all day. I fell asleep."

Roger high-fived me.

"Fucking porn star," he said. "I don't know how you landed a bitch like Natalie. If I were you, I'd bang her two times every night."

"Jesus," I said.

"I'd bang her so hard," he said. He tried to high-five me again but missed my hand. He laughed and pounded the table.

"Roger should eat," Natalie said.

We stood him up, and he put his arms over me and Natalie's shoulders. We headed for the door, but the bar manager rushed over, waving us down.

"He never paid!" he said.

Everyone in the bar looked up from their drinks. All the customers were white, and most of them were middle-aged or older, but the workers—the manager and waiters and bartenders—were Hawaiian and Korean and Filipino. Natalie followed the manager to the cash register and cleared up Roger's bill with her credit card.

FORTY-SEVEN

Out we stumbled into the sublime darkness of the Hawaiian night. Hotel lights illuminated a small beach of white sand. Natalie squealed and took off running toward the water lapping ashore. Avril sighed and rolled her eyes and chased after her. They knelt and put their hands in the ocean. They took off their sandals and danced in the water. Natalie wore a short silver dress that glimmered in the moonlight. She took out her iPhone and snapped a selfie.

"Bitches be crazy," Roger said.

"It's the little things that make Natalie happy," I said.

"Obviously." Roger snorted, then laughed really loud. "The thing about girls is you can't trust them. Girls are liars. Sluts. You can't trust Natalie. It's nothing personal, Nate. You can't trust anyone." Roger laughed really loud again. Pounded me on the back. It was supposed to be friendly but hurt a little. Natalie and Avril continued dancing in the water. Waves rolled in, causing foam to swirl around their ankles.

"They're happy here," I said.

"You know what makes *me* happy?"

I opened my mouth to answer, but he cut me off.

"Drinking," he said.

"You must be very happy."

"Today is the happiest day of my life."

After Natalie and Avril finished playing in the ocean we walked down Ali'i Drive. The road curved along the coast, bordered on one side by a low seawall. The sidewalks were packed with tourists just like us. A few people walked on the seawall and looked at the ocean. Lampposts lit up the street.

"This is where the tourists go," Natalie said.

"The Hawaiians buried magnets underground," Roger said. "Tourists magnets."

"I'm a tourist," Avril said. "I don't feel anything."

"It's not a slut magnet," Roger said.

We navigated the crowded sidewalks. Sketchy kids in ball caps moved in packs as couples held hands and old people meandered slowly along. The crowd was mostly white people, which seemed strange to me. We passed a store selling ugly T-shirts and beach towels and flip-flops. Suddenly everything made sense. White people love ugly T-shirts and beach towels and flip-flops.

"We should come back here later," Natalie said. "For souvenirs. I should get something for mom."

"It's too early to think about souvenirs," Avril said. "We just got here."

"I never buy souvenirs," Roger said, weaving a little as he walked. "I'm an asshole."

"That's why everybody likes you," Natalie said. "I'm tired of people who are simple and kind. I can't go to the grocery store anymore without some nice guy letting me in front of him in line. I've had all I can take of nice people."

"Nice people are boring," Avril said.

"You girls are lucky to be with me and Nate," Roger said. "We're assholes."

"We drink too much," I said.

"That's a red flag," Roger said. "That's the highway to the danger zone."

We walked by the Fish Hopper restaurant. It had a large, elevated patio full of diners who seemed to be having a lot of fun. Natalie looked at the patio, then back at me, then back at the patio. I followed her up a short flight of wooden steps to the entrance.

"Looks expensive," I said.

"I'll put it on the card," Natalie said. "Dad wants us to have a good time."

We walked upstairs and talked to the hostess. She was Hawaiian and pretty. She smiled. She took us to a table by the railing so we could see the ocean. A busboy, also Hawaiian, wiped off the table as we approached. He smiled just like the hostess. Workers at swanky restaurants always smile. When you go to a crappy restaurant like Applebee's, the waiters never smile. I don't know anything about working at restaurants, but one thing I know for sure is that the people who work at swanky restaurants smile so much because they're relieved not to be working at some hellhole like Applebee's. That's what I would do.

The waiter arrived—smiling—and we ordered drinks. A few minutes later he brought them to the table and asked if we were ready to order. Natalie tried to order a chicken sandwich, but Roger interrupted.

"Get some fish," Roger said. "This is Hawaii. People eat fish in Hawaii. Goddamn. Eat some fish before you piss off the volcano god."

"I don't know what to order," Natalie said.

The waiter recommended Ahi. He said it was the catch of the day. He was extremely polite. All of us ordered Ahi.

"I can't believe we're in Hawaii," Natalie said.

"I'm so drunk," Roger said. He drank a Jameson and ginger ale. "I don't care where I am. I could be in Baltimore, and it would still be awesome. Baltimore is the worst place on Earth."

"Everything here is so exotic," Natalie said.

"Everybody here is white," I said. "I feel like I'm in Iowa. Everybody here is a tourist."

"Some of them must be from Europe," Natalie said. "Exciting."

"It's like the Nazis won World War II and made everybody white," I said. "There should be brown people in Hawaii, but everybody's white."

"That's what's great about Hawaii," Roger said. "It's Americanized. It's like a foreign country that America owns, so there's no culture shock."

I looked around the restaurant at all the white people eating fish. Brown people took orders and bused tables. When the food showed up, we ordered another round of drinks. I was really very hungry, and once I started eating I relaxed and stopped feeling weird about all the white people. I tried the ahi and liked it. I hoped it wasn't something endangered.

Beyond the patio, streetlights splashed on the road and the shiny tops of cars swishing by. Waves broke against the seawall, sending foam exploding over the edge. I ate and talked to Natalie. Sometimes I glanced at Avril, and sometimes she glanced back. When the check came, I wrote a big tip and put it all on Natalie's credit card. I enjoyed spending other people's money. Maybe working at the IRS wouldn't be so bad. I needed a job and a real income. Back in Murfreesboro, I worried a lot about money. Everybody in Murfreesboro worried about money. Worrying about money seemed very normal, the natural state of things. I wanted to be rich and never worry about anything forever.

FORTY-EIGHT

After dinner we merged back into the crowd of tourists meandering down Aliʻi. I held Natalie's hand, and the night felt warm, and the air smelled salty like the ocean, and the whole scene might have been romantic except Roger wouldn't shut up.

"Let's rent a boat," he said. "Tonight. Go out on the water. Dump some chum. Fish for sharks. Spear fishing. Spear fishing on a boat. Chum for tiger sharks and spear the fuck out of them."

Avril rolled her eyes but didn't say anything. She followed a few steps behind the rest of us, her arms crossed over her chest. We passed more tourist shops and restaurants. An old man sat in the doorway of some business that had closed for the night. He looked Hawaiian. He had a long beard that would have been white if it hadn't been so dirty. As we passed, he coughed and spit a glob of something out of his mouth. He said something I couldn't understand and held out his hand. We ignored him and kept walking.

"I hate beggars," Natalie said.

"Hawaii is full of bums," Roger said.

"They only come here because people give them money," Natalie said. "The suckers who give money feel good about themselves, but it only encourages more begging. The suckers are part of the problem. A lot of Hawaiians make a living asking people for money. And not a bad living, either. Not in a tourist trap like this. It's all stupid. Don't give homeless people any money."

The more Natalie talked, the more I wanted to go back and give that guy a five-dollar bill. But I didn't. I kept on walking with everyone else.

"We should fuck with a bum tonight," Roger said. "Act real friendly and get him drunk. Then when he passes out, toss him into the ocean."

Natalie laughed. She looked at Roger and made eye contact, and he laughed. Natalie and Roger shared a special moment together laughing about bums.

FORTY-NINE

We left the sidewalk and entered a damp alleyway. Natalie used her phone to navigate. She took us to a building that looked like a warehouse. Electronic music emanated faintly from inside. A large sign over the entrance spelled *Sunlight* in plastic yellow letters. A small group of people huddled beneath it. We joined the huddle. Natalie rifled through her wallet and handed me some cash. A bouncer, big and Hawaiian, leaned against the wall and looked bored. Sometimes he talked to girls on their way inside. At the door, I paid with Natalie's cash. We went inside, and the place looked like any other club except with a lot more wooden tiki figures.

The bartender was Hawaiian and pretty. She said *aloha* just like the clerk at the hotel, emotionlessly, as if repeating the word ad nauseam at her place of work had stomped all life and meaning out of it, like if she said it one more time she might put a gun in her mouth and blow her brains out all over the bar. I ordered fruity drinks and paid for them with Natalie's credit card. We found a table in the back. We sat down and sipped our drinks. My friends went to the dance floor. I remained seated and continued drinking. My drink tasted sweet and good. I watched my friends dance. First Avril and Natalie danced together, then Natalie danced with some Hawaiian guy with big muscles. He wore a sleeveless shirt to show off his muscles. He had the right idea. If I ever developed big muscles, I would only wear sleeveless shirts. I'd take all my regular shirts and rip out the sleeves.

A sweet, rummy flavor coated the inside of my mouth. My drink tasted like pineapples and sugar. I watched Natalie and Roger dance close and whisper. I finished my drink and burped sugar and pineapples. I stood up and went to the dance floor. The music sounded weird, some mash-up of electronica and Hawaiian, something I'd never heard before. I touched Natalie from behind, and when she saw me she looked surprised. Roger danced by himself for a while. Then he danced with a white girl with dreadlocks.

"Funny seeing you here," Natalie said.

"You're a good dancer," I said.

"I know."

She moved away to dance by herself. I didn't follow, didn't want to bother her. I didn't want to get in the way of her having fun and dancing with whomever, maybe Roger or another asshole with his sleeves ripped out. We'd been dating for a long time and understood the importance of space, spending time with other people. I found Avril dancing alone. She smiled at me. We danced. Orange light from tiki torches flickered across her skin.

"Move to Japan with me?" I asked.

"Do you even know how to use chopsticks?"

"Move to Japan with me and eat McDonald's?"

Avril told me I was funny. She said we didn't talk enough.

"Move to Japan and talk to me," I said.

"I want to see you tonight."

"I don't know."

"Tomorrow?"

"Maybe," I said. "I don't know."

We danced close. I enjoyed the soft pressure of her tits against my chest. I felt good. I felt a lot of other things too. I felt guilty about Natalie. I felt confused. I felt like I'd screwed up my whole life and didn't know how to fix it.

Lights flashed, painting Avril blue, then yellow, then blue again. I wanted to stay on the dance floor with her forever.

"Tomorrow," I said.

FIFTY

We stayed at the club for an hour before returning to the hotel. Me and Natalie went to our room, and she flopped onto the bed. It was very swanky with expensive blankets and sheets. Natalie belonged there, with her silver dress and smooth legs, her hair splayed out over the pillows like she'd been arranged on the bed by some famous designer for a photo shoot in *Vanity Fair*.

I opened a sliding glass door and stepped onto the balcony. The air felt warm, and the sky glowed with silver moonlight. Everything looked sharper and more colorful than it did back home, as if I was observing the world through a powerful lens. I held onto the railing and leaned forward to see the sand below and, further off, the sea. The surf made a noise like fire from a jet engine. Suddenly I wanted a cigarette. I didn't smoke much but would have liked to smoke on that balcony above the beach.

"Hail, ancient ocean," I said.

I wanted the ocean to hear me. I wanted it to like me and be my friend. I wanted the ocean to know that no matter what happened while I was in Hawaii, I would remain loyal to it. Secretly loyal.

I went back in the room and lay down with Natalie. She told me to turn off the lights. I got up and fumbled around for the switch.

I turned off the lights and went back to bed. I found Natalie's body in the dark. We kissed. I helped her slip out of her dress. I kissed her again and pawed her tits. Natalie's were the only tits I'd ever known. I felt ownership over her tits. She took off her bra. Moonlight struck contours of her body as she sat up in bed. I put my mouth around a nipple and sucked. She arched her back and moaned. She reclined against the bed. I moved myself over her. She nestled her head into a pillow. We kissed. I reached for her crotch.

"God Nate, I can't tonight," she said.

"Jesus," I said.

"I want to. Seriously. I want to fuck," Natalie said. "I'm just so tired, Nate. I'm drunk."

"Jesus," I said. "Jesus fucking Christ."

"Tomorrow, I promise," she said. "Fuck me tomorrow. I promise."

"How long has it been? A month? More than a month?"

"Tomorrow," she said.

She stroked the side of my face with her hand.

"We're like old people. Married people," I said. "Actually we're worse than married people, because married people do occasionally have sex."

"I'm tired," she said. "The plane ride. Jet lag. God, I drank so much. I'm tired, Nate. Let me get some sleep. We'll fuck tomorrow."

"You weren't tired at the club."

"I danced too much. I'm exhausted."

I stopped talking. Natalie fell asleep. In a few minutes I heard her snoring. I lay beside her. I rolled away. Her snoring continued and grew louder. I hated her, but the hatred didn't make me want her any less—it made me want her more. I thought about Avril. Maybe the best thing for everyone would be for me and Natalie to stop having sex forever. Maybe it was too late for us. I tried to count in my head how many days it had been since I'd had sex. I counted up to twenty-six or twenty-seven before I got confused and gave up.

FIFTY-ONE

I stayed awake for a long time. I lay on my back and looked out the window at the moon, noticed how it lit the sky around it in a halo of blue. I wondered why earthlings didn't have colonies on the moon. It seemed like the sort of thing rich people would want. Someday in the future, I suppose rich people will cover the moon with luxury apartments and strip malls and Taco Bells. But there's no efficient way to grow food on the moon, so they'll ship it up from the Earth, and everything will be very expensive, so only rich people will be able to afford it. As conditions on Earth get shittier—climate apocalypse and nuclear war—more and more rich people will escape to the moon. And someday even the moon will be overcrowded, so all the rich people will have to escape to some new and more fashionable planet and leave us poor people behind to suffer. And then the new planet will fill up and become unlivable, and the rich will find another and another. That will be the story of the human race. We'll fly out into the universe, colonize all the nice planets and fill them with people and chemicals and smog. Humans will keep spreading forever, terraforming planet after planet into useless garbage.

I dwelled on humanity's fate for long hours before drifting asleep. I'd only been in Hawaii for a day, but already it had impressed me as a very nice place. I felt sorry that rich people were filling it up with chemicals and garbage and smog.

FIFTY-TWO

I slept for a while and woke up sometime during the night. I started thinking about a weekend in high school when Natalie's parents went on vacation. I'd made some excuse to my own parents so I could stay over with Natalie in her big McMansion. This wasn't long after we'd started having sex. Every night that week before her parents left, we talked on the phone about how we'd fuck our brains out all weekend. And we did fuck. We fucked in the foyer. We fucked on the stairs. We moved upstairs and fucked in her bed. It was the first time we'd ever fucked in her bed, and our sex there became soft and intimate.

Afterward we talked for a while and messed around under the covers, and then we went downstairs to get vodka from her parents' liquor cabinet. We mixed vodka and Diet Pepsi. In another room I noticed the first three *Alien* movies on Blu-ray. They were still wrapped in their original packaging, like her dad had bought the movies but never bothered to watch them. I unwrapped them and played the first one, from the 1970s. And of course it was really good, so afterward we watched the second and third. We kept meaning to pause the movies and have more sex, but instead we drank vodka and Diet Pepsi and watched aliens burst out of chests.

We watched Sigourney Weaver run down hallways and set monsters on fire with a flamethrower.

Later I sat with Natalie on the floor of her parents' closet as we flipped through photo albums. She showed me pictures of her mom. Her real mom, who divorced her dad when Natalie was only a kid. Natalie had lived with her mom until she was eleven, when her dad sued for custody and won.

"Mom and I lived in a trailer outside Pulaski," Natalie said. "I don't tell people these things. Sometimes at the end of the month, there wouldn't be money left over for groceries. A guy at the gas station would let mom buy milk and peanut butter on store credit."

Me and Natalie talked again about having sex, but we were tired from drinking and staying up late. We went to bed and kissed for a while and then stopped. I must have fallen asleep because I remember waking later on that night to Natalie's voice.

"What do you want to be when you grow up?" she asked.

"I don't know," I said. "I've never wanted to be anything."

"Maybe you'll be a lawyer," she said. "Or a doctor. Or a stock broker. Someone who will make a lot of money."

"Sure," I said.

"Good," she said. "You're smart. You'll be good at whatever you do. You'll make a lot of money."

I rolled over in bed and looked at her and saw how the lights from outside the window illuminated strands of her hair. I really had no idea what I wanted to do with my life, but making a lot of money did sound like a good idea. And it made Natalie happy. Anyway I was only a kid in high school, and the rest of my life seemed a long way off—difficult to imagine—some fantasy world forever out of reach. The future was a dream, no more real than the cozy ones we experienced that night as we slept together for the first time in the same bed. A dream of embracing, and warmth like an ocean, and never letting go.

FIFTY-THREE

I woke up to light shining through the windows so bright it stung my eyes. An air conditioner hummed. I sat up in bed and looked out through the glass and saw an enormous blue ocean, one that grew darker and bluer as it receded into the distance. Seabirds with long white wings skimmed the surface.

I asked Natalie if she wanted to go downstairs for breakfast. She said she wanted to eat at a restaurant she'd seen while we were out last night.

"It's cheaper at the hotel," I said.

"I'll put it on the credit card," Natalie said.

She called Roger and Avril, and later we met in the lobby. Avril wore a purple dress, the kind they sell cheap at Target. Roger wore a T-shirt and khaki shorts. I also wore a T-shirt and khaki shorts. Roger's shirt had a picture of a shark and the words *Bite Me.*

The four of us walked down Ali'i Drive, which was crowded again with white people. We followed the sidewalk near the ocean. Sailboats navigated the bay. A few puffy clouds floated far out over the water, but the rest of the sky was clear.

Roger boosted himself onto the seawall. He walked along beside us, sometimes looking out to sea and sometimes down on us to talk.

"I'm still a little drunk from last night," he said. "Don't be surprised if I fall off and die."

"Don't be surprised if nobody cares," Avril said.

He stared down at her.

"Jesus, Avril. Your tits are hanging out," he said. "Jesus, have some class."

The restaurant was elevated like the seafood place from the night before, providing an easy view of the bay. The hostess was Hawaiian. She seated us near the railing, and a breeze blew through the dining room. After she left, we opened our menus. Natalie said she wanted a cinnamon roll. We scanned the menus. The restaurant didn't serve cinnamon rolls.

"Fuck this place," Natalie said.

"Why did you want to eat here?" I said.

"I wanted to eat breakfast by the ocean," she said.

"It's a nice view," Avril said.

"The whole island has a nice view," Roger said.

"Let's leave," Natalie said. "I want a cinnamon roll."

"No way," Roger said. He pounded his fist on the table. People at nearby tables turned to look. Most of them were white, but for the first time since I'd been on the island I saw a Hawaiian couple eating at a restaurant instead of working. The woman had a purple flower in her hair. The guy wore a T-shirt and khaki shorts. "I want bacon," Roger said. "Fuck your cinnamon roll. I want bacon, and I want it right now."

That settled it. We all ordered eggs and bacon. Me and Roger got hash browns, and the girls ordered rice on the side.

"Did you notice the Spam on the menu?" Avril asked. "Spam and eggs?"

"Hawaiian food is gross," Natalie said. "They'll fry a couple eggs and throw them on top of a pile of rice and a hamburger patty. And Spam. Spam on everything. Spam sushi." Natalie made a vomiting noise. "Hawaiian food is the worst."

The Hawaiian couple sitting nearby quietly rose from their seats and moved to a table across the restaurant. A sharp dagger of jealousy stabbed my chest. It was so easy for them to escape.

The food arrived, but I didn't feel hungry. My stomach was queasy from all the drinking the night before. I took a few bites and stared out to sea. The restaurant really did have a great view. I noticed the blue water and green fronds of palm trees. Greens and blues appeared especially strong in Hawaii. Maybe if I looked at them for too long without blinking, the vividity would scorch my retinas or cause my head to explode. I imagined myself diving into the bay and swimming and swimming for two thousand miles to Japan. There, I would drag my tired body from the ocean and begin a new and better life, one marked by mossy Shinto temples and quiet meditation.

"What are we doing today, besides drinking?" Roger asked through a mouthful of eggs.

"Hapuna beach," Natalie said. "It's the best. The guidebook says so."

"Are we taking an Uber?" Roger asked.

"It's like thirty miles," Natalie said. "And there won't be any Ubers to take us back."

"Why didn't we rent a car at the airport?" Roger asked.

"I know a place to call," Natalie said. "They'll deliver a rental to the hotel."

"Won't that be expensive?" I asked.

Natalie shrugged. She had the credit card.

Roger scraped some eggs and bacon into a last bite. He chewed thoughtfully.

"Don't get some rice burner."

FIFTY-FOUR

Natalie ordered a Mustang convertible, and a guy from the agency drove it to the hotel. Natalie didn't let me see how much it cost. When the agency guy handed her the paperwork, she folded it and stuffed it in her purse. The Mustang had a red paint job and leather seats. It wasn't an Italian sports car or anything, but still it was the nicest car I'd ever been in.

Roger drove because he was the only one of us who could work a stick. Natalie sat up front—she'd paid for the car and felt entitled. This left me and Avril together in the back. She wore a large pair of plastic sunglasses, and the wind blew her fake-red hair all over her shoulders. Beneath her dress she wore a bikini. Orange straps ran from her shoulders down her back.

Roger wanted to head straight for the beach, but Natalie said she needed some things from Target. We drove through the city. It looked like any other city in America except with better scenery. The landscape was flat near the coast, but as you went inland the city climbed straight up a cliff, where the houses looked cute and yellow, like something you'd see on a *Lifestyles of the Rich and Famous* episode set on the Mediterranean coast. Pretty soon we drove by McDonald's and PetSmart and Wendy's and Costco.

Once we got to Target, the girls filled our cart with sunscreen, aloe, moisturizers, beach towels, and sunglasses. Some Hawaiian and Japanese people moved through the aisles, but mostly the people shopping at Target were white. We walked through rows and rows of products on shelves. I could get lost in Target and wander for weeks, never finding my way out. There probably existed an alternate nightmare universe where I'd spend the entire vacation shopping at Target.

Natalie dragged me to the women's apparel section to help her choose a bathing suit. Standing in the bathing suit section made me feel like a creep. I might as well have been standing in the underwear section. I glanced from side to side. Tried not to look pervy.

"Why do you need a new bathing suit?" I asked. "Your old bathing suit is fine."

"My old bathing suit is old."

"You bought it special for the trip."

"I want a bathing suit from Hawaii."

Natalie picked out an American flag bikini that strapped around her back. Natalie's breasts were small enough that she could wear this type of bikini without flopping out of it. Natalie always talked about how she wanted plastic surgery to make her boobs bigger. She said she'd asked her father about it, and he said he might pay for it someday.

We caught up with Roger and Avril down another aisle. Roger put a Super Soaker in the cart.

"Watch me fuck up some little kid with this," he said.

FIFTY-FIVE

The drive to Hapuna Beach took most of an hour even with Roger flooring it the whole way. With the top down, the wind made tremendous noise and battered my face. I sat in the back with Avril, and occasionally I'd reach over and touch her hand. At these times, she would glance at me, then look away and smile. In the front seat, Natalie played *Candy Crush* on her iPhone.

A few miles north of the city, I got a good look at Mauna Kea, the tallest mountain on the island. The volcano is one of several that created Hawaii Island by lifting the seafloor above the surface of the ocean. It hadn't erupted in four thousand years. It made a lot of excitement when it was young, but it grew up and became cold and dead like any other mountain. Now there was nothing for it to do but erode until the end of time.

The landscape north of Kona looked nothing like I'd expected. No rainforest or tropical flowers. The highway ran through an immense swath of volcanic desolation. The land was black rock, all cracked and broken. Pale yellow grasses thrived among the stones. I didn't know how anything could survive out there. It seemed like anything alive would die in about a half hour.

I leaned forward and shouted to Natalie and Roger.

"It's like *Mad Max*," I said.

"What?" Natalie held a hand to her head to keep the wind from blowing her hair around so much.

"*Beyond Thunderdome*," I said.

Roger turned his head and shouted.

"The wind makes it hard to drive."

But at first I misunderstood him. The noise of the wind was thunderous. It garbled Roger's voice like one of those speakers that make you sound like Darth Vader. Roger's words sounded like a prophecy.

The one who prepares us to die.

FIFTY-SIX

Hapuna Beach looked like something out of a postcard or tourism video, and when I laid eyes on it I believed I had at last found the real Hawaii. A band of white sand fronted the ocean. Palm trees swayed in a breeze coming in over the water. I saw beach umbrellas and children building sandcastles and parents drinking beverages from coconuts and hundreds of people playing in the surf, laughing, skin glistening. There at the beach, all colors achieved peak intensity—the water was the bluest blue, the sand the whitest white.

"Boom," Roger said, claiming a spot.

The four of us spread towels on the sand and stripped down to our bathing suits. We walked to the ocean. The wind blew strongly, occasionally sending pockets of sand airborne. I felt self-conscious about my whiteness. I was much whiter than any of the Hawaiian or Asian people on the beach. I was whiter even than most white people. My skin was apparently incapable of tanning. I felt ridiculous, like an invasive plant or weird animal, an ostrich.

I stepped into about an inch of water as it flowed over the sand. I stood still, trying to recreate a memory from my childhood. I realized, suddenly, I hadn't been in the ocean since I was five years old, when my parents took me to visit my grandparents in Florida. I remembered standing in the surf and talking to my mom, and the movement of sand under my feet made me feel like I was sliding backward. And I told this to my mom and she laughed. At Hapuna, I stood in the sand and tried to feel it again. A dying wave washed over my feet. I felt the old sensation, just like when I was a kid, the feeling of moving backward while standing still.

I caught up to my friends at the shore break. Waist-high waves rolled in hard, strong enough to knock us around. I held hands with Natalie, and we pushed through the break to a calm place where the water rose and fell more gently. A man rode a sailboard in the distance. The wind blew him across the surface of the ocean, and sometimes he'd launch into the air.

"This is perfect," Natalie said.

"It's not what I expected," I said. "It's better."

"I knew you'd love it," she said.

We walked further, into deeper water. The sun shone brightly on her wet hair. Her eyes reflected the sky and ocean. I saw her with new clarity, the way I might have when we were younger. Maybe this was the real Natalie. Maybe the one I'd lived with back home was only a blurry copy. I wanted to know her again, her true self. Then Roger swam up behind us and dunked her.

"Iceberg! Right ahead!" he shouted, wrapping his arms around her body, jerking her up before pulling her under. They surfaced seconds later. She sputtered and laughed. She slugged him on the arm.

"You bitch," she said, all smiling and radiant.

"You can't handle me," he said, shaking his head, flinging water like a dog. "Shit. The surf out here. I mean, shit. Do you think I could learn to surf this week? I want to go surfing."

"You'd have to wake up early and stop drinking," Avril said.

"Never mind," Roger said.

We stayed in the water for a long time. Natalie looked pretty, and Roger didn't complain about anything or act like a dick, and the saltwater made Avril's breasts especially buoyant so they peeked above the surface like twin pearl-white islands. I floated on my back, my body rising and falling with the waves. I squinted at the sun. I looked toward the beach and all the tiny people. I saw the green of the trees, and, beyond, a great red mountain rising to the sky, a mountain larger than anything in my life. It felt nice to be in the ocean. We floated together in the warm water until everything felt right with the world and I felt my weightless soul slipping out of my body. Around that time, Natalie said she was bored.

FIFTY-SEVEN

I sat on my towel and worked sunscreen into my skin. The sun, which had felt pleasantly warm before, now ran down on me like wildfire. I envied all the people sitting beneath beach umbrellas. I rubbed lotion on my arms and thought about skin cancer. Anybody who brings an umbrella to the beach is a genius.

"You'll never tan like that," Natalie said, looking up from her iPhone.

"I'm gonna burn."

"You're using too much," she said. "You won't get any sun."

"I burn easy. I burn in Tennessee in the winter."

"He's super white," Roger said. "Nate is the whitest guy I've ever known."

I asked Natalie to rub sunscreen on my back, but she told me to get lost. I turned to Roger and Avril.

"Don't even ask," Roger said from behind a pair of sunglasses.

"Give it here," Avril said, reaching for the tube of sunscreen. "Only because nobody else will do it." She made a big deal of acting like it was no big deal. I rolled onto my chest, and she put her hands on my back, and they felt good, and she kept them there longer than absolutely necessary.

"You'll just make him whiter," Natalie said.

"I'm very thorough," Avril said.

"I'll bet you are," Natalie said.

FIFTY-EIGHT

I reclined in the sand and watched the waves come in, and when that got boring I checked out all the people on the beach. Most of them had very nice tans. I was unused to seeing so many attractive, well-tanned bodies. I'd spent my whole life looking at pasty, white Tennesseans. It is true that tanning beds were popular among Tennesseans who didn't want to look so white. Sometimes you'd see people who spent too much time in the tanning beds. They didn't look real. They looked all dried out like beef jerky. They looked like fake people wearing leather skin suits, something they'd stitched together to hide their real selves. Tanning beds were a great way to get skin cancer. I rolled over, looked up at the sun. Squinted. The sun looked huge and horrible in the sky. Someday the sun will scorch the earth. Someday the sun will give everybody cancer.

FIFTY-NINE

Avril sat up and complained about being hungry. Me and Roger agreed that we were hungry. Natalie didn't say anything. She never talked about being hungry. Even if she'd been lost and wandering in a desert for a week, after the rescue she wouldn't ask for anything but a salad with dressing on the side. I put on my T-shirt and rubbed more sunscreen onto my face. We all got up and went to a snack bar.

Me and Roger ordered hot dogs. Avril and Natalie shared a big order of curly fries. Natalie tried to pay with the credit card, but the Hawaiian girl behind the counter explained she could only take cash. Natalie muttered *shithole* under her breath—quietly enough so the girl behind the counter might plausibly not have heard her, but loud enough so Natalie could be certain the girl did, in fact, hear her.

"No worries," Roger said. He opened his wallet and pulled out a pair of twenties. I glanced in the wallet and saw it was thick with bills. "Always carry cash," he said to Natalie, in a voice like Superman after rescuing Lois Lane. "Nobody says no to cash."

We ate outside at a cement table in front of the stand. A Hawaiian woman and her kid walked up to the stand and ordered fries and two small cokes. The kid tugged on her sarong and told her he wanted a cheeseburger. His mom tried to tell him no, but then he started crying and tugging again. She snapped at him and told him a cheeseburger cost six dollars, and this shut him up, like maybe he had an idea of how much six dollars was, and to him it was an astronomical amount of money. He stopped crying. He made a sniffing noise, like he was struggling not to cry.

"Jesus," Natalie said under her breath. "Buy the kid a cheeseburger."

The Hawaiian woman glanced at Natalie and looked away.

"Not everybody has your dad's credit card," I said. I put a curly fry in my mouth. It tasted fantastic. I don't understand why people eat regular fries when curly fries taste so much better.

"You're always trying to make me feel bad," Natalie said. She ate a curly fry. "There's nothing wrong with having money. Everybody wants to own things. You want an iPad? A new car? They cost money. That's how the world works."

Roger laughed until he coughed up little chewed bits of pink hot dog. I didn't understand the joke. A big blue umbrella over the table shaded us from the sun. The afternoon would have been sweltering except for all the wind. I held onto the paper wrapper of my hot dog to keep it from blowing away. Natalie ate a few more curly fries, then pushed the plate to Avril.

"I'm done," Natalie said. "I'm ready to pop."

Avril shrugged and ate the rest of the fries.

SIXTY

When we got back to the beach, Natalie and Avril lay on their towels to tan, and me and Roger went into the ocean. But first I applied more sunscreen.

"You really are ridiculous," Roger said.

"You won't be laughing after you die from skin cancer."

"Cancer is something that happens to other people," he said, and he laughed like he'd made a joke. "Poor people." He laughed harder.

We stepped into the water and pushed past the surf break. We swam around, and Roger tried to do a handstand underwater, but the movement of the waves tipped him over.

"Let's get drunk tonight," Roger said, treading water.

"Crazy drunk," I said.

"I want a real Hawaiian drink, like from a coconut," he said.

We floated on our backs, bobbing up and down in the gentle waves. The sun felt nice on my chest. Not nice enough to make me forget about skin cancer, but still, pretty nice. After a while we resumed treading water.

"What do you want to do when you grow up?" I asked.

"Fucking get rich."

"I mean *how* will you get rich?"

"I'm a business major." Roger shrugged. "I'll do business."

"Cool," I said. "What will you buy with all your money?"

"All this." Roger glanced back toward the beach. "I'm gonna make so much money I can live in a place like this."

"That's a lot of money."

"I've been places like this," he said. "On vacation. My dad ain't good for much, but he pays the bills, you know? And he loves taking us on crazy vacations—Bahamas, Cabo, the Keys. That's the kind of dad I want to be. Just like him, I mean, but better. Like if I could take the good stuff about him and double down on it, and forget about all the rest, all the grief he gives mom. I mean . . . I just mean I'm gonna make bank, and when I have a kid of my own, give him a good life."

"I don't want kids," I said. "Too much pressure."

"I gotta make bank." Roger smiled. He really was very handsome, and some quality of the sunlight and water amplified his looks. "Girls only fuck guys if they're loaded. That's the whole game. Gonna make some money, drive a Maserati, buy a fucking mansion. Gonna live the good life. Stick my dick in a bunch of girls, marry a hot bitch. That's life. That's all it is."

"Gotta make bank," I said.

Roger looked toward shore.

"Check out that one," he said. "That's the kind of bitch you should fuck once you make bank."

We watched a white girl and her boyfriend hold hands as they walked into the water. When they got to the surf break, a wave knocked the guy down.

"What a fag." Roger laughed and floated on his back. "Jesus. Learn to walk." The couple moved farther into the ocean and swam. The girl had strawberry-blond hair and wore a green bikini. She was close enough for me to see the freckles on her cheeks. She was only of normal attractiveness, but somehow her presence on a beach in Hawaii made her more desirable.

"I'd fuck every one of her holes," Roger said. "I'd fuck her cunt, ass, mouth. Jesus. We should double-team that bitch, you and me, Nate. Girls like her want it and don't even know. Let's do her a favor. Invite her back to the hotel. Fuck her like she won't forget it. So even after she goes back home to Iowa she'll never forget it."

I floated on my back and tried not to think about the girl. I tried to forget what Roger had said. Roger always talked too much. Hawaii was the most beautiful place in the world, and Roger could fuck it up just by talking.

I heard someone shouting, and I looked up and saw a group of Hawaiian guys riding body boards. The Hawaiian guys were tall and brown. The sun gleamed off their water-slicked chests. The Hawaiian guys looked like the heroes in a Marvel superhero movie. They stood in waist-high water, and whenever a wave came they'd hop on their boards and ride.

"Looks pretty faggy to me," Roger said.

We treaded water and watched the body boarders. Swells came in regularly. The Hawaiians stood at the spot where the waves broke. After a while the boarders noticed us watching, and one of them waved us over.

"Try it," he said, holding out the board to me.

"No, sorry," I said. "We were just watching."

Roger told me to stop being a bitch. He shouted to the Hawaiian guy that we'd give it a shot. We swam over, and the Hawaiians gave us their boards. They told us where to stand and wait for the waves. Me and Roger crouched in the shallow water, holding the boards in front of us. We twisted around to look for waves. None came. We stayed in the water for a long time. It was a little embarrassing, really, because the Hawaiian guys must have thought we were the lamest white people of all time. Finally a wave came, and we tried to catch it but ended up just flopping around in the water. The Hawaiian guys laughed. One of them came over and gave us some tips on how to hold the boards and when to jump for the waves. The advice helped. Next time a wave came, me and Roger both caught it and rode it all the way to the beach. I loved it. Riding that little wave on that little board made me feel like the king of the goddamn ocean. We went back out into the water and spent a half hour taking turns with the Hawaiian guys on the boards. They were interested in where we visited from. The Hawaiians were a lot better with the boards than me and Roger. Every kid on the beach was better than me and Roger. Anyway it was fun. I wanted to stay in the water and never come back. I wanted to become one with the ocean. I wanted my soul to leave my body and become liquid, and I wanted my empty husk to sink to the sandy bottom and be covered by all that water.

SIXTY-ONE

Later me and Roger sat on the beach with one of the Hawaiians. His name was Kamaka. He had a thickly muscled surfer body and a black mustache. He patiently answered all of Roger's dumb questions about surfing. Kamaka offered to teach him. Kamaka said he knew a good beach. Banyans. He told us he was a tour guide. I asked if he worked for a tour company. He shook his head *no*. He said he worked for himself.

"I can show you all around the island," he said. "I'm kama'aina. Nobody knows the island like me. The best beaches, best surf spots, best waterfalls—you name it. I'll hook you up. You can own me for $100 a day."

"Deal," Roger said.

Kamaka and Roger bumped fists. The three of us walked along the beach, heading back to the spot where we'd left the girls. Kamaka told us about the island. He was very informative. He told us about Kilauea volcano. He said the air in Kona and the west side of the island always looked hazy because of volcanic gas. He said the gas comes out of a vent and hangs around Kona like fog. He called it vog. The gas is highly poisonous.

"If the vog settled over some house in a low spot, it could kill everybody inside. Suffocate them. Poof. Dead. Just like that," he said. "It's never happened. But maybe someday."

He told me the other side of the island looked completely different. All jungle and rain and tropical flowers.

"It's because of the trade winds," he said. "They come off the ocean and drop rain when they hit the mountain. Back east, it's always raining. It's pretty over there. You guys should see it. Lots of flowers. Your girls would love it." Then he motioned toward the beach and the reddish mountain in the distance. "Over here, everything's dead."

The three of us approached Natalie and Avril. They were lying on their beach towels and talking to some guys. The guys were the bro-iest looking bros. First of all, they were white, with blond hair and big muscles, and they wore board shorts, and they nodded their heads and laughed a lot. One of the bros was checking out Avril's tits. He had light-blond stubble and a Punisher skull tattoo on his shoulder. The Punisher tattoo looked stupid. It looked like every other Punisher tattoo I'd ever seen, and I'd seen a lot of them, because every douchebag gets the exact same tattoo of a Punisher skull or barbed wire. Normally I wouldn't mind if a person stared at Avril's tits—they were, after all, spectacular. It just bothered me to see her getting checked out by a guy with such a lame tattoo. Me, Roger, and Kamaka stood around and watched the girls talk to the bros. I expected the girls to make introductions, but they kept on talking and ignoring us.

"We're back," I said after being ignored for a long time.

Natalie sighed loudly and introduced us. The bros had brotastic names—Cory, Slater, and Bodhi. Natalie informed us they were from California, pronouncing the state-name slowly and emphatically, as if California was important and we should be impressed. All the guys nodded to each other. Nobody shook hands. Natalie said the bros had a suite in our hotel.

"Isn't that a coincidence?" she said, like it was the most amazing thing in the world. She said the bros had invited us to a party that night in their suite.

"This is Kamaka," I said, motioning to him. "He's going to show us around the island for a few days."

"Oh," Natalie said.

She tilted her head down to observe him over the top of her sunglasses. She told him it was good to meet him, but she said it like it really wasn't good at all.

"Kamaka is my surf instructor," Roger said. "We're going to Banyans."

The bros nodded their heads. They liked Banyans but preferred Pine Trees. Kamaka and the bros talked about surf locations, places I'd never heard of, places with evocative names like Magics and Kahaluʻu Bay. Kamaka said he learned to surf at Honoliʻi. The bros had never surfed Honoliʻi. It was on the east side of the island.

"It's a different world," Kamaka said.

I asked Kamaka where he lived. He said he had a place back east in Hilo, but this week he and his friends were staying at the Seaside Hotel in Kona. He told us the Seaside was basically across the street from the Grand Liliʻuokalani. I told him he should come to the party. He said he'd think about it. Kamaka and Roger exchanged phone numbers.

Pretty soon, Kamaka and the bros left. The girls said they wanted to sunbathe some more. I sat on my towel. I wiggled my feet in the sand. I admired the beach and palm trees and ocean. It all looked nicer than any other place I'd ever been. Far out to sea, the blue of the ocean merged with the blue of the sky. I thought about Murfreesboro and its dreary December bleakness. I thought about the cold, gray rain. How could a place as miserable as Murfreesboro exist?

I picked up my phone. I touched the screen to bring it to life. I navigated to Twitter and read some tweets by President Trump.

The president was bad at capitalizing words. So bad it de-pressed me. I didn't want to be depressed anymore. I tossed my phone onto the sand. Fine white grains settled on the black sur-face. I looked at the yellow-white sun in the western sky. The sky was blue and cloudless, the bluest sky I'd seen in my life. Suddenly I didn't care about Trump. I liked Hawaii, and being there made me happy. I had no desire to return to the mainland. Couldn't care less about Congress or the national debt. A warmth welled up in-side me, spread through my chest. I was in love with Hawaii. It was stupid for people to live anywhere else.

SIXTY-TWO

After a while we felt tired and hungry. Roger drove us back to Kona. Me and Avril sat in the back seat. The rocky landscape raced by in a blur of yellow and black. Avril pretended to sleep. She leaned into me, drowsily allowing her hand to rest on my leg.

"You two look comfy," Natalie said from the front seat.

Avril shuddered.

"She's asleep," I said.

"Awfully comfy," Natalie said. Then she went back to playing with her iPhone.

We were starving by the time we got to Kona. Avril perked up and said she wanted to try authentic Hawaiian food, but as soon as Roger spotted a Wendy's he pulled into the drive-through. We took the food to our hotel rooms. I sat cross-legged on the bed and ate a spicy chicken sandwich. The same sandwich I'd have ordered from Wendy's back home. I consumed it quickly without tasting it. Afterward, me and Natalie lay beside each other on the bed.

"We should fuck," I said.

"Sure," Natalie said.

"Fuck right now."

"Right," Natalie said. "Let's do it."

Then we fell asleep.

SIXTY-THREE

In my dream, Natalie stood naked in the ocean. She told me she tasted like salt. Water rose and fell up to her chest, revealing and concealing her breasts in steady rhythm. Giant palm trees towered over her. Green fronds swayed in the trade winds. The sky and water were blue, but the water was a deeper blue. Dream Natalie licked herself and rose from the water.

I awoke in a dark room. I thought I was back in Murfreesboro. Then I remembered.

"I taste like salt," Natalie said.

I rubbed my eyes. She lay beside me on the bed. I couldn't make out the details of her face.

"Salt from the ocean."

I sat up and blinked. Natalie got off the bed, flipped a light switch. The light in the hotel room was dirty yellow. I saw my reflection—pale and blurry—in the glass balcony door. Natalie said she needed a shower. She stripped, pulled out the band that held her ponytail. Her hair fell against her shoulders, which were red, a little, from the sun. The longer I looked, the more I wanted her. I considered trying to join her in the shower but didn't. I knew what she would say.

I tried to fall asleep again. When I gave up, I grabbed the TV remote. I watched what I thought was a commercial, but it kept going until gradually I realized it was an infomercial. The program advertised a cat litter box that cleaned itself. The ideal customer for the self-cleaning cat litter box would be someone who wanted to have a pet but didn't want to be responsible for its wellbeing. A man and woman did the selling. They acted like they were having a conversation, but their voices were flat, and their lines sounded scripted. The man and woman looked vaguely attractive but not attractive enough to get the good acting jobs on movies and TV. I usually didn't watch infomercials—because I like to think I have a life, and because sitting on a couch all day and buying stuff is skanky. It's the same with the internet. About half of the internet is stuff to buy. The other half is porn. I like buying stuff, and I like porn, but after a certain point it just gets skanky.

"We should get something to eat before the party," Natalie shouted from the bathroom as she turned off the shower. She came out of the bathroom looking slick and wet. She toweled off in front of me to watch the infomercial, then rooted through our luggage for clothes to wear. She wasn't bashful about nakedness. We'd been together for years. I could remember back to high school when she wanted to fuck whenever we were alone. Nowadays I only turned her on as much as your average piece of patio furniture. Possibly less. Natalie pulled a tight pair of blue jeans over her ass and buttoned them. She watched the infomercial. She scratched her head.

"You know," she said, "those automatic litter boxes are a smart idea."

SIXTY-FOUR

Me and Natalie walked along Ali‘i. I put my arm around her, and I think she liked it, even though she didn't really care about me anymore. She took the gesture to mean I claimed her for my own—she was desirable, worthy of possession—and I, in turn, belonged to her. Natalie believed deeply in ownership.

The moon cast its silver light across the ocean, and a succession of waves rolled in, causing the image of the moon to twist and flow. I told Natalie I liked Hawaii.

"Of course you do. Everybody likes Hawaii. If you can't be happy in Hawaii, you should give up on life," she said. "But I wish we'd gone to Oahu. I wish you could see Honolulu at night from the top of a skyscraper. It's beautiful. And, I mean, it's civilization. Kona is fine, but it's one of those towns that thinks it's bigger than it really is."

"Fuck Kona," I said, even though I liked it quite a lot.

We walked past a guy playing guitar on the sidewalk. We smiled at him, and he smiled back, either because he thought it was sweet that we were in love or because he'd seen enough happy couples over the years to know what we were really about. A guy walked up to us with long hair that hadn't been washed in a long time. He smelled like cigarettes and vomit. The guy asked if I had a dollar. I lied and told him I was broke. Me and Natalie walked past him. Before we got far I heard him muttering under his breath.

"Yeah," he said. "You look broke."

I was glad I hadn't given him anything. I would save my money for a nice, polite homeless person, like in the movies. Homeless people in movies are always secret musical prodigies or rich people suffering from amnesia.

"What an asshole," I said.

"What do you expect?" Natalie asked. "Homeless people are mentally ill."

"Not all of them. Some people just lose their jobs and end up on the street. It can happen to anyone. After you lose your job, everything goes to shit."

"Try not to get fired from the IRS," she said. "Be an IRS superhero. Get into management, so we can live in a big house and drive BMWs."

"I hate the IRS," I said. "What if I wanted to be a rockstar? What if the only thing that mattered to me was the music?"

"What do you know about music?"

"Hypothetically. Like what if I was born to play the guitar, but I don't know it because I never tried?"

"Then I'd find some other man." Natalie laughed, but the laughter sounded weird—sharp and high-pitched—the way people force themselves to laugh even when nothing's funny.

SIXTY-FIVE

We walked past tourists and all the shops set up to take advantage of tourists. I didn't like to think of myself as a tourist. I mean, that's objectively what I was, but what sense was there in dwelling on it? Tourists are out-of-touch people who live in upper-middle-class suburbs in the Midwest. Tourists are old couples who worked away the best years of their lives, and now that they've retired with a fat IRA they decide they want to see the world—only when they get to Paris or wherever they can't enjoy it because they're too old and used up to feel anything.

Natalie pulled me into some cheesy T-shirt and memento shop where she browsed a display of ceramic sea turtles. They were small, about the size of a silver dollar, and there were a lot of them, all in supposedly cute poses, like rolled over on their backs or breaking out of their egg shells.

"We should buy these," Natalie said. "The whole set."

"Why would we do that? We'd get home and you'd never take them out of the box."

"I love them," she said. "They'll remind me of Hawaii."

"How about we buy just one of them?"

Natalie pouted before choosing one that was curled up and trying to bite its own tail. She paid for it with the credit card.

"I feel stupid buying one little thing on credit," she said after we left the store with the ceramic turtle wrapped in a small paper bag. "The stores have to pay fees to the credit card companies. It's not worth it unless you spend a lot of money. When you buy something small, the store owner loses money. Then they cut corners. They stop giving Christmas bonuses to the workers. Think about that, Nate. Think about the workers."

I wanted to argue but didn't care enough to actually say anything. We entered another area of touristy shops, anchored by a restaurant with a line of tables set up beside a railing overlooking the bay. We read the menu on a sign out front. The restaurant served fish and some other dishes that didn't sound terrible. We went inside and asked for a table near the water. We ordered fruity drinks.

Tiki torches lit the restaurant and gave off a fake Hawaiian vibe. It looked like any restaurant on the mainland trying to pass itself off as Hawaiian—with lots of coconuts and angry-faced Polynesian gods carved out of wood. The waiters wore plastic leis around their necks and especially gaudy Hawaiian shirts. The fake Hawaiian vibe was strong in Kona. The fake Hawaiian vibe was all I knew. It seemed real to me, more authentic than anything genuinely Hawaiian.

We ordered seafood and drank our fruity drinks. This and going to beaches appeared to be the point of Hawaii. Natalie ate bluefin tuna. She asked if I wanted a bite. I told her not to eat bluefin tuna because they were going extinct.

"Fisheries are collapsing," I said. "It's a problem. People won't stop eating bluefin tuna."

"You can't expect me to feel guilty about fish," Natalie said. "Possibly cows, but never fish."

"Someday there won't be any more bluefin tuna. Someday some rich white person will eat the last one. Or a rich Japanese person."

"Then we'll find some other fish to eat," she said. "Salmon or mahi."

"Mahi is safe. I think. But I don't know. It's hard to keep track of everything endangered."

"That's why I hate environmentalists." Natalie's face glowed in the flickering torchlight. "They always tell us what *not* to do. 'Don't drive cars. Don't eat red meat. Don't eat any meat.' If the environmentalists had their way, we'd all be weird vegetarians. We'd all have pasty skin and yellow eyes. We'd have no muscle mass. We'd waste away to nothing."

"Sometimes people shouldn't do things. Sometimes people should stop, or everything turns out shitty. Species go extinct."

"Calm down," she said. "There are plenty of fish. You act like we're running out of everything."

"We really are running out of everything."

The ocean looked scary at night. I imagined swimming in it. I imagined jellyfish and stingrays ascending to the surface. Me and Natalie stopped talking. We ate our meals. Before she finished, she asked if I wanted the last bite of bluefin tuna. She held it out for me on the tip of her fork, and it hung there, glistening in buttery, garlicky sauce. I ate it. The fish tasted delicious. Immediately I felt bad for enjoying it, but I reminded myself that it wasn't my fault that the fish tasted so delicious. I imagined myself swimming in the ocean. Imagined a tiger shark emerging from the deep—a giant. It would stare at me with its beady red eyes. The eyes of the tiger shark would hold me in contempt. The tiger shark would shear off my arms and legs with its razor-sharp teeth. The tiger shark would clamp its mouth around my torso and drag me into the bloodstained murk, and as the last bubbles of air escaped my lips, I would feel a strange sense of peace. I'd marvel at the quiet wisdom of the universe, because at long last I'd received exactly what I deserved.

SIXTY-SIX

We ordered more drinks. We'd drunk plenty already, and the drinking improved my mood. I'd been sitting across from Natalie in the booth, but after the waiter took away the plates I moved to sit beside her. Moonlight lit up her hair, and behind her the lights from town reflected off the water of the bay. At that moment, my life didn't seem so terrible.

"Do you like living in America?" I asked.

"I don't understand what you mean."

"Would you rather live in America or somewhere else?"

"I never really thought about it," she said. "I guess I like it here. I guess it's the best country in the world. America is a lot of fun."

"It's only fun because your dad is rich," I said. "Because he pays for your car and your iPhone. Not everybody can afford to watch *Succession* on HBO and buy Apple products."

"Sucks for them." Natalie tipped up her drink.

"It does suck," I said. "It sucks to be poor in America and miss out on all the fun everybody else is having. It sucks to be poor anywhere in the world. I think my life is pretty shitty, but compared to the way people live in Sudan, it's great. My life is Willy Wonka's Chocolate Factory. Do you see how none of that is fair? The world isn't fair. America isn't fair. Capitalism isn't fair. All of life is fucked and broken."

"Capitalism is the best thing that's ever happened to the world," Natalie said. She took a drink and gazed toward the bay. "No other economic system in human history has raised so many people out of poverty. I learned about it in economics class. Poverty is disappearing all over the planet, and it's all thanks to capitalism."

"Capitalism is a pyramid scheme that only works as long as markets keep growing," I said. "Someday, everyone in the world will have bought all of the plastic shit they'll ever need, and they'll stop spending so much money, and then the whole system will blow up, and everybody will be fucked forever."

"That's a dumb science fiction plot," Natalie said. "Capitalism is winning. You and all the other socialist weirdos are bitter because capitalism keeps winning."

"The problem is bigger than capitalism." I waved my hand emphatically. "Think about all the problems. What about global warming? What about peak oil? Crude oil is a finite resource. What happens when we run out? There are too many problems."

"If we run out of oil, we'll switch to something else," Natalie said. "If there's nothing else, then we'll do without. Make less electricity. Stop driving cars. Life goes on. Life is much more simple than you think it is."

The ocean, past the light of the tiki torches, faded entirely to black and dissolved into the night. A gust of cold wind blew a salt scent into the restaurant. I shivered and stared into the distance, trying and failing to discern the line of the horizon. I thought about the planet and how big it was. I thought about all the people in the world and how they were so far away.

"What about food?" I asked. "Soon there will be nine billion people. We're wearing out the soil, converting farmland into desert. I read about it in a book by Jared Diamond. He says we're fucked."

"If we can't grow food, people will starve," Natalie said. "That sucks, but it's nothing new. People have starved before."

"Says some rich American girl who knows she won't be the one starving," I said. "It must be nice for all the world's problems to be someone else's problem."

A waiter approached our table and overheard our conversation. He walked away, rapidly.

"People suffer every day," Natalie said. "They suffer and die. People are suffering and dying right now. There's nothing you can do about it. They will suffer. They will die. So you might as well stop worrying and get on with your life. Do what makes you happy."

"That's how douchebags think."

"Grow up," Natalie said. "Smile more."

"Why does growing up mean becoming a douchebag?"

"You're human," Natalie said. "The job of every human is to be happy."

SIXTY-SEVEN

Before we left the restaurant, Natalie texted Roger to ask him what time the party would start. He texted back and told us it already started and to bring more alcohol.

"Why do you always text Roger when you want to know something?" I asked. "Why not text Avril?"

"Avril thinks she's better than everybody else."

"It's weird how you text him all the time."

"It's weird how you stare at Avril's tits."

"You're obsessed with her tits," I said.

"Have you *seen* them?" Natalie gestured wildly with her arms. "Oh, right, look who I'm talking to. Of course you have."

"Your tit obsession is getting out of hand." I made a comedy face like *Jim Carrey in Ace Ventura: Pet Detective.*

"You're not as funny as you think you are."

"I think I'm awfully funny." I grabbed my glass, which was mostly empty, and tipped it up to consume the last drops of alcohol.

"I'm tired of her," she said.

"She's your friend. Sometimes friends get tired of each other."

"I don't have friends," she said, looking at me the way adults look at children after they fall down and scrape their knees.

I paid at the restaurant with Natalie's credit card. We left and walked to a liquor store where we used the card again, this time for a bottle of rum and one of champagne. The guy behind the cash register was Hawaiian, and I noticed him looking at Natalie while he rang us up, how his eyes lingered on her tits, even though they were very small. Actually I didn't mind much. Guys always looked at Natalie. I used to look at her that way, too. But that was a long time ago when I was still a real person living a real life.

SIXTY-EIGHT

Back at the hotel, we took the elevator to the top floor to the bros'
suite. On the way up I asked Natalie to have sex in the elevator.
I didn't actually want to have sex. I just wanted to hear how she
would reject me.

"Are you drunk?" she said.

The penthouse suite was much nicer than me and Natalie's
room. From the balcony you could see across the bay and all the
lights from the city. I could tell Natalie liked it. She looked aroused
for the first time in months. She looked like she wanted to have sex
with the suite.

Avril and Roger stood by the bar in the kitchen. Avril tried to
tell him about some movie, and Roger tried to ignore her. Avril
wore a bright pink tank top and a short leather skirt that showed
off her legs.

All of the bros acted really happy to see Natalie. They crowded
around and agreed with everything she said. Natalie complained
about stuff she didn't like about Hawaii. She complained about
slow drivers. She complained about homeless people. I followed
Natalie and the bros to the balcony. I stood beside her and tried to
join the conversation, but whenever I said anything—which wasn't

often because I didn't have much to say about homeless people—
nobody listened. Pretty soon I got tired of everybody talking over
me. I went to the bar to drink with Roger. I checked the fridge and
found a jug of tropical punch Kool-Aid. I mixed a rum punch.

"You shouldn't let those guys talk to Natalie," Roger said. He
drank a Heineken.

"It's just talk."

"Any one of those guys would give it to her if they got the
chance," Roger said. "They'd all give it to her at the same time."

Avril coughed. She'd been drinking some fruity drink, but then
started coughing like it had gone down her windpipe. Briefly we
made eye contact. Avril started telling me about the movie. It
didn't sound like a very good movie. I looked into her eyes while
she talked. I looked and looked and wouldn't look away. Really it
was too much eye contact, but Avril didn't seem to mind.

Kamaka and his two friends entered the suite. They saw all the
white people. They moved as a group to the bar.

"Howzit?" Kamaka asked.

"How's what?" Roger asked.

Kamaka laughed. "Don't worry about it," he said, glancing back
at his friends. They all laughed.

"We're all getting drunk tonight," Roger said.

"Go slow," Kamaka said. "In the morning we surf."

"I surf better when I'm drunk," Roger said.

"You'll get eaten by a shark," Avril said. "Drink up."

"The shark will smell the alcohol in my blood from miles away,"
Roger said. "The shark will eat me and get drunk off my blood."

I turned to Kamaka and asked about sharks. I asked how often
they eat surfers. He shrugged and said it happens but only rarely.
Surfers see sharks all the time, and sometimes surfers feel them
brush past their feet, but not many people get bitten. He said usually when people do get bit, it's only a little nip from a reef shark.
He said they were nothing to worry about. Tiger sharks are the
ones to watch out for. Tigers are the bad sharks.

"That's how I want to die," Roger said. "Eaten by a shark. Print it in my obituary. I want every girl I ever fucked to know I got eaten by a shark."

"If a shark eats you, I'll give you your money back," Kamaka said. "Tomorrow we surf at Banyans. It's a good place to learn. Probably no sharks. I'll rent some boards and meet you in the lobby in the morning."

Roger nodded. He asked Kamaka what time.

"Anytime you want," Kamaka said. "Early is better than late."

"Make it noon," Roger said.

"Banyans gets crowded on weekends," Kamaka said. "Better to go early."

"I don't do anything before noon," Roger said.

"Sure thing," Kamaka said. "You're the boss. I'll rent the boards and meet you in the lobby at noon."

I drank another rum punch. Kamaka and his friends downed green bottles of Heineken. They told me again about the island's best surf spots. I nodded my head a lot and said words like *yeah* and *cool* because I didn't know much about surfing. One of the guys wore a black T-shirt with the words *Defend Hawaii* on the chest. Beneath the words was an illustration of an AK-47. Kamaka and his friends went to the balcony to talk to the bros about surfing. Roger grabbed another beer.

"Who do they think they're defending it from?" he asked, using a bottle opener to pop off the cap.

"Assholes like you," I said.

"I don't know why everybody here has an attitude about America. If it wasn't for us, some other country would own Hawaii. Probably China."

"I'm sure Kamaka and his friends would be fascinated by your insights."

"America is the best country in the world," he said. "Hawaiians should thank us for adopting their shitty little kingdom."

"We're not really the best country," I said. "That's just some-thing Americans teach their children to believe. Every country in Europe has better schools. Every industrialized country in the world has a better healthcare system."

"Why the fuck do I need a doctor?" Roger flexed his bicep and kissed it. "I'm Superman."

"America acts like it's all about freedom and liberty, but it's not," I said. "It's about fat people driving SUVs. The only thing politicians do anymore is make it easier for people to get fat and drive SUVs."

"I hate fat people," Roger said. "If I ever get fat, take me out back and shoot me."

"You guys are boring," Avril said.

She opened a Heineken. Roger walked away. He talked to some Hawaiian girl who had been standing by herself. Avril took a swig of Heineken. She touched my arm.

"Thank you for being slightly less terrible than Roger," she said.

"That's my slogan," I said. "Slightly less terrible than Roger."

"Yeah," she said, grinning, "but sometimes you whine like a bitch."

"That's my other slogan."

"All you ever say is *America sucks* and *I'm so depressed*," she said. She made air quotes and did an impersonation of my voice that sounded high-pitched and annoying. "But a week from now you'll fly back to Murfreesboro and apply for a job with the IRS. And someday you'll propose to Natalie, and you'll have a bunch of kids and live in a stupid house, and you'll be the most normal, boring American male of all time. That's your future. You'll take up golfing."

I took another sip of rum punch. I put down my glass on the bar. Liquid swirled in the glass. Maybe it would keep spinning and spinning forever.

"I don't know," I said. "That could be a good life."

"A good life would be one where you sail a boat for Greenpeace to save the whales," she said. "Or go to law school and become a non-evil lawyer, the kind who sues the corporations that scam people out of their houses."

"Okay," I said. "I'll do that."

"You won't." She shook her head and looked down, a little, until her hair partially obscured her face. "I know you. You'll go home and find some small way to make yourself useful to the global industrial civilization. You're just like everybody else."

I drank more rum punch. It tasted sugary and nice, but less nice than before because Avril was insulting me. I asked her what I should do.

Avril finished her Heineken and set the empty bottle on the bar. The bottle cast a green shadow across the marble surface.

"Let's get out of here," she said.

This felt like an important moment in my life, like a million little moments had led up to it. I had a decision to make. I thought about my life, imagined it as one long conveyor belt carrying me through a noisy factory. The machinery of the factory shaped me into something I did not wish to become. I wanted to make whatever choice would allow me to escape from the factory. I wanted a new life. I wanted to be a different person with a better future.

"You first," I said. Her eyes were green, the greenest color in the world. "I'll come later. To your room."

Avril brushed against me as she left. Her hair smelled like flowers.

I mixed Natalie another drink and took it to her. She was still talking to the bros. She said the beaches were too crowded in Hawaii. She said Hawaii needed more private beaches.

"I'm tired," I said. "I'm leaving."

"I don't want to go," Natalie said.

"Stay," I said. "I'll walk on the beach. I'll see you later."

I kissed her and left. I entered the elevator by myself. The doors closed. I stood facing the elevator buttons glowing blue and red. I didn't know what to do. Fluorescent lights hummed. I asked myself what Jean-Pierre Léaud would do. Probably he would marry Natalie and find a job drying flowers in the courtyard outside their apartment. He would tell Natalie how satisfied he was with their small life. But then he would get her pregnant and feel pressure to find a new job to earn more income. Soon after finding this job, he would attend a business meeting where he would meet and fall in love with Mademoiselle Hiroko. The affair would be brief and passionate.

I pushed the elevator button that would take me to Avril.

SIXTY-NINE

I stood in front of Avril's door and admired its absolute whiteness.

"Burn down your life," I said to the door.

I knocked, and when it didn't open immediately wondered if I was at the wrong door.

Avril opened it. "Come in before somebody sees you."

"There's no one. They're at the party. They're drunk."

"So am I," Avril said.

"Good. So am I."

"Good."

Avril's room was laid out exactly like me and Natalie's, with two queen-sized beds and a balcony overlooking the bay. Even the artwork on the walls was the same—a matching pair of Japanese-style prints of tropical plants. Avril had done something different with her hair. It framed her face in a new way, making her appear friendlier and happier.

We stood close, not more than an inch apart. She looked into my eyes and exhaled quietly out of her mouth. I kissed her. I put my hands on the sides of her face near her jaw and kissed her again, harder, and Avril pulled away, smirking, and got on the bed on her knees. I turned out the lights. I knew if the lights stayed on everything would be weird. I knew I would think about what I was doing and with whom. My brain was tired from thinking.

I sat beside her on the bed as she took off her shirt and bra. Her breasts glowed white in the moonlight from the balcony. I kissed her again and put my hand on one of her breasts. I deserved them. Deserved to have sex with someone who wanted me. I put my hand up her skirt and touched her. We kissed again, and some circuit tripped in my head, and any doubt or guilt disappeared. I didn't worry anymore or think. Avril leaned back. I took off my clothes. She opened her legs for me. I pushed inside her, and she felt exactly how I wanted her to feel.

SEVENTY

Avril lay beside me in bed. I felt tired in a good way, the way I'd felt at Hapuna after swimming in the ocean.

"I'm glad we did that," Avril said.

"So am I."

"I needed that."

"So did I."

"Will you tell Natalie?"

"Fuck." I rolled away from her.

"Will you?" she asked.

"Never," I said, speaking to the wall.

"Good," she said.

"I'm a robot." I moved my arms like C-3Po from *Star Wars*. "I obey my programming."

"Be a good robot and keep my secrets," she said.

I rolled toward her, looked into her eyes. I spoke in a robot voice.

"The job of every human is to be happy."

SEVENTY-ONE

Later we moved onto the balcony. I wore my T-shirt and boxers, and when I sat on a white plastic chair I felt the coldness of the plastic. Avril wore nothing but a pair of red panties. She sat in the chair beside me. The lights of the hotel tinted her skin yellow. I looked at her yellow breasts, fuller and heavier than Natalie's. Looking at them turned me on. Any pair of breasts that didn't belong to Natalie would have done it for me. The chair must have felt cold against Avril's bare skin, but she gave no indication.

"I take it you're not one hundred percent satisfied with the state of your life," she said.

"Robots don't feel emotions," I said. "That's the nice thing about being a robot. Also they're crazy strong and can punch through metal."

"What would it take for you to be happy?"

"Norway," I said. " Everybody is happy in Norway. I read about it on the internet. Norwegian society provides a generous social safety net, so nobody has to be poor and suffer. Even janitors and fast-food workers have it good in Norway."

"Norway is insufficiently Marxist," Avril said. "People get lazy off the free healthcare and the five weeks of vacation. They sit around watching *Dr. Who* on the BBC Norge. That's how the capitalists win. They give just enough to make everyone fat and sleepy. Capitalists turn people into slaves who shop at IKEA and never make class war."

"I don't want to make class war," I said. "I just want to be happy."

She asked me to consider the possibility that class war would make me happy. I briefly considered and rejected it. Class war sounded like a lot of work.

"It's nice in the mountains," she said, looking not at me but toward the dark ocean.

"What mountains?"

"The Cascades."

"Why the Cascades?"

Avril shifted to look at me. "Because that's where they make class war."

"Who?"

She smirked and looked again over the ocean. "Come with me. In the summer. I'll introduce you."

"What's so great about class war?"

Below us, waves roared as they crashed against the beach. They'd been hitting that sand for thousands of years. The waves will go on hitting for the next thousand and the next. The ocean will never stop.

"The great thing is that we're going to win," she said. "And the prize is a new world. One without rich people or poor people, without private property or systems of hierarchy. No blue collars or white collars, no managers, no slaves—just people. No nations, armies, wars. No kings, no presidents. No shortages or scarcity. No hunger or poverty. No police, no jails. No laws at all. No punishment. No discipline. No rules. The idea is to have fewer consumers, more creators. Less work. More play."

"I don't think that's real."

"Come with me, Nate. To the mountains. We'll watch the cities burn. It will be beautiful. You'll be happy. Honestly happy for the first time. Happy to have front row seats for the birth of the new world."

SEVENTY-TWO

Eventually we moved back into bed. Avril slid under the covers. I held her. I told her I needed to go back to my room, and she said she understood. I kept thinking that any minute now I'd get up and leave. Somehow I kept staying.

"How long have you wanted to break up with Natalie?" Avril faced away from me, and in the darkness the question seemed to come not from her but out of the void.

"Since the beginning."

"Really?" she asked, turning to me. Her voice grew clearer, as if she had been on the verge of sleep but now was waking up.

"No," I said. "It's hard to know. But I've wanted to for a long time."

"Sure—but when did you *know*?"

"It didn't happen like you're imagining it," I said. "My life isn't some movie. Really I'm a boring person. Me and Natalie dated for a long time, and it felt comfortable. I guess every once in a while I'd have a moment when I'd recognize we were wrong for each other, but I wouldn't do anything about it, and the longer we went on pretending everything was fine, the more wrong it became. But those were just moments. They would pass."

"Describe one of these moments."

"I took a film class this year. We watched *Two or Three Things I Know about Her*."

Avril said she'd never heard of it.

"So I'm sitting in the classroom, and the movie is about this woman who lives in a nice apartment in Paris, and she shows off her closet full of clothing and kitchen full of consumer products. All these *things* are really important to her. She's not religious; she's not romantic—she's the perfect consumer. She lives for no greater purpose than to acquire more and better things. Later in the movie she needs more money to buy stuff. She becomes a prostitute."

"And this made you want to break up with your girlfriend?"

"The thing that struck me about the woman is how logical she is. She understands the world and how to thrive in it. All that separates her from real people like you and me is that she's shed her illusions. She knows there's no room in the world anymore for God or love or family, because we replaced them with Costco hot dogs and Walmart. We built this world, and now the world is building us, turning all of us into her—perfect little capitalist robots."

"And the woman in the movie reminds you of Natalie?"

"No," I said. "The woman in the movie reminds me of myself."

SEVENTY-THREE

I slipped back into me and Natalie's hotel room at two in the morning. I tried to be as quiet as possible but woke her anyway.

"Where were you?" she asked, her voice groggy like she was barely awake.

"I went to a bar." I slipped into bed beside her. "On Ali'i. The one with the tiki statues and weird lights."

"That place is terrible," Natalie said, and even through the grogginess she laughed a little.

"It was full of tourists," I said. "You should have seen it. It was embarrassing."

"Why did you go there?"

"To get drunk."

"I like being drunk."

"Everybody likes being drunk," I said.

"I like being drunk with you," she said. She moved close and draped her arm over my chest, and the weight of it felt familiar and reminded me of when we were younger and in love. Those had been good days, and I regretted that there would be no more of them.

SEVENTY-FOUR

At breakfast my head hurt. Everybody's heads hurt. These hangovers sewed themselves into the fabric of the vacation. I wondered if, years later when looking back, all I'd remember about Hawaii would be the hangovers. The hotel provided an enormous breakfast buffet that did not include cinnamon rolls. Natalie was pissed about the rolls. Roger enjoyed the meal but kept complaining that it wasn't complimentary.

"For what we're paying for these rooms, you'd think they could throw in some bacon and eggs."

Natalie offered to put his meal on the credit card. The prospect of someone else paying for breakfast cheered Roger tremendously. I forked food into my mouth without tasting it. Watery eggs and rubbery bacon. Across the room, a long line of guests lined up at the buffet, hungry for mediocre hotel food. I recognized the look in their eyes. I'd seen it on farms back home. The hotel guests looked like the pigs that farmers herded to the trough, fat animals horny to stuff their round bellies with nutriment, enough to sate them until lunch. Fat animals who didn't know that the meal came with a hidden cost, didn't know that there are only so many times you can gorge yourself on slop before you get trucked to the slaughter house.

Roger put an elbow on the table and rubbed his forehead.

"This hangover. Shit. I feel like death."

"I could vomit," Natalie said. "Really. I could do it."

"I can't surf like this," Roger said. "How can I surf like this? I'll fucking die."

"Call Kamaka and tell him we don't want to go surfing today," Natalie said.

"We'll go to a beach or something," Roger said. "We'll sit in beach chairs and drink beer until our heads stop hurting."

"We could go snorkeling," Avril said. "Snorkeling is easy."

I imagined Avril's form gliding effortlessly through the water—her buoyant tits, her smooth, white skin. I made glancing eye contact from across the table.

"Let's do it," I said.

"Let's go hard," Avril said

Natalie said snorkeling sounded fine. Maybe we would see a turtle or dolphin.

"Snorkeling," Roger said. "Perfect. I'll vomit underwater. Puke all over a coral reef. That's always been my dream. To barf on something beautiful."

SEVENTY-FIVE

At noon, Kamaka pulled up to the hotel in a rusty pickup hauling five surfboards in the bed. Roger had not bothered to call and inform him about the change of plans. When Kamaka got out of the truck, Roger told him that we wouldn't need the boards because we wanted to go snorkeling instead. Roger did not say it in any way that could be construed as apologetic.

"I've already got the boards," Kamaka said. "I paid to rent them all day."

"Return the boards and get your money back," Roger said. "Me and my friends want to go snorkeling. We need you to rent snorkels, masks, and fins."

"Daylight's burning," Kamaka said. "Let's surf. Come on. Surfing a Hawaiian beach is a once-in-a-lifetime experience, something to tell the grandkids about."

"We want to snorkel. We don't need surfboards." Roger pronounced each syllable slowly and deliberately. He reached into the bed of Kamaka's truck, hoisted one of the boards and pointed to it, as if Kamaka might not have understood what a surfboard was. "Return the boards and get your money back. Then rent the snorkel gear and get back here, ASAP."

Kamaka nodded.

"Understand?" Roger asked.

"Sure, sure, whatever," Kamaka said, and he nodded again.

"No," Roger said, approaching Kamaka and speaking slowly and loudly. "Do . . . you . . . understand . . . me?"

I considered telling Roger to relax but didn't. I looked at Natalie. She shrugged. I looked at Avril. She formed her hand into the shape of a gun and mimed blowing her brains out. We all stood on the black pavement of the hotel parking lot. The sun felt hot on my skin, and sweat beaded on my forehead.

"Loud and clear, boss," Kamaka said, plucking nervously at his mustache. "Whatever you want. I work for you."

Kamaka hopped into his truck. When he tried to start the engine, it revved a few times and quit. He tried to start it a few more times. On the fourth try the engine turned over, and Kamaka drove out of the hotel parking lot.

"Jesus." Roger said. "Another dumb Hawaiian."

SEVENTY-SIX

About an hour later, Roger drove the rental Mustang south down
the Belt Road toward the region of Ka'u. Kamaka sat in the passenger seat to give directions. Me and Avril sat in the back with
Natalie between us. Avril watched the passing scenery, the palm
trees and bluffs.

Kamaka was navigating us to a place called Two Step. He said it
was more than an hour away but worth it, a great spot for snorkeling. It was across the bay from a historical site, Pu'uhonua, which
he said was worth checking out.

"That way you get a little history with your vacation," he said.

Natalie rolled her eyes.

I held Natalie's hand at first, but soon she took it away to mess
with her hair. She and Avril both wore short khaki shorts, and
their bare legs glistened in the sun. Natalie pulled out her iPhone
and played *Candy Crush*. After a while, Avril turned to Natalie and
asked her what kind of animal she would be, if she could be any
animal in the world. Natalie put down her phone and thought it
over for a few seconds before declaring it a stupid question.

"I guess I could be a zebra," Natalie said. "Zebras are pretty. But then again they live in Africa. I don't want to live in Africa. It's the worst country in the world. Zebras get eaten by lions."

Avril mouthed, *country?*

"I'd for sure be a lion," Roger said. "I bet zebras taste delicious."

Avril said she would be a wolf. She told us some random wolf facts. The vikings drank the blood of the wolf to invoke the animal's spirit in battle. The smallest wolf is the Arabian wolf. The Norse gods chained the great wolf Fenrir to Yggdrasil to prevent him from consuming the Nine Worlds. Avril knew a lot about wolves.

"Wolves are dirty," Natalie said, shaking her head so her hair whipped in the wind. "Wolves stink. They attract fleas. They're a menace to ranchers because they kill livestock."

"This is the gayest conversation." Roger craned his neck to look back at us and smirk. "I mean by a lot. No conversation in the history of the world has been this gay."

Avril told him to shut up.

Roger turned to Kamaka. "Isn't this conversation gay?"

Kamaka shifted uncomfortably in his seat. He stared in the direction of the ocean. He didn't look like he was having a great time. He probably wanted to be somewhere else. I figured we were the worst people he'd ever taken on tour.

SEVENTY-SEVEN

When we entered the district of Ka'u, the landscape rapidly changed from bare stone to green grass and jungle trees. Jagged cliffs rose above the inland side of the road, and the highway curved and twisted around them.

"The whole southern part of the island is different than Kona. It rains here sometimes, and there aren't so many good beaches. Not a lot of people live here. And there's the volcano. Usually if haoles make it to Ka'u, it's to see the volcano."

The highway twisted past gas stations and bars and shabby wooden tourist shops. Eventually Kamaka told Roger to turn onto a small road that ran in a semicircle down to the bay. We parked in a gravel lot and exited the car. The sky was cloudy and the same color as the gravel.

"Are you sure it's safe to get into the water?" Natalie asked.

"It always looks like this," Kamaka said. "Always gray skies."

"Where's the beach?" Roger asked.

Kamaka pointed to an enormous shelf of black lava rock jutting into the bay. A handful of people had put towels on the rock shelf and were attempting to sun themselves beneath the cloud-covered sky.

"This *is* the beach," Kamaka said.

"It's awful," Natalie said. "We drove an hour for this?"

"Wait till you get in the water," Kamaka said. He walked around to the back of the Mustang. Roger used his key fob to pop the hood, and Kamaka took out the snorkel gear. "It's a different world underwater. Just wait. There's no better place."

Natalie gave me a doubtful look. She gave the same look to Roger. He shrugged. I took two sets of snorkel gear so Natalie wouldn't have to carry anything. We made our way onto the rocky area near the water, where we spread out our towels. I attached my snorkel to a rubber strap on my mask and did the same for Natalie's.

"Across the bay is Pu'uhonua," Kamaka said. "When you get tired of snorkeling you should explore."

"The beach looks nice on that side," Natalie said. "Why are we sitting on rocks when we could be on a beach?"

"It's a historic park. They don't let people use the beach," Kamaka said.

"That's stupid," Natalie said. "Why waste a beach?"

"To preserve the history and culture of the island and its people." It was a statement, but Kamaka said it more like a question. "Also as a refuge for sea turtles. They sleep on the beach, where nobody can bother them."

"Turtles are dumb," Roger said. "Seems like by now they'd all have been eaten by sharks."

"They're endangered," Kamaka said. "It's against the law to mess with them. And the coral, too. The coral is endangered. It's very fragile. When you go underwater, don't touch it. Even the oils from your fingers can hurt it."

We walked onto the lava shelf and found a spot to put down our towels and gear. We went to the edge of the shelf, where the water of the bay lapped against it. I wiggled my feet into a pair of flippers. I stood up and tried to walk and felt like the biggest dork in the universe. I waddled over to Kamaka, who stood by the water. He told me to sit on a step that had been cut into the rock. I could see another step below it, just under the surface of the water.

"Two steps," Kamaka said.

He told me to be careful. He pointed out some circular areas that had been worn into the step. Each had become home to a tiny sea urchin bristling with sharp spikes.

"Don't touch," he said. "They'll hurt you bad."

I put on my mask and pressed it to my face until I felt suction. I breathed through the snorkel. Kamaka told me to wait for the next wave to come in, push off from the step and let the wave carry me into the bay. I followed his instructions carefully because I didn't want to die. I kept my eyes on the ocean, watched a wave break against the steps. As it washed back out I pushed off and sort of belly flopped into it. The water felt cold. It churned and bubbled. I couldn't see past the bubbles. Then the water cleared, and I saw the reef. The sight of it forced my brain into a hard reboot. I had never seen a coral reef, and this one seemed too beautiful to exist in the real world. I looked at the fish and corals. The water was perfectly clear. I noticed that the colors—pinks, blues, purples, yellows—were at maximum vividity. Everything in Hawaii was vivid, but the reef was the most vivid by far. I felt sorry for all the people back home who would never see the reef.

I turned my head and saw that Roger and the girls were in the water. The four of us swam together, almost in formation, as schools of fish scattered and cruised among outcroppings of coral. I took a huge gulp of air and dove deep, kicking with my fins, exhaling slowly to save my breath the way I'd seen people do on Shark Week on the Discovery Channel. I approached a globular bloom of pink coral.

A black-and-white spotted blowfish swam in front of my mask. I relaxed and let myself drift, suspended in the water. The fish paddled along with quick flicks of its fins. It hardly seemed to notice or care about my presence at all. The coral forest possessed an alien beauty. I came as a guest to an unfamiliar world, and I hoped not to disturb it. I'd always liked to think of myself as the sort of person clever enough to not believe in God, but there among the coral, I sensed something weird—maybe something like what a believer would experience in a grand cathedral—an uncanny awareness, but also something else, an understanding that no prayers or worship were asked of me, because the coral forest was a living prayer, a hymn of time and matter, the creation song that all of nature had been singing since that first day when the spirit of God moved upon the face of the waters.

Then I was out of breath. Time to go. I swam upward in what I like to imagine was a graceful arc. I pumped my legs. My lungs burned for air. As I struggled through the water, the surface appeared so far out of reach that I thought for sure I would drown. Sunlight danced above me. I kicked hard. Reached. Churned my arms through the water. Surfaced.

"This is wild," Roger said. He'd pulled his mask up to his forehead and was treading water with Natalie and Avril.

I gasped for breath, chest heaving.

Natalie touched my shoulder.

"I want to go down like you did," she said. "I want to see the coral up close."

I nodded. I concentrated on inhaling and exhaling slowly. I floated on my back to rest. After a couple minutes I felt ready to dive again. Me and Natalie secured our masks and went down. Natalie led. She looked especially beautiful underwater, with her hair flowing in a trail behind her and sunlight illuminating her white skin. The muscles of her legs flexed as she kicked, and the tension of her bathing suit pulled her breasts tight against her chest. We swam close to the coral. We hovered and observed the shapes and colors—mottled orange globes, purple formations like otherworldly trees. After a few seconds, I started back to the surface, but Natalie stayed behind. She reached out a hand toward the coral. I swam back, motioned for her to stop. She ignored me. A thin growth of coral extended like a twig. She touched it, rubbed it between her thumb and forefinger. A small piece snapped off, and she dropped it, and it drifted slowly toward the bottom of the bay. Natalie looked up and swam fast for the surface.

"I didn't know I could hold my breath that long," she said once she'd pulled off her mask. She breathed heavily. She kicked her legs to stay afloat.

"You can't touch the coral," I said.

"Sorry." She shrugged. "I guess."

"You killed it," I said.

"I wanted to know what it felt like. Not the dead stuff. I wanted to feel a real one. One still living."

"You can't do that."

Natalie scrunched her face.

"So serious," she said. "You're no fun anymore."

I didn't say anything. She paddled nearer to me, then darted forward to kiss my face.

"So what did it feel like?" I asked.

"Weird," she said, looking down at the water. "Rough. Not like you'd expect. Sandpapery."

For the next quarter of an hour, the four of us swam around the reef. Later we climbed out of the water and took off our flippers and collapsed onto beach towels, all of us out of breath and jabbering about coral and weird tropical fish. Kamaka asked what we thought about the place. He seemed genuinely happy we liked it. He was the first genuinely happy person I'd seen in a long time. It meant a lot to him that we liked Two Step.

I wanted to bask in the sun, but there was no sun, and the lava-rock surface beneath our towels was uncomfortable. Sharp points of rock jabbed my back through the towel.

"As beaches go, this one is fairly shitty," Natalie said, once Kamaka was out of earshot. He hung out with some Hawaiian guys in wetsuits. They would talk and then point at things in the water and laugh.

"It's nice underwater," I said.

"Sure," she said. "This is actually the best place I've ever snorkeled. But, I mean, as a beach it's not so great."

"Look at those divers," Roger said. "How much do you think all that gear costs? A wetsuit, air tanks—what would that be, a thousand dollars? Do you think I have time to learn to dive this week?"

"Maybe stick to surfing," Natalie said.

"I'd be a great diver," he said. "I'd plumb the depths."

Roger asked if anyone wanted to go back in the water. Me and Avril said we were too tired, so he and Natalie went off together. Avril lay on her back. The clouds reflected in her sunglasses. I sat up and folded my arms around my knees. I looked at my white chest and wished for more sun so I'd tan.

"Will you fuck me tonight?" Avril asked.

"Maybe," I said. "Probably."

"You should fuck me."

"I feel bad about Natalie," I said.

"I've been thinking about that," she said. "I guess you should tell her. Once we're back home. Then she can make up her mind. That's fair. That's decent. Allow her to make a decision."

"I still feel shitty."

"It's not like you and Natalie are married. She's not your wife. You're a free person, and you can do whatever you want. That's what you don't understand. That's why you're always depressed."

"I still feel shitty about it."

"Then stop fucking me. Let my cunt go to waste." She grabbed her crotch. "Do whatever you want. Nobody can make you do anything."

She took off her sunglasses and looked at me with her green eyes. Wisps of red hair scattered across her face. I thought about my life. I imagined it again as a conveyor belt through a terrible factory, a large and terrifying machine that worked day and night to make itself larger and more terrifying. I wondered, idly, what kind of person I would have become if I'd done certain things differently a long time ago.

"I don't love Natalie," I said. "I used to. I really did. I cared about her more than anything in the world. I'd stay up at night thinking about her. Natalie made me happy. She loved me. She was the best thing in my life."

I watched Natalie and Roger swimming in the bay. I wondered what they were seeing in the water—probably something amazing like a manta ray or shark. Avril put her sunglasses back on and lay down. I looked at all the people on the lava shelf. Most of the people were couples. The sight of other couples made me feel strange, neither happy nor sad. I looked out to sea. I looked at Natalie and Roger again, swimming side by side. She was pretty; he was handsome. They looked good together—looked perfect.

I leaned toward Avril.

Kissed her.

Her lips tasted like the ocean.

SEVENTY-EIGHT

Later all of us lay on the lava rocks in another attempt to soak up what little sun filtered through the gray blanket of clouds. Kamaka asked if we wanted to check out Pu'uhonua. Nobody said anything. He looked at each of us individually, his imploring eyes growing sadder with each rejection. I suppose he had nurtured a desperate hope that somehow we would be different and better than the average tourist, but at last we'd revealed ourselves. We were just like everyone else, white people whose torpid minds produced nothing but apathy toward the history and culture of his homeland. When he turned his eyes to me, his gaze penetrated all the way down to the formless void at my center, the grand nothingness that had birthed all other aspects of my person. I sat up and scratched my head. I hardly knew Kamaka, but he seemed like a decent guy, and we'd treated him badly. I didn't want him to hate me.

Pretty soon the two of us were walking around the bay to Pu'uhonua. On the way, Kamaka rattled off the history of everything, like a real tour guide. Kamaka had visited Pu'uhonua many times and knew all about it. He told me the area used to be a place of refuge. In old Hawaii, the punishment for breaking a Kapu law was death. But people could be pardoned if they fled to sacred Pu'uhonua. The refuge area was on a peninsula that reached into the ocean.

"Weird," I said.

We stopped by a hut with a thatched roof. The hut was guarded by tiki gods carved into wooden poles in the sand around the building. The tiki gods looked fearsome, the type of gods who feasted on human souls.

"I mean it's arbitrary," I said. "Why should anybody be forgiven just because they were able to get here? Doesn't make sense."

"Does the U.S. justice system make sense?" Kamaka asked. "If you're rich, you can pay a bunch of lawyers to keep you out of jail. If you're the president, you can break whatever laws you want, and apparently nobody can touch you. The justice system is full of courts and lawyers that make it look fair, but mostly it just puts black people and poor people in jail."

"Yeah the courts suck," I said. "Actually the whole country sucks. I mean, relatively. Like I'd rather live in the U.S. than China, you know? But it still sucks. Everybody back home is thoroughly brainwashed, and they think it's the best country in the world. But in a lot of ways, the United States is really a very mediocre country."

"China sucks," Kamaka said, nodding thoughtfully.

"How do you really feel about America?" I said. "Is it okay for me to ask? I think if I was Hawaiian, I would hate America."

"It's complicated," Kamaka said, rubbing his mustache between his thumb and index finger. "I don't like that a bunch of white people showed up and took over, and I can't say I love what you've done with the place. I have some friends involved in the Hawaiian sovereignty movement, and I think the movement is great, and I want to see where it goes. But—for real—I don't see Hawaii declaring independence anytime soon. The U.S. has problems, but it's not the worst country in the world. Like I'd rather be here than Russia."

"Russia sucks."

"Fuck Russia," Kamaka said. "Fuck Putin."

"Fuck Putin in the face," I said.

I liked Kamaka. It was good to meet somebody who shared my contempt for Vladimir Putin. We walked by a small beach. Four or five turtles lay in the sand. They were green with white spots on their flippers.

"These guys have the right idea," Kamaka said. "Chilling on the beach. Living a good life. Turtles don't worry about the government. Turtles don't worry about Putin."

"They might worry if they knew they were going extinct," I said.

"It's better not to think about it."

"You have to think about it," I said. "It's important. We all need to think about it."

"No," he said. "It makes me angry. When I think about what people are doing to the turtles, it makes me want to murder everybody."

SEVENTY-NINE

We talked about turtles again on the drive home. The conversation did not go well. Roger drove with Kamaka beside him. Kamaka went into tour-guide mode and explained why sea turtles were endangered in Hawaii. He said sometimes the turtles were killed for food but most died from eating plastic trash floating in the ocean.

"They mistake the plastic bags for food," Kamaka said. "They choke to death on plastic."

Roger was not impressed.

"If they're too stupid to tell the difference, they deserve to go extinct," he said. "Turtles are too dumb to live."

"How could turtles understand plastic bags?" Kamaka asked. "They didn't invent them. They didn't dump them in the ocean. It's not their fault."

"Why do we need turtles anyway?" Roger asked. "I mean what good are they? Good for eating, I guess. But there are a thousand things that taste better. I don't give a fuck about turtles. If I saw a turtle on the highway, I'd run that motherfucker over. I'd get out of the car and piss on its ugly turtle corpse. That's my opinion."

Kamaka stared straight ahead through the windshield. His shoulders rose and fell as he sighed.

"I'm just about pau," he said.

"What?" Roger asked, shouting to be heard over the wind.

Kamaka didn't answer. He must have been really angry. Nobody said anything for the rest of the drive. Kamaka looked like at any moment he might start murdering people.

EIGHTY

Back at the hotel, me and Natalie lay on the bed in our room. We looked at the ceiling. We did not touch each other.

"Do you want to get something to eat?" I asked.

"Later," she said.

"Do you want a shower?"

"Later," she said, "before dinner."

"What do you want to do?"

"I don't know."

"Do you want to sleep?"

"No," Natalie said. "I don't want to sleep."

I kept looking at the ceiling, which was plaster and marked by a series of flowing ridges, like waves. I rolled over. Natalie's body was splayed out beside me on the bedspread. She wore her stars-and-stripes bikini. I took note of her white legs and butt and the graceful curve of her back. Her pink lips parted ever so slightly as she breathed.

"Do you want to have sex?" I asked.

"No," Natalie said. "I don't want that."

EIGHTY-ONE

Later Natalie grabbed the remote and watched TV. She flipped to a news station, where some expert told an anchorwoman that the government had already borrowed more money than it could ever repay. Natalie changed channels. She watched an old rerun of *My Two Dads*. Light from the television bleached her skin like she suffered from tuberculosis. Back then, I watched a lot of documentaries about diseases. I watched a lot of everything.

I tried to sleep but couldn't. I started thinking about that weekend in high school—it seemed so long ago, like another life or a story I'd read about something happening to someone else—when her father and stepmother went on vacation, and I stayed over at their house, and we'd planned on fucking continuously for two days straight but mostly just drank vodka and watched *Alien* movies.

I remembered how on the second day we went out for sandwiches at some fancy-shit deli on the fancy-shit side of town, and on the way back it rained, and as I drove through her neighborhood a cat—I remember it was mostly black but with some brown or gray patches almost like stripes along its back—ran in front of my car, and I slammed the brakes and skidded down the wet street. And we heard a thump—felt it, too—a soft noise, and hollow. Natalie and I looked at each other. We got out in the rain and found the cat. One of its back legs was twisted and bleeding. It hunched in the street and yowled.

"I don't know what to do," I said. I didn't feel old or responsible enough to handle the situation. I felt helpless, like a child lost in a crowded department store. I looked around, hoping some grownup would swoop in to save us.

Natalie picked up the cat and cradled it in the bottom half of her T-shirt. I was sure it would bite her, but it didn't. I drove us home, and when we got inside Natalie took the cat to her bathroom and told me to search the internet for veterinary clinics nearby. She put the cat in her bathtub and tried to wash out the wound, but the cat freaked out and scratched her and ran away and hid under her bed. For the rest of the day, Natalie knelt by the foot of the bed and tried to lure it out. She whispered to it and sang and offered it tuna, but the cat wouldn't budge. When I reached under the bed to pull it out, it screeched and tore at my hand and drew blood.

That night, Natalie slept on the floor and whispered to the cat, pleading again for it to come out. I sat with her for a while but eventually gave up and climbed into the bed. Around midnight the cat began yowling. This continued until about 3 a.m., and after that I fell asleep. As soon as I awoke, groggily, in the morning, I got down on the floor beside Natalie, who still slept. She woke up and asked about the cat. I reached for it until my hand closed around something cold and stiff. I slid its body out from under the bed. We looked at the cat and its twisted leg and how the blood had dried and matted in its fur.

"I wanted to help," Natalie said.

"I know," I said.

"I wanted to make everything better."

EIGHTY-TWO

The bros threw another party in the penthouse that night. Me and Natalie showed up together, but as soon as we arrived she ditched me and went out on the balcony to hang out with them. I stood by the bar and fixed myself a rum punch. I felt like I was trapped in time, living the same day over and over. The bros had three different kinds of rum—Malibu, Captain Morgan, and Diplomatico. The bros weren't good for much, but they did keep on hand an impressive supply of rum. I checked inside their fridge. They had a six-pack of Mike's Hard Lemonade. Seeing it made me think about Natalie. She liked Mike's Hard Lemonade, even though it's terrible. She drank it all the time. Roger leaned against the bar and drank whiskey from a rock glass.

"Look at that piece of ass," he said.

He motioned with his glass to a Hawaiian girl sitting on the bed with one of the bros. She wore a black bikini top and cut-off denim shorts. She looked athletic, like she'd played sports in high school—volleyball or swim team.

"You should hit that," Roger said.

"I'm unavailable."

"Then why is Natalie flirting with those guys outside?" he said. "I feel bad for you. Really. I feel depressed for you."

"You're a great friend," I said.

I finished my drink in one mighty gulp. I thought about how my friends never drank my rum punches. I felt sorry for them. They were missing out on a great drink. Rum punch is a sadly underappreciated libation.

"Let's be honest for a second," Roger said. "There will come a day when Natalie will cheat on you. I hate to say it, but it's the truth. And it's not because she doesn't love you. I know she thinks you're a great guy, blah-blah-blah. But people are people, and people enjoy having sex with other people. Natalie is the kind of girl who will always have opportunities, understand? Face it, Nate. Face reality. Natalie is going to cheat on you. She's probably cheating already."

The more I talked to Roger, the more I wanted to jump off a building. I opened the fridge and grabbed a Mike's Hard Lemonade. I brought it to Natalie on the balcony. She accepted it and resumed ignoring me. She and the bros talked about business. One of the bros was working on his MBA. He said his dad had an MBA, and his older brother had an MBA, and they both made tons of money.

"My dad fires people all the time," the bro said. "He says he hates it, but I can tell he loves it. Deep down."

Natalie asked the bro if he was going to be a CEO like his father.

"Obviously," he said. "The CEO sits at the top of the pyramid. That's where the cash is. Think about it: the CEO does the least amount of work and makes the most money. That's how the system works. The lower you go, the more work you do and the less you get paid. All the way at the bottom are people who work at fast-food restaurants and Walmart. They work like dogs and get paid like dogs."

"I don't understand why anybody would work at Walmart," Natalie said.

"You'd have to be really stupid," the bro said.

From the balcony I could see the ocean and the warm lights of the city. I wanted to be in the ocean, swimming with dolphins. I wanted to be anywhere other than the balcony. I went back inside. Avril had arrived. She leaned against the bar wearing a tight T-shirt, and her nipples poked little bumps through the fabric. I opened the fridge and took out the jug of Kool-Aid. I mixed myself another rum punch.

"Hawaii sucks," I said.

Avril shrugged and sipped her drink.

"I hoped Kamaka would be here tonight," she said.

"Roger pissed him off," I said.

"Roger sucks," she said.

Roger sat on one of the beds with the Hawaiian girl. Roger told her how he snorkeled at Two Step. The girl looked bored. He told her he saw a dolphin, which wasn't true. As soon as he mentioned the dolphin, the girl started paying attention.

"Have you ever eaten a dolphin?" Roger asked. He sipped from his glass of whiskey. "I bet dolphins taste like the best thing in the world."

Avril leaned against me. She slid her glass beside mine on the bar and placed her hand on top of my own. Hers felt warm like she'd been lying in the sun.

"This party sucks," she said.

EIGHTY-THREE

Me and Avril faced each other on the bed in her hotel room. All the lights in the room were on, creating an overwhelming brightness. I considered turning them off, like the night before, but then I looked at Avril and wanted them on. I enjoyed seeing her and didn't want to miss anything.

"What will you do to me tonight?" Avril said. She pulled her shirt over her head. She reached behind her back to unlatch her bra, and her tits flopped out, and I stared at them.

I didn't answer. I didn't know what I wanted to do to her. But I did want her. I'd never wanted anybody so much in my life. I removed my shirt and tossed it to the floor. We stood on our knees, chest to chest, our legs sinking into the plush mattress. I moved toward her. Kissed her. She pressed her tits against my chest. I pushed her onto her back and mounted her and sucked one of her tits and entered her. I did all the same things I used to do with Natalie. They felt different with Avril—better. It was good to be with someone who wanted me. I observed her as we fucked—her face and the way her body moved. I hoped these new images entering my brain would replace my memories of Natalie. We kept going and going, and by the end I couldn't picture Natalie at all.

Avril was all I wanted. All I would ever want. I noticed the shape her mouth made when she came, and then I came, and then it was over and I felt like we'd gone to war together and survived.

EIGHTY-FOUR

Later we sat on the balcony. A breeze blew in from the ocean, and boats lit up the harbor beneath the purple-black sky. I thought about what we'd done. I felt like a different person than I'd been in the bedroom. I felt like a traveler who had returned to the real world from a place of magic. The memories were foggy, slipping away like a dream.

"We should do that more often," Avril said.

"Every day," I said. "Twice a day. Three times."

"Run away with me," she said. "Come to the mountains this summer. We'll save the world."

"I don't want to save the world." I said. "People don't deserve to be saved. Everybody back home votes for Trump and cheap oil and guns and Whoppers-with-cheese and a big stupid wall to protect them from brown people and the rest of the world and reality. I'm done. I want out."

"I'm your way out," she said. "Come with me and make class war."

I told her I didn't want class war. Or any other war. She asked if I wanted a better world. I told her it depended on what she meant by better. I didn't want some bleak communist nightmare.

"Not the old communism," she said. "A new communism for a new world."

"Everybody hates communism," I said.

She told me I was grouchy. She told me to relax—sit on a beach, soak up some sun, get my energy back. Then go home and make class war.

We stayed on the balcony for a long time. My body and brain felt sluggish. I wanted to fall asleep in my chair and stay there for about a week. I looked at the clouds. I looked at Avril's fake-red hair whipping in the wind from the ocean. The air smelled like salt and felt cool but not cold. I had this idea that I was on the verge of a great change. For the better? Worse? Maybe some weird change I couldn't even imagine. I closed my eyes and listened to my own breathing, and then, softly, I heard Avril breathing too. Even high up in the hotel tower I heard waves crashing against the shore.

EIGHTY-FIVE

I didn't come back to my room until late. I unlocked the door with my key card and went inside and ran my hand up the wall to feel for the light switch. Immediately I heard noises. A girl said *shit, shit, shit*. A guy said *goddamn it*. My hand found the switch. Fluorescent light flooded the room. Roger fucked Natalie from behind on the hotel bed. He had his hands around her waist and rammed her hard. I could tell they were deep into the fucking because even after they realized the lights were on they kept at it for a few thrusts, like they'd built up a lot of momentum. Roger's face went all rubbery when he saw me. His expression morphed from surprise to anger to horror to shame. His mouth wiggled like the mouths in claymation cartoons. Natalie tried to cover her face with her hands, which seemed unnecessary considering her ass stood up in the air where nobody could miss it. I saw everything. I saw her tiny black asshole and my friend's glossy cock penetrating her cunt. Roger's mouth wiggled some more.

Things hadn't been right between Natalie and me for a long time, so walking in on her and Roger didn't affect me the way you might think. I didn't fly into a murderous rage. Blood vessels didn't pop in my brain. My world didn't dissolve in a red haze, and I didn't wake up in the morning atop a pile of their mutilated bodies. I felt instead like I watched them from a great distance, and nothing they did was of any consequence or even mattered to my life. I might not have cared at all except Natalie appeared to enjoy it so much.

EIGHTY-SIX

The first thing I did was go for a walk. I took the stairs down to the lobby because I couldn't stand the idea of getting into some elevator and waiting around. Just the thought of being in some claustrophobic elevator drove me crazy. I passed someone from the hotel staff in the stairwell. A maid. She carried pillows. She stared at me, but I ignored her and kept going down the stairs. I'd paid for a hotel room and could use the stairs if I felt like it. Or Natalie paid. Or her father. It didn't matter who paid. I didn't want to think about it.

Even late at night, people still milled about the lobby. A cute couple held hands on a loveseat. They were older, so I assumed they were married. I always assume old couples are married, because the idea of old people dating grosses me out. Anyway, I'll bet that guy never walked in on his wife getting fucked. They'd probably been married for forty years, and it never happened once. Some people have all the luck.

I took the sidewalk along Ali'i. A lot of people were out on the street. I remember how the temperature felt perfect. Back in Murfreesboro, everybody was dying of hypothermia. Even though Hawaii was destroying my life, I still felt lucky to be there.

I climbed onto the seawall. I stood atop it and stuffed my hands in the pockets of my shorts and watched the waves below. They broke gently against the wall with a sound like static from a TV. I imagined sometimes the waves would be bigger. I imagined if I stood on the wall during a storm the waves would drag me out to sea and drown me somewhere deep. I wondered what it would feel like to drown in the middle of a storm, with waves exploding all around me, rain falling like a bombardment of artillery, lightning transforming night into day. It didn't seem like a bad way to go.

Some old-timers fished on the pier. They were far away, but because of the lights on the pier I could see them pretty clearly. They looked like real Hawaiians. Without meaning to, I made up a little story about them in my head. They were friends who'd gone fishing in the same spot for decades. All of them were single because of tragic circumstances, like infidelity or their wives died in car wrecks or were lost at sea. I wanted to stay in Hawaii forever and become a fisherman. I would fish with the old men on the pier, and they would accept me and become my new family. I didn't want to go home.

I thought about my next move. I thought about Avril. It would be easy to go to her and spend the night, but I knew that in the morning certain things between us would be set into motion. I didn't know if I wanted to be Avril's boyfriend. I didn't want to be anybody's boyfriend. I didn't want to be anybody's anything. I wanted to drown in a storm. I wanted to punch a shark in the face. I wanted to lift one out of the ocean and hold it in the air until it suffocated. And I would laugh. I would kick the shark as it lay dying, and I would laugh.

I walked along the seawall. I didn't fall into the ocean, but if I had, that would have been okay. Later I walked on the sidewalk and found a bar. The bar was tacky with colored lights and plastic tiki statues. I sat down at the bar. The bartender was a woman. She wore a coconut bra and a grass skirt. She wasn't Hawaiian. She was white and roughly sixty-five years old. She asked what I wanted to drink. She called me *honey* in an exaggerated Southern accent.

I ordered a Kona beer. I drank it and stared at the wall behind the bar. It was decorated with bottles of alcohol. I waited around for a while after I finished my beer. The bartender asked if I wanted another. I was the only customer at the bar. I told her I didn't want another. She told me I couldn't sit at the bar unless I was ordering.

"Punch a shark in the face," I said.

She pretended not to hear. She wiped the bar with a dirty rag. She wiped a lot harder than necessary.

"I'm not running a homeless shelter," she said.

This time she didn't call me honey.

I paid and left the bar. I stood on the sidewalk out front. Across the street, the lights of a seafood restaurant winked out, and then the tourist shop next door. I thought again about Avril. The idea of going to her didn't seem so depressing anymore. I rooted around in my pocket for my phone. I dialed her number. She answered. Sounded groggy. I told her I needed a huge favor.

EIGHTY-SEVEN

Avril opened her door immediately after I knocked. She asked if I was okay. She looked at me the way a mother might look at a child with a broken arm. Her expression should have comforted me but actually made me feel worse, the most pathetic man who had ever lived.

"I'm fine," I said.

She grabbed my arm and pulled me into the room. Hugged me. She put her hand on my forehead as if taking my temperature. And all of the pulling and hugging felt good, even though, basically, I wanted to die. She sat me down on the bed. My legs hung over the side, and I swung them, intermittently, like a kid. She sat cross-legged beside me. I talked to her a little but avoided her eyes. I stared straight ahead toward the door to the balcony. We appeared pale and ghostlike in the glass, as if a gust of wind or mean word could destroy us.

"Everything is over," I said. "My whole life. Everything. I don't know what to do anymore."

"You hated your life," Avril said.

"My life was great," I said. "I had a girlfriend. She had a rich father. My girlfriend wanted to marry me and be a mother to my children. Her father would have showered us with money forever."

"You were bored," Avril said. "Your girlfriend was an Instagram slut, and she bored you."

"Maybe I'm the one who's boring," I said. "Maybe I didn't deserve my life. I'm not good enough. Maybe that's why it's gone."

"You wanted to run away. You wanted to move to Norway."

"Norway is for losers," I said. "Norway is for sad people who can't cope, people who can't make it in America. Norway is for pussies."

"You're being weird," Avril said.

We sat on the bed and talked for a while, but nothing that either of us said made me feel better. The more we talked, the more I wanted to jump off the balcony. Later she switched off the light, and we went to bed. I stayed far to the side of the mattress and made sure not to touch her. I didn't want her anymore. I wanted my life back. I stared at the ceiling in the dark and thought about how much I wanted my life back.

EIGHTY-EIGHT

I woke up at one of those weird hours like 3 a.m., when everybody is usually asleep and there's nothing good on TV. I rolled over and put a hand on Avril's waist. I couldn't see much in the dark, but I could tell when her eyes opened because they appeared brighter than the rest of the room. I kissed her and moved my body against her. She woke up fast. I kissed her neck and shoulder and tits. I slid my hand between her legs. She got on top of me. I lost myself in her hair and lips and skin. My whole life was gone, disappeared into her hair and lips and skin. We fucked, and I thought about the future. I thought, *this is my new life.*

In the morning we awoke and fucked again and showered together. Avril packed her luggage. She called a rental car company. She read her credit card number over the phone. I felt lucky to always be loved by women with credit cards. Later I returned to my room, and Natalie, mercifully, was gone. I packed a few things. I went downstairs and found Avril, and we took possession of a new car and new lives, and if we thought about the past at all it was only briefly and tinged with relief, a gladness that all of that was behind us, over and done, because we weren't the same people we used to be.

We were new people.
Free people.
And happy.

PART

FOUR

THE
SWIMMING POOL
WILL REMAIN
CLOSED
INDEFINITELY

EIGHTY-NINE

ME AND AVRIL stood on a crowded ledge overlooking an active volcano. I draped my hand over her shoulders as we peered into the crater. The prospect of seeing a pool of lava excited me, but as it turned out, there was nothing to see. The lava was nowhere near the surface. The crater was just a big hole in the ground.

"I expected the volcano to be much more awesome," Avril said.

"There should be lava."

"And explosions," she said.

"They say the vapors are toxic," I said. "If a big-enough vapor cloud blew toward us, we would all die."

"I guess that's something," she said.

About a hundred people stood with us on the overlook. I guess the volcano would have seemed more impressive if me and Avril had been alone. If we'd trekked for days through deep jungle. If we'd worked for it. Bled and starved for it. The tourists sucked all wonder and magic from the volcano. It was no more exciting than spotting Mickey Mouse at Disney World.

After losing interest in the crater, we worked our way through the crowd and entered the volcano museum and gift shop. We looked at a diorama of the volcano and the whole island. We stood in front of a monitor and watched a video about volcanoes. Bright-hot lava flowed into the ocean, generating clouds of white steam.

"Now that's the volcano shit I want to see," I said.

"Real-ass volcano shit," Avril said.

We made our way through the museum, but we had to move slowly because of all the tourists. Hawaii attracted the most boring varieties of white people. Everyone looked like a loan officer from a bank in the Midwest.

Me and Avril looked at a painting of Pele. The goddess's face materialized out of a plume of ash above the volcano. I put my arm around Avril again. It felt necessary, somehow, that I touch her constantly.

"I bet Pele hates this tourist bullshit," I said. "I bet she's just biding her time until the island fills up completely. Then she'll make the volcano erupt and bury them in lava."

"If the volcano erupts right now, you'll die along with everybody else," Avril said.

"Worth it," I said.

I looked at the painting again and noticed Pele's nearly imperceptible smile, as if she understood something we tourists could never know. I wanted Pele to reveal all her secrets to me. I wanted her to love me. I wanted to be her mighty champion.

"Hail to thee, oh volcano goddess," I said, waving my arms dramatically. Some tourists stopped to look. "We appeal to thy tender mercies, oh volcano goddess."

Avril tugged my arm to pull me away.

"Don't be weird," she said.

We crossed into the gift shop. We played with stuffed-animal dolphins. We looked at Hawaii-themed magnets, keychains and coffee mugs. Avril pressed buttons on a machine that played music from various CDs. The machine played a song that sounded like ukuleles and a woman singing sadly in a language I did not understand. I perused a shelf of books. I flipped through a field guide to the fish of Hawaii. I looked at photos of butterflyfish, yellow tang, triggerfish, grouper, stingrays, goatfish, and Moorish idol. I read about the official state fish of Hawaii, humuhumunukunukuāpua‘a. I tried to pronounce the name but failed.

"Soon you will belong to me," I said to the fish.

I put down the field guide and picked up a book about Hawaiian mythology. I showed it to Avril.

"I'm gonna buy this," I said. "It's important to understand the gods."

"We don't have much money," Avril said. "We have to be careful."

I looked at the book and weighed how much I wanted it. I glanced around the store, at all the crappy plastic merchandise. I remembered how nice it was to travel with Natalie and her credit card. If we'd wanted, we could have bought out the entire gift shop and put it on the card. Avril's credit card wasn't like Natalie's. It had a smaller credit limit, and the father who paid it off every month was much less understanding. I slid the book back onto the shelf.

"Don't you want it?" Avril asked.

"No," I said. "I don't want any tourist shit."

NINETY

We drove around the volcano park until we saw a sign for something called the Thurston Lava Tube. We parked and walked along a sidewalk leading downhill through a rainforest. A metal railing ran along the sidewalk to prevent people from falling to their deaths down the hill. All the plants and leaves in the rainforest looked extremely green. The vividity once again imparted a sense of unreality, as if more than geographical distance separated Hawaii from the mainland. As if I had crossed a dimensional barrier and entered a new world of warmth and beauty.

"Those plants are weird," Avril said.

We stopped and looked at a stalk that rose straight out of the ground and curled into a tight green spiral at the tip.

"Looks like a tentacle," I said. "Some Cthulhu bullshit. Like if a dog walked by, it would grab him and squeeze him to death."

"It's not big enough to kill a dog," she said.

"A small dog," I said. "A cat."

"In a million years, these plants will evolve and become large enough to eat humans," Avril said.

"We're lucky to be alive at this point in history, before the plants turn against us," I said. "After we go to war with the plants, everything will be fucked."

"If we burn the plants, there will be no oxygen," Avril said.

"We'll learn to make new oxygen from machines," I said. "But only the rich will be able to afford the good oxygen, the clean stuff. Everybody else will buy discount oxygen at Walmart, and it will smell like sulfur and farts."

"The future will be worse than the past," Avril said.

We descended into a rainforest of flowers and alien-looking plants until we came to the mouth of the lava tube. It looked like a cave, only its diameter was almost perfectly round. A metal bridge led into its mouth. Beyond the entrance, the tube went dark. Me and Avril peered inside it.

"Everything bad in the world is at the bottom of this tube," I said.

"Abominations," Avril said. "Bahamut and Leviathan."

"This is where the Earth Mother was wounded and bled out," I said. "This is where she died."

"The Earth Mother bleeds manatee blood," Avril said. "She weeps koala tears."

We crossed the bridge and entered the tube. It wasn't as dark inside as I'd expected. The air felt cool and damp. The tube was perfectly cylindrical, with shallow ridges patterning the walls.

"Some giant shoved his penis into the ground," I said.

"That's what killed the Earth Mother," Avril said. "Fucked to death by giants."

We held hands in the dark. Soon a family of tourists approached from behind. Me and Avril parted so they could pass between us. They looked like nice, red-cheeked Americans, people who drove Ford trucks and attended church on Sunday. People who wore Wranglers and ate apple pie. Friendly people with good intentions who nevertheless fill landfills with garbage and the oceans with plastic bottles. They looked like regular, normal people. The most normal people in the world.

"They have no love for the Earth Mother," I said.

"They are the giants," Avril said. "The giants of Omaha, Nebraska."

After exploring the lava tube we returned to the entrance. I squinted from the sudden brightness. I felt a vibration in my pocket. I pulled out my cell phone and saw I had a message from Natalie. I looked at the phone. I looked at Avril. I looked at the dark mouth of the lava tube.

"The future will be worse than the past," I said.

NINETY-ONE

"I just want to know if you're still alive," Natalie said. Her voice over the phone sounded sad, but I couldn't tell if she was actually sad or merely trying to sound that way, like she knew the situation demanded sadness, so she'd fake it for the sake of appearances. "You and Avril disappeared. Me and Roger were worried sick." In addition to sounding sad, Natalie sounded more than a little annoyed.

"We're alive," I said.

"Where are you."

"We're in Hawaii," I said. "We're alive and having fun. A tropical adventure."

"It's been crazy here without you."

"Go to a beach," I said. "Hawaii is renowned for its many picturesque beaches."

"I haven't left the hotel. Roger's been drunk all day. We've both been drunk."

"I don't want to talk about Roger."

"Roger feels terrible," she said. "He understands how bad this is. Did you know that you're his only friend? His only real one. Roger feels like shit. He knows he fucked up."

"Poor Roger," I said.

"I just want it to be over," she said. "All of it. The vacation. Everything that happened last night. All of it. I want to forget. I want to go back to Murfreesboro. I want my life back. Our life. You know? I want to be with you again and forget everything."

I paced while we talked. I noticed another of those weird plants with coiled tendrils. I imagined it whipping out and curling around my neck. I imagined the tentacle suffocating me until I drifted off into an eternal, dreamless slumber. It didn't seem like a bad way to go. I listened to dead air for a minute before she spoke again.

"Is Avril there? Are you with Avril?" She spoke rapidly, like a salesman trying to make a deal.

"We're together," I said.

"Have you fucked her yet?" she asked. "Just, honestly, I want to know. Is that it? Are you fucking Avril?"

I lowered the phone and looked at Avril. She sat on the metal railing above the walkway with her feet hooked around a lower rail. Avril formed her hand into the shape of a gun—two fingers representing the barrel—put it to her temple and pulled the trigger to blow out her brains.

"The Earth Mother knows your heart," I said into the phone. "The Earth Mother is not amused."

NINETY-TWO

Me and Avril found a hotel that night on the outskirts of Kona. It didn't look like a very nice hotel, but neither did it look like a place where we'd be raped to death in the parking lot. The hotel was a big square around a central courtyard with a swimming pool. The pool had been drained. A construction crew tore into the concrete with jackhammers. The air of the courtyard grew thick and white with concrete dust. When we checked in, the woman behind the counter talked loudly to be heard over the jackhammering. She told us the pool was closed for repairs.

Avril paid with her credit card. After running her card through a machine and signing the receipt, she gave me the bad news.

"Maxed out," she said.

"That didn't take long."

"I didn't expect to pay for a rental car. I didn't expect another hotel room. I don't have unlimited fucking money."

"Four more days until we fly home," I said. "How will we live? What will we eat?"

"Would it kill you to pay for something once in a while?" she asked. "Anything? Would it kill you?"

"Maybe if you call your dad, he'll wire you some money."

"Maybe you're out of your fucking mind," she said. "He's already gonna lose his shit when he sees the credit card bill. He'll pay it—he's my dad, after all, and paying credit card bills is what dads are for. But before he pays he'll absolutely lose his shit."

Our room was small and smelled of mildew. Cheesy artwork depicting a woman doing hula hung on the wall. The print was badly faded, as if it had hung on the wall since the early 1970s. Avril sat on the bed and used the remote to turn on the TV. It was boxy and black with a rounded screen, the kind parents keep in their basements. I pulled a curtain aside to look out the glass balcony door. The balcony was large enough for maybe half a person to stand comfortably. It overlooked a highway and a crummy neighborhood behind it. Every third house along the street looked like a meth kitchen.

Avril switched off the television. She lay on the bed and moved her arms and legs as if making a snow angel. I lay beside her, propping my head up with my hand. We looked at each other.

"Well," she said.

"Here we are," I said.

We looked at each other for another minute.

"What do you want to do?" I asked.

"I don't know," she said. "I don't feel like anything."

"Do you want to have sex?" I said.

"Yes," she said. Then, "No. I don't know. I feel weird."

"That's natural," I said. "When life is good, we should feel good. When it's weird, we should feel weird. It's normal to feel this way."

"I don't want to feel weird anymore."

"Everything is fine," I said. "We'll go away. Move to Norway. Everything will be better in Norway."

After that I fucked her. I put her on her knees to fuck her from behind, the way Roger had fucked Natalie. Avril's ass was bigger than Natalie's, and the size of it made me feel lucky to be alive. I fucked Avril hard and thought about Natalie. It was just as much fun to think about either of them. I flipped them back and forth in my head, fucking Avril harder and harder. I'm not sure which one I was fantasizing about when I came, maybe both at once. Anyway it was the biggest, hardest orgasm I'd ever experienced, and it probably ranked among the top ten in the history of mankind.

NINETY-THREE

That night we ate dinner at a seafood place in Kona. It was in the tourist district but noticeably less fancy than the Fish Hopper. It reminded me of the place where I'd eaten with Natalie the night before, only worse and tackier—more tiki statues, coconuts, and flickering torches. The hostess was a young Hawaiian woman, and she seated us at a table by an open window with an expansive view of Kailua Bay. I kept glancing toward the entrance to see if Natalie or Roger would wander in. It was stupid to look. Natalie and Roger would eat somewhere nicer.

It was difficult for me to accept that I was no longer Natalie's boyfriend. So much had happened in a single day. My life had veered off in a strange new direction. I gazed at the water and lights along the bayside. None of it belonged in my life. A moment from someone else's life had been spliced into mine, a happier person living a life of adventure and excitement.

"This isn't so bad." I nodded toward the bay.

"Better than Murfreesboro," Avril said.

"You can go up and down every street in Murfreesboro and never find an ocean as nice as this one," I said.

"That's the problem with Murfreesboro," Avril said. "Terrible oceans."

"The worst."

"I want to order a drink," Avril said. "Can we afford drinks?"

"We can each have one drink," I said. "On the way back to the hotel we'll buy whiskey. Cheap."

"What's the point of taking a vacation to Hawaii if we can't get drinks by the ocean?" she asked.

A waiter brought out menus and explained the daily specials. Me and Avril listened politely even though we couldn't afford the specials. The waiter ran down the list like he was bored, like he was counting the minutes until his shift ended and he could go home and smoke weed. I wanted to go to his house and smoke weed with him. Going to some Hawaiian waiter's house and smoking weed would have been a meaningful experience to tell people about later. Not that it was likely to happen. He probably hung out with people much cooler than me.

I read the menu. I flipped past the *entrees* section and looked for *sandwiches*, to save money. I considered ordering a fish sandwich until I noticed the words *market price*. I couldn't afford *market price*. I ordered a chicken strip appetizer.

"I keep thinking about Norway," I said after the waiter took our orders and left. "Everyone in Norway makes bank."

"A meal at McDonald's costs $25 in Norway," Avril said.

"We won't eat at McDonald's," I said. "McDonald's is gross and makes you fat. McDonald's makes you dead."

"I've never known anyone so obsessed with Norway," Avril said.

"I just want to be happy," I said. "The problem with America is that someone's always at the bottom of the pile getting fucked. Usually it's me. I'm tired of everything being about who's got the biggest car, biggest house. America is the McDonald's of nations."

"Will you really move to Norway?" Avril asked. "Or just talk about moving to Norway?"

I shrugged. I looked out at the bay. I remembered an article I'd read on the internet about jellyfish. The article said *jellyfish blooms* are out of control. Human beings overharvested the fish species like salmon that eat jellyfish, so the population is exploding. Scientists don't know what realistically can be done to stop it.

"Jellyfish blooms," I said.

"What?"

"Nothing," I said.

The waiter brought our drinks. Avril's glowed fluorescent green in the tiki lights. I sipped my rum and pineapple juice. My plan was to go slow and nurse it all night. Our waiter's hair was spiked and black. I couldn't decide if he looked more like a marijuana user or methamphetamine user. Meth is a problem in Hawaii. Meth is bad. It's also extremely uncool. If you're determined to abuse illegal drugs, you should abuse the coolest drug available to you. Cocaine is incredibly cool.

"I'm mad at Natalie for fucking Roger," I said as soon as the waiter was gone.

"You fucked me twice before Natalie ever fucked him," Avril said.

"Who knows how long they've been fucking? What if she's been fucking him for years?"

"Anybody who fucks Roger has my sympathy," she said.

"That's a lot of people."

"The drunk ones don't count," Avril said. "Roger's only had sex with two or three people who were sober. I guarantee."

I sipped my drink. I tried to stop thinking about Roger's sex life.

"Jesus," Avril said. "That night at C.J.'s party. Freshman year. Do you remember? I was blasted."

"Mountain Dew and vodka," I said.

"Do you want to know what happened after they took me upstairs?" She leaned in, spoke low and conspiratorially. Part of me wanted to know. Part of me didn't. Avril stared with a strange intensity. She didn't wait for me to answer. "I was so drunk I barely knew what was happening. I remember C.J. fucking me from behind. C.J. was really hairy. Then Roger shoved his dick in my mouth. I don't remember everything, just bits and pieces. I remember Roger's dick smelled awful. His pubes, I mean. That's where the stink came from. It smelled like he'd just finished fucking somebody. I don't know. Maybe it was me he'd fucked. Maybe I smelled my own cunt on his dick. I don't know. I was drunk. The other thing I remember is the bed. How the sheets kept popping off the corners of the mattress. The mattress smelled musty like it belonged to someone's grandparents. After the guys finished, I lay on the bare mattress for a while before passing out. I remember it was covered in stains. I thought the stains must be from other girls they'd fucked, just like me, and I wanted to get up and find a towel to wipe down the bed, because I didn't want to leave another stain. I didn't want any part of me to remain on that bed. But in the end, I didn't do anything. I lay on the mattress until I passed out. I was really drunk."

The waiter arrived with our food, and I ordered another round of drinks even though we couldn't afford them. I stared toward the bay again. I imagined what it would look like full of jellyfish, if they were jammed in so tight you could walk all the way across, stepping from one gelatinous blob to another. I wanted to stroll among the jellyfish. I would sing to them, and they would raise their tentacles as I passed, as if waving to me, recognizing a long-lost brother. Waving and gurgling. Gurgling and waving. Waving to welcome me home.

NINETY-FOUR

On our way out of the restaurant, Avril told me she needed to use the restroom. I waited by a railing overlooking the ocean. The water was dark except where the light from the tiki torches illuminated it. In the distance, I could make out the curve of the bay, all the way to the fishing pier. I took my phone out of my pocket and opened Twitter. I scrolled through some tweets. They were terrible. I liked that they were terrible. Twitter should always be terrible.

Good morning to the man who hates me and thinks my work is frivolous trash

My roommate poops 50-60 percent more often than me and actually I'm jealous

Drank a White Claw might die soon

I looked out to sea. I thought about how big the ocean was, how full of life. I thought about how old it was. I wanted to dissolve in its waters. I wanted to become part of the ocean.

I looked at my phone again. I read another tweet. Someone had tweeted *my boyfriend's back* and attached a photo of the McDonald's McRib sandwich.

I tapped like.

I tapped retweet.

NINETY-FIVE

Me and Avril fucked in the hotel that night. Afterward we held each other beneath a cheap bedspread on a stiff mattress, and she fell asleep, and I almost fell asleep but couldn't. I got out of bed, careful not to disturb her. I found my phone on the desk. I tapped the screen to bring it to life and checked my messages. There were none. I'd hoped for another message from Natalie. I hated her, but part of me still belonged to her. It hurt my feelings that she didn't care enough to text me. I felt the hurt—physically—as a great emptiness in my chest.

I opened twitter. I read a tweet from President Trump.

Google loves the communist Chinese but not the U.S. Terrible!

The tweet raised my spirits, in a way, because it reminded me that however low I sank, I could never be dumber or more pathetic than this president of the United States. His gross stupidity provided great comfort in my time of suffering. There in the hotel room, I experienced a revelation about the people who voted for Trump and idolized him. They were losers. They voted for him because they were so far down the hole that even some slick Manhattan real estate shyster could look like a winner, someone loud and mean who had never once in his life told a good joke.

They admired his showy demonstrations of wealth and the power he appeared to wield on his network television reality show. And in their heart of hearts they recognized him as one of their own—a loser. In Trump, the grumpy American fascists found a perfect straw man for their hatreds and resentments. Trump voters put on their biggest, fakest smiles and called him a winner while secretly taking comfort in the belief that if such a monumental loser could become president, perhaps some hope still remained for themselves. Even though no hope did remain—they were losers. I tapped my phone to turn it off. I felt bad for all the Trump voters. I felt sorry for them, sorry their lives were miserable, sorry for their hopelessness and failures.

I walked across the room to the balcony door and peered through the glass. Ramshackle houses as far as the eye could see. I summoned the ocean in my imagination, a dark horizon of water lit dimly from the bluish light of the moon. I imagined the garbage vortex spinning somewhere out there. I wondered if someday it would be gone, if the whole ocean could be clean again. I thought about Avril and Natalie and all the ways I'd failed them.

NINETY-SIX

Since I couldn't sleep, I put on a pair of shorts and left the room to take a walk around the hotel. I closed the door gingerly on my way out, careful not to wake Avril. I roamed the hallway. It was boring, with old carpet that looked like it had never felt the caress of a vacuum cleaner. The walls were decorated sporadically with faded art prints of sea turtles and volcanoes. I took the elevator down to the lobby. There was no music in the elevator. I slipped my phone out of my pocket and scrolled Twitter to avoid being alone with my thoughts. Someone had tweeted, *So much fucking noise*. I tapped the screen to like the tweet. I scrolled through some others. I tried to imagine the lives of the people who write all the tweets. Probably not the greatest. Probably no abundance of comfort and joy. I wondered how long all the sad people in the world would go on tweeting. Someday, some lonely person will send history's final tweet.

The elevator doors slid open, and I entered the lobby. I leaned against the railing around the pool construction. Tiny white particles from the construction hung in the air like a chalky mist. For all I knew, they were the kind of particles that cause lung cancer. I imagined what it would be like to have lung cancer. Immediately

I stopped. I promised myself not to think about lung cancer ever again.

The bottom of the pool was torn up and jagged from where construction workers had jackhammered it. The longer I looked at the broken pool, the sadder I felt. The hole reminded me of the garbage vortex. The hole reminded me of my entire life.

A young Hawaiian guy wearing a hotel name tag came over to me. He smiled. He leaned against the railing.

"Sucks about the pool," he said.

"Yeah," I said. "I don't know. I probably wouldn't have gone swimming anyway. Pools are gross."

"Ha ha, yeah," the Hawaiian guy said. "Super gross. Especially this one. It's supposed to get cleaned every day but doesn't. The people who own this place are assholes. The pool sucks."

I asked if he liked living in Hawaii. He told me he loved it. It was the best place on earth. He said the only things that sucked about Hawaii were that it was expensive and hard to find work. The best job he'd found was on the night shift at the hotel. I wished him luck finding a better job. I told him I didn't know what kind of job I wanted or how to get it.

"Jobs are hard," he said.

"Yeah," I said.

He asked if I wanted to buy weed.

I thought about it.

I told him I didn't want to buy weed.

NINETY-SEVEN

In the morning, me and Avril took the rental car to South Point. We drove through Ka'u along the Belt Road until we turned south onto a crumbling strip of pavement that alternated between two lanes and one. A dust cloud rose behind the car, and the landscape flattened into fields of wind turbines and cattle.

"Weird to see cows in Hawaii," I said.

"Weird," Avril said.

"I guess I expected something more exotic. Water buffalo. Muskoxen."

"Why does it matter?"

"It's just weird."

At South Point we walked out to the cliffs and stood on one of several old boat hoists. A metal ladder stretched down to the sea. I peeked over the end of the platform and saw the water churning far below. The sight made me dizzy. I imagined falling. I imagined landing on the rocks. I backed up a few feet and sat down. Avril walked to the edge of the platform, bracing herself by holding onto a metal beam. Periodically she would let go, until the wind and heights made her teeter.

"Please stop doing that," I said.

"It's fun," she said. "I won't fall."

"The current will suck you to Antarctica."

"I won't fall," she said.

She let go of the beam. Wind and sunlight played in her hair. She balanced for a while before her legs began to wobble and she grabbed the beam.

"It wouldn't be a bad way to go," she said.

"I can think of better ways."

"For a few seconds, it would be like flying. I'd see the sky, and the water rising up to meet me. And then I'd never have to think about anything again. My body would become part of the ocean."

She let go and balanced at the end of the platform for a long time, teetering a little, until a strong gust of wind rocked her. She yelped and grabbed the beam.

"Please stop doing that," I said. "Please."

"It would make a good Facebook post. The final post. After I go over the edge, you could take a picture from the cliff and notify my friends and family that this was where I died. I jumped off the hugest, most beautiful cliff in the world and became one with the ocean."

"Jumped or fell?"

She took her hand off the beam.

"Jumped," she said, her arms outstretched, delicately, like the wings of a bird. "It's no good if your death is some dumb accident. You have to mean it. Death is too important to leave to chance."

NINETY-EIGHT

The path from South Point to the beach stretched for more than two miles through dusty terrain that brought to mind—despite my never having been there—the Australian Outback. Me and Avril made our way along a deeply rutted trail dug by the tires of four-wheel-drive vehicles. It was a windy, dusty trek beneath a blazing sun, and we, like the dozen people we encountered along the way, made it in our bathing suits.

"Weirdest hike ever," Avril said.

"It's like a science fiction movie," I said.

"That woman is carrying a beach ball."

"A weird science fiction movie," I said. "Low-budget from the 1970s."

After a half hour of walking, we arrived at the edge of an enormous crater overlooking a pristine bay. We descended the crater along a narrow path worn smooth by years of abrasion. At the bottom was a beach of olivine crystals. The green sand gave way to a turquoise sea, and all of this was framed by the stone walls of the crater, sun-bleached and textured like dead wood. We found an empty spot on the beach and spread out our towels. Everything looked beautiful. Waves rolled in. Waves rolled out. A handful of

Hawaiian children rode body boards, and their skin glistened in the surf.

"Someone took the most beautiful beach in the world and stuck it on the planet Tatooine," I said.

"Don't make jokes," Avril said. "Don't ruin this. It's perfect. Let me enjoy it. I've never been anywhere perfect."

We stayed on the beach for a long time. We sunned ourselves and rolled over onto our backs. I got a twinge of that same feeling from when I swam down to the reef at Two Step. Like when I was a kid and my parents took me to church. There were times when I sat alone in the sanctuary and felt something strange—maybe even holy—a crisp silence hinting at a deeper wisdom or presence.

"I'll never go home," I said.

"Right," Avril said. "Norway."

"Or stay in Hawaii," I said. "Make money somehow, enough to live on."

"Just go home and finish school," she said.

"If I go back, I'll be stuck forever. I'll print out a bunch of résumés and get hired at some boring company that makes boring products and destroys the planet to make a small group of Republicans insanely wealthy. I'll commute to work in rush hour traffic. I'll wear dress shirts and slacks. That will be my life. Dress shirts and slacks."

Avril rolled toward me. Smiled. Ran her hand down my arm. I looked at her face and red hair and sunglasses and the roundness of her breasts and the tension of her bikini against them. The sunlight on her skin shined so bright she glowed. Avril looked perfect. I closed my eyes and imagined living a life with her—a happy one marked by excitement and adventure.

A life of fulfillment.

Sincerity.

Gentleness and quiet pleasures.

A life I didn't deserve.

NINETY-NINE

We lay on the beach and lost track of time and even forgot the meaning of the word. A single bead of sweat traced a salty path down my forehead. The hot sun beating down and the warmth of the sand enveloped me pleasantly. Back home, everybody was freezing in the middle of winter. Everybody wore their thickest coats and scraped ice off windshields. I was glad to be in Hawaii. I reached out to Avril, held her hand, entangled her fingers in mine. I felt happy to be in a warm place and in love.

A few couples and families populated the beach, with wide areas of empty sand between them. Compared to the crowds at Hapuna, the green sand beach felt peaceful. Instead of screaming kids, I heard only the rumble of surf and occasional cry of seabirds overhead.

I turned to Avril and told her I loved her. It had been years since I'd said those words and meant them. There had been a time when I spoke them sincerely to Natalie. But we'd persisted in using those words until long after all meaning had leached out of them, reducing them to a boring ritual and, eventually, a painful reminder of what we'd lost.

Avril blushed and told me she loved me too. And I believed her. It felt nice to be loved. I had forgotten what it was like. Somewhere along the way I'd stopped believing that it was even possible for anyone to love me.

Avril said she wanted to get in the ocean. We walked down the beach, and the hot sand burned our feet until we reached the water. It was cool but not cold. We kept going until it rose to our chests. Hawaiian kids played nearby. Everybody at the beach looked happy. I'd never seen so many happy people in my life.

Avril stood facing me in the water, and I held her around her hips. The cliffs of the crater curled in a semicircle around the beach. Avril asked what I meant when I said I loved her.

"I mean I love you," I said.

"But what do you mean?"

I didn't know what to say, so I kissed her. Avril's lips tasted like salt. Sometimes love is just that. Sometimes love is the taste of salt on her lips.

Later we floated on our backs, rocked by gentle waves. I reached for Avril's hand. I gave thanks for that moment. I took comfort in knowing that even if later everything blew up, all my suffering would be worth it for that moment. I held onto Avril, and loved her, and drifted with her on the water, eyes closed, overcome by the strength of the light.

ONE HUNDRED

Evening had fallen by the time we got back to the car. We returned to the Belt Road and took it east toward Hilo, driving slowly in the dark because I didn't know the road. I imagined sudden turns sending us flying over a cliff into the ocean. But as usual I worried too much. The road curved gently along the southern flank of the island.

My phone vibrated. I checked it while driving and saw a text from Natalie: *We need to talk.*

"What was that?" Avril asked.

"Nothing," I said. "Just some email."

I drove for another hour in the dark. My stomach growled. I hadn't eaten since breakfast. I'd planned on stopping at a restaurant off the highway, but there were no restaurants. Eventually we came to the town of Kea'au. We spotted a shopping center off the highway with a McDonald's. I parked, and we went inside and ordered combo meals from the Value Menu. I ordered the two-cheeseburger meal, same as I would have back home.

It was late, and we were the only people eating in the lobby. The cheeseburgers tasted sort of good and sort of bad. Usually I avoid McDonald's, because I respect myself, but occasionally I really will get a craving for it. Sometimes all I'm hungry for is mediocrity. The food from McDonald's has a neutral quality, like air or water or low levels of background radiation.

"How much longer will we drive tonight?" Avril asked. She held a waxy cardboard cup and sipped Diet Coke through a straw.

"It's not much farther to Hilo," I said.

"What's in Hilo?"

"Civilization," I said. "Hotels."

"We don't have money for a hotel."

I took a bite of cheeseburger. I ate some fries.

"There's only a few more days till we fly home," I said. "I'll try not to spend much. We'll do free stuff. Beaches."

"The flight will be awful," Avril said. "We'll have to sit with Natalie and Roger the whole way."

"Call the airline and change our seats."

"It costs money," she said.

I ate more fries. I sipped diet coke. I felt a vibration from my phone and saw another text from Natalie: *I want to see you again.*

"More email?" Avril asked.

I detected a weird tone in her voice.

On the way out of the restaurant I took my tray to a trash can. It had a hole in the top, wide enough for trash but small enough so people can't throw away the trays. I tipped up the tray and let my trash slide into it, and it reminded me of my whole life. A guy behind the counter said something to us—maybe in pidgin—and I couldn't understand.

Me and Avril got in the car. I started the engine but then just sat there with my hands on the wheel. Avril looked at me. Touched my leg.

"We should sleep in the car tonight," I said. "I don't know any of the hotels in Hilo, and even if I did we couldn't afford them. Let's drive and find some quiet place. I don't know."

"It's okay," Avril said. "I guess. Aren't you afraid of being murdered?"

"The murderers will probably let us go after raping us a little."

I started down the dark highway and eventually made a left turn onto a dirt road leading up a hill. There were a lot of houses at first, but I kept driving until they disappeared. The road narrowed to one lane. Trees grew all around, some close enough for their twigs to knock against the side of the car. The night was clear. The sky looked enormous and full of stars.

"I liked the beach today," Avril said. "I've never seen anything like it. Even if everything else about this trip sucks, I'm still glad I saw the beach."

"It's weird that it's always been there, but we didn't know, never even imagined."

"I wonder what Roger and Natalie did today," she said.

"Drowned, I hope."

"Roger and Natalie are my only friends, and I hate them," she said.

"Make new friends," I said.

"It's not that easy," she said. "I'm no good with people. They get on my nerves. People are boring and selfish. All anybody wants is to make money and get married and poop out a few kids. Everybody wants to drive an SUV. They want to pretend global warming isn't happening. They want to eat meat. They want to watch reruns of *How I Met Your Mother* and *Big Bang Theory*. I hate it. It takes me forever to make friends."

We drove further up the hill. The forest smelled damp. I turned down a muddy road bordered by trees, then pulled through an open gate into a field and stopped. I turned off the engine and killed the headlights. The stars and moon shone brighter and bluer in their absence. I'd never seen so many stars in my life. Moonlight lit up a cloud moving toward the horizon, making it appear silvery and alive, a giant serpent from the ancient past. I heard a sound like birds chirping. I'd never heard so many birds at night. Eventually I realized it wasn't birds. It was frogs. The frogs sang a weird song, and I liked it.

Me and Avril climbed over the front seats to get to the back, and she laughed when I bumped my head on the dome light. She got on top of me, and I kissed her, and her hair smelled like the ocean, and we kissed again and fucked quietly in the back seat. Afterward I noticed how the moonlight lit up her skin. Her skin looked just like the cloud.

"It will be weird to go home," Avril said.

I thought about Murfreesboro. For the first time since leaving, I missed it and wanted to return. I tried to imagine a new life with Avril back home. It was difficult, fuzzy like a dream. Natalie was much easier to picture. A vision of her rose ghost-like from my memory. I saw Natalie lying naked on an expensive hotel bed. I imagined fucking her one last time. My old life had seemed inescapable—but now that I was free, it didn't seem so oppressive. My old life had been comfortable, like a well-worn pair of jeans that fit as perfectly as my own skin. I missed Natalie and her credit card. I wanted to throw her down and fuck her on a pile of her father's money. It wouldn't be so bad to commute to work every day and wear dress shirts and slacks, not if I came home every night and fucked her on a pile of her father's money.

ONE HUNDRED ONE

In the morning we drove back down the hill to Kea‘au and got breakfast at the same McDonald's. We ate in the car as we drove to Hilo, not because we were in any hurry but because eating in a McDonald's lobby for two consecutive meals would have made us want to kill ourselves.

It didn't take as long as I'd expected to arrive in Hilo. We drove past shopping centers, car dealerships, and a mall with a movie theater. It was like any other town in America, except for the palm trees and strange architecture. The houses had peculiar metal roofs, long and shallowly sloping. I made a left on Kamehameha Boulevard and drove along the waterfront. People kayaked and rode paddle boards in Hilo Bay. I noticed that nobody was swimming. The sky looked gray and turbulent with clouds. The water in the bay churned brown and murky. The sand of the beach was black, the remains of ancient lava rocks. I parked the car, and me and Avril walked along the shore. We sat on a grassy rise above the sand.

"What a weird town," Avril said.

"Did you see those big trees along the road?"

"Gigantic."

"It's kind of beautiful here," I said.

"Definitely," she said, looking out to sea. "Definitely beautiful."

"And something else. I don't know what."

"Weird," she said.

"Why isn't anyone swimming? Why isn't anyone sunbathing on the beach?"

"Very weird here," she said.

I saw a pile of stones on the beach. They were all about the size of my fist and buffed smooth by the ocean. I stepped on top of them.

"I'm standing on a pile of miracles," I said.

"This is nothing like Kona," Avril said. "Practically a different island."

"A weird island."

"I want to go to a beach," she said. "A real beach. Not this weird beach."

"I don't know where they hide all the good beaches."

Avril pulled out her phone and swiped her fingers across the surface. I sat in the sand. Avril crouched beside me and searched on her phone. Brown waves rolled onto the sand. In the bay, a small island was connected to land by a pedestrian bridge. Men fished off a nearby pier. To the north, a green hill sloped down, reached far out to sea before slipping beneath the water. We stood up and wandered along a row of canoe halau. Racing canoes were stored on racks inside them. These were big canoes requiring an entire team to paddle. I tried to imagine what the bay would look like filled with canoes. I wanted to see hundreds all at once, colorful vessels cutting through the water as far as the eye could see. I wanted to travel back in time and see the bay as it had been before white people had come to the island.

"I found something," Avril said. "There are beaches south of town."

"Good beaches?"

Avril made a face.

"Beaches where we won't get infected by crypto bacteria?"

"I don't know," Avril said. "I don't know anything about crypto bacteria."

ONE HUNDRED TWO

We drove south out of town. Avril navigated with Google Maps, but we didn't really need it because only one road ran in that direction. It took us past a port with a lot of industrial warehouses and facilities that looked as bleak and dirty as anything in Murfreesboro. Soon, jungle trees replaced the brownfield. We rounded a curve and passed a series of beach parks and expensive homes before pulling into a parking area shrouded by palm trees.

A sidewalk led us across a grassy lawn decorated by palms and shallow pools of water. From there we took a dirt path to a small black-sand beach where parents swam with their kids. The water looked clear and much nicer than the brown stuff in town. An apartment building towered over the treetops behind us, granting its tenants a commanding view of the bay.

"How much do you think it would cost to live here?" I asked.

"More than you've got," Avril said.

We passed through a stand of trees and arrived at another beach, backed by an enormous shelf of lava rock. A few people lay in the sun or swam in the water, while others climbed on the rocks. Me and Avril camped down with our beach towels. I raised my arm to shield my eyes from the sun.

The water was calm because much of the cove was protected by a ridge of lava rock jutting out of the water. Huge waves exploded against it. Toward the mouth of the cove, people surfed in rougher waters. The cove looked to be the southernmost arm of Hilo Bay. Looking north from the beach, the city was hidden from view, but I could see all the way to the land beyond it, a green triangle sloping lazily out to sea. The clouds that had hung overhead had dispersed, and when I looked inland I could see all the way to Mauna Kea. The landscape of the island rose for miles, transitioning from green to brown to the snow-capped peak.

"I could die here," Avril said.

"Let's die here," I said.

ONE HUNDRED THREE

We lay on our towels on the black sand and looked at the water and talked about going in but instead just kept lying there. The sun felt hot, and I hoped to get a good tan even though the truth was I never tanned. I was a burner. My skin would turn red for a few days before going pale again and producing a new freckle. Suddenly the sun disappeared. I opened my eyes. A big Hawaiian guy loomed over us. His arms were gigantic, crossed over his chest.

"Howzit?" he asked in a thunderous voice.

I removed my sunglasses and blinked.

Kamaka's mustached face grinned down on me.

"Bro," he said. "What brings you tourists to my side of the island?"

"We're tired of Kona," Avril said.

"There are too many tourists there," I said.

Kamaka laughed.

"Fuck tourists," Avril said.

"Tourists are the worst," I said. "They don't respect the 'aina."

"No, they most definitely do not." Kamaka crouched down in the sand beside us. "So where are your friends? The asshole guy?"

"Dead," I said. "I mean I hope."

"I hate that guy," Kamaka said. "Did you know that? Fucking Roger. I'm gonna destroy that guy."

"Everybody hates Roger," I said. "Even Roger hates Roger."

"And the blond girl? Nancy?" Kamaka asked.

Avril laughed viciously.

"A shark ate her," I said. "We are all saddened by her passing."

Kamaka shook his head. He told us we were crazy. He said he was in Hilo visiting his girlfriend, but in a few days he would go back to Kona and try to find more work as a tour guide. He said he didn't make much money at it, but it was better than getting some lame job behind a desk. Kamaka laughed again and seemed unusually talkative. He told us he didn't want to be one of those guys who goes to work every day in an Aloha shirt and khaki pants, who sits in some cubicle at a county office and pushes paper. He said he didn't even have the connections to get a job with the county, so it didn't matter. I told him that if he saw Roger in Kona, he should punch him in the face. Kamaka grinned. He looked out to sea. He reached into the pocket of his shorts and pulled out a joint and a Bic lighter. He looked at the joint, then raised his eyebrows at me and Avril. He lit the joint and took a drag and exhaled and passed it to me. I took it and held it to my lips. The joint excited me. I hoped the weed in Hawaii would be some insane-powerful gourmet strain. But when I smoked it, it just felt like normal marijuana.

Kamaka pointed inland to Mauna Kea. "See that mountain?"

"Awfully nice mountain," I said.

"I bet it's one of the top ten mountains of all time," Avril said. "Top five."

Kamaka told us about the observatories at the peak. A lot of big-time astronomy happened up there. But Mauna Kea is one of the most sacred sites in Hawaiian culture, and Hawaiians didn't want a bunch of crap built up there. A few years ago, a group of universities proposed building another observatory, a massive one featuring the biggest telescope in the world. This made a lot of Hawaiians very angry. They didn't want the sacred mountain to be desecrated again. They held protests. They set up a camp on the mountain and blocked construction crews from reaching the summit.

"A telescope seems okay," I said. "I mean it's not like they're digging a garbage dump. It's for science."

"That's the prevailing haole opinion," Kamaka said. He sighed and scratched his mustache. He said when the telescope was first announced, he didn't know much about it or care if it got built. But then the protests started, and that's what made up his mind. Kamaka said he got obsessed with news footage of the protests and all the videos on social media. Videos of police officers arresting all these old Hawaiians, kapuna with their hands bound by zip ties, old ladies who looked like his grandmother being put into police vans. Interviews with Hawaiian police officers who were torn up inside because even though they respected what the protesters were doing, they arrested them anyway. The protesters stayed on the mountain for months until the state backed down and sent the cops away.

"You can think whatever you want," Kamaka said. "I hope they never build that fucking telescope."

I asked Kamaka if he was native Hawaiian. He smirked. He said only a tourist would ask that question. He said anybody who lived on the island could tell he wasn't all-the-way Hawaiian. He said he was hapa, and then he paused to see if I understood, and I had no idea, and I waited for him to explain, but instead he looked away and frowned. He took a hit off the joint and coughed up smoke.

I liked hanging out with Kamaka. I felt like a space traveler who'd journeyed light years from planet Earth to some sleek and technologically advanced civilization. And I'd met some ultra-chill alien who didn't mind slumming it with me for the weekend. But soon I'd have to return to my shitty home planet, and afterward if he ever thought about me again it would be only to write a few sentimental lines in his space blog. A few lines about me and my interstellar misery.

ONE HUNDRED FOUR

The three of us lay in the sand and didn't speak for a long time. I closed my eyes. The sun felt pleasantly warm, and I almost fell asleep. When I opened my eyes, Avril's face floated above mine, blocking the sun.

"Let's stay in Hawaii forever," I said.

"I don't get why people live anywhere else," Kamaka said.

"Hawaii is expensive," Avril said.

"I could work at the mall," I said. "Fold shirts at The Gap. That's easy." A breeze blew, tousling the limbs of trees at the edge of the beach. "We'll rent one of those off-the-grid cabins in Puna. They're only a few hundred bucks a month. We'll buy a scooter and ride it to our minimum-wage jobs. We'll never leave Hawaii, and life will be one long vacation."

Kamaka sat up. He grabbed his ankles and pulled forward to stretch.

"You guys are hilarious," he said. "But for real—don't be poor like me. I never have money for gas. I can't take my girl out to a movie. Can't pay for drinks at a club. Can't even get into the club. You don't want that. If you can get a good job—do it. Work that career. Make money."

"You live on a tropical island," I said. "You surf every day. You live the best life."

"Someday you'll want a family," he said. "You'll want a house and a car—a nice one that people won't laugh at. Someday you'll want all the basic stuff everybody takes for granted. It's not bad to want those things. It's actually good. People in poor neighborhoods try so hard to live regular lives. A poor person will work his whole life, and usually at the end he's still poor."

"Don't listen to Nate," Avril said. "He talks big, but it's all talk. He'll tell you how he's going to move to another country and have adventures, but after a while you learn not to take him seriously. A few days from now he'll go home to Tennessee. Back to his old life. His boring life. There's nothing Nate loves more than his boring fucking life. Don't let him fool you. He's completely normal."

Kamaka sat up and told me to look down the beach. A few soft waves rolled into the sand. A strange object jutted out of the water. It looked like a rock at first, but something about it appeared strange and un-rocklike. A turtle's head and fins emerged. The creature began to crawl onto the sand. The three of us stood up and walked toward it. I knelt down and looked at its alien face. The turtle was a monster, larger than five feet from head to tail.

"Can I touch it?" I said.

"Look but don't touch," Kamaka said.

The turtle raised its head. It stared at me through black eyes.

"It's like a dinosaur," Avril said.

"It *is* a dinosaur," Kamaka said.

The turtle waddled toward me. The scales on its face looked dull and worn from decades in the ocean. Its eyes were black. The turtle looked at me and opened its mouth. Its beak was serrated like the edge of a knife.

I tried to transmit a psychic message.

"I'm sorry humans pollute your waters," I imagined saying with my mind.

I'm sorry you humans are cursed to live on land, came its imaginary reply. *You will never know the sea like I do. Is that why your species is killing itself? Because you don't know the ocean? I fear there will come a day when no turtle will even remember the human race. It's funny meeting you, here on my beach. I will try not to forget you.*

ONE HUNDRED FIVE

Kamaka took us to a Mexican restaurant in Hilo called Casa de Luna. The restaurant was open to the street on two sides, providing diners with a panoramic view of the town.

"Is the Mexican food any good in Hilo?" I asked.

"Some places," Kamaka said. "Not here. Mostly we'll drink tonight. This place is good for drinking."

We got a table and ordered drinks. Kamaka recommended a local beer called Hapa. I watched people passing on the sidewalk. Big Hawaiian guys held hands with their girlfriends. Skateboarders rolled along in their hoodies.

Our waitress was pretty, with long brown hair pulled back into a ponytail. She looked like a college student. I could imagine her in a library, wearing glasses and reading Foucault. I thanked her when she brought my beer. I tried to think of something else to say, but my mind went blank. I should have asked if she was in college. I should have asked her about Foucault. Hapa was a brown ale and tasted good. Kamaka told me the brewery was across town.

"You look like a beer guy," Kamaka said. "I bet you drink all that fancy beer."

"He does," Avril sipped a margarita. "For a revolutionary anti
-capitalist, Nate spends a lot on beer."

A different waitress brought our food. She looked sort of young
but with a lot of premature wrinkles, like she smoked too much.
She set down our plates and asked if we needed anything else. Her
breath smelled like old coffee and ashes. I didn't bother asking if
she was in college.

Kamaka ate a quesadilla. Avril got fish tacos, and I got regular
tacos. My tacos tasted bland like they hadn't been seasoned—just
plain meat wrapped in a soft tortilla shell. Hawaii, in most ways,
was a wonderful place, but those tacos were unforgivable.

My phone rang. I felt it vibrate in my pocket. I pulled it out
to check the display. Natalie. I put the phone on the table and
watched it ring and vibrate. I looked at Kamaka. I looked at Avril.
The phone pulsed again. Moved. It vibrated across the table like a
living thing.

ONE HUNDRED SIX

I stood on the sidewalk with my phone pressed against my ear. I heard Natalie's voice through the speaker and looked down the street at all the weather-beaten buildings with long metal roofs rusting and sagging. It was strange to hear her voice in Hilo. Natalie's voice belonged to snow-covered lawns and old brick university buildings with ivy crawling up the walls. It was for long Tennessee highways, where if you drive with a girl and hold her hand at night, the road seems to go on forever, and you wish it would, you wish you could go on driving and holding her hand forever.

I told Natalie it was good to hear from her. This was a lie. Hearing from her was not good. It wasn't bad, either. I just didn't feel much of anything. I knew myself well enough to know that later on I'd feel a lot of things, and most of them would hurt. I told Natalie about Hilo. I told her about the beach and the turtle.

Natalie cut me off. She apologized about the other night. She apologized over and over. She called herself a slut. She called herself a whore. I told her not to feel bad. I told her about me and Avril. Natalie cried, a little, and then for a while didn't say anything. I told her she was better off with Roger. They had a lot in common. They really had a chance to make it. Maybe they could be happy.

A Japanese man and woman passed me on the sidewalk. They held hands and smiled at each other. Or at least I thought they were Japanese. Something I'd learned about myself in Hawaii was that I was very bad at determining anybody's ethnicity. They could have been Korean or Taiwanese. I really was clueless about that stuff. The only people I could identify with any confidence were white people. I wondered, idly, if Japanese people were as bad about infidelity as white people. Probably. People everywhere are probably just like everybody else.

"I don't want to be with Roger," she said. "I don't love Roger. I could never love him. I want you back. I want our old life. I was happy with you. I want to be happy again."

"Everything's weird now," I said.

"I want to see you again."

"It won't matter."

"I'm coming to Hilo tomorrow."

"Don't," I said. "Don't do that."

"I'll get a hotel room. A nice one. By the ocean."

"There's no point."

"I'll be your Christmas present. You'll unwrap me."

"Stop."

"I'll crawl on the floor and eat your cock."

"We can't do that anymore."

"Fuck my face."

"Be serious."

"Fuck my throat," she said. "Fuck my cunt and my ass. I give them to you. I give my whole self. Own me. Destroy me. Pin me down and make me feel you. Fuck me on the balcony. I want to feel the sun on my back as you fuck me. Fuck me and own me, like you've always owned me. I want you to look up at the ocean and sky. Look at the ocean and sky and fuck me."

ONE HUNDRED SEVEN

That night, me and Avril stayed at the cheapest motel in Hilo. I paid for it with most of the rest of the money in my bank account. I didn't have enough left for any more hotel rooms. I didn't know what we would do. We were fucked. I told Avril how fucked we were, and she smiled and told me we were fine. I worried too much. Avril told me she loved me and we would be fine.

I parked the car in the dumpy parking lot in front of our room. I pulled the keys out of the ignition and told her again we were fucked. We got out and went around to the trunk for our luggage. The door to the room beside ours was open, and a man sat in the doorway on a bucket. He smoked a cigarette. He saw me looking at him and smiled and waved. From the other side of the parking lot, a pair of deep voices yelled angrily. I didn't stick around to watch. They sounded like they were about to murder each other.

"Let's go inside and try not to get murdered," I said.

The room was dark, even though it was still daylight outside. I switched on the lights, which helped a little, but the room remained partially dark. The room felt warm like somebody had forgotten to turn on the air conditioning.

"Turn on the air before we sweat to death," Avril said.

We looked around the room but didn't find a thermostat.

"We are so fucked," she said.

We put away the luggage and got on the bed, which squeaked and felt stiff like a plank of wood. I estimated that the mattress was about a thousand years old, and all the cushioning had been worn away by the many people who'd had sex on it over the centuries. I was afraid to get under the cover. I didn't want to know how the sheets looked or felt. The air in the room felt moist and stank of old cigarettes.

I turned on the TV. We didn't have cable, and the antenna only picked up a few staticky channels. I turned off the TV. Me and Avril turned to our phones. I read a news story about global warming. The year was on track to be the hottest on record. A climate scientist said the reality of global warming already was worse than what had been predicted. She said the only hope for human civilization was for countries all over the world to radically curtail greenhouse gas emissions. She warned that this was not happening—emissions actually were increasing. She said the nations of the world were not showing any willingness to make the necessary sacrifices. I decided to tell Avril that Natalie was coming to Hilo in the morning, and that I would spend time with her alone. I opened my mouth to talk, then stopped.

Evening turned to night. Street lights shone through the window and illuminated a pale, bluish rectangle on the bed. The blueness washed over Avril as I prepared my lie. I told her about Natalie. I told her I needed to talk to Natalie because we had a lot of emotional baggage to sort out. We'd been dating for many years, I explained. It was complicated.

"Yesterday you didn't want to talk to her," Avril said. "You couldn't say her name without calling her a bitch."

"She's been important to me for a long time," I said, with forced calm and fake rationality. "She knows me better than anyone in the world. I don't want to hate her. I just want everything to be over. The relationship, I mean. There's a lot for me and Natalie to talk about."

I weaponized sincerity. And the lies were easy to tell because they were partly true and also I didn't know what was real anymore. Ever since I'd been in Hawaii, my life had felt hazy, like a dream. I'd cheated on my girlfriend. Abandoned her. I wanted her back.

"I guess it's for the best," Avril said.

The plan was for her to take the car to the beach again in the morning. This would give me a few hours alone with Natalie. I imagined what Natalie would look like on a soft bed in an expensive hotel. I imagined her taking off her clothes, slowly, a piece at a time, dropping them on a clean, hygienic floor—not the garbage dump where me and Avril were staying.

"I don't see how we're going to get through this and not hate each other," Avril said.

I didn't listen. I thought about Natalie, her white skin. I thought about how she'd feel beneath me. I imagined how she'd close her eyes as I fucked her, how each thrust would bring me closer to the life I'd had once but lost.

ONE HUNDRED EIGHT

I had trouble falling asleep because of some party raging in the parking lot. The kind of party where everybody binge drinks and occasionally screams. Finally I almost fell asleep when I heard glass smashing right outside the door.

Avril stirred beside me but didn't wake. In the dark, she could have been Natalie. Always before it had been Natalie sleeping beside me. I didn't know anymore who I wanted to sleep with. I loved Avril—or believed I did—and in some ways I still loved Natalie. Anyway I didn't deserve them. I wasn't a good person. I wasn't even a neutral person, either. I was bad. A bad, bad person.

I rolled over and took my phone from the nightstand. I wrote a text to Damon, who must have been back at his parent's home in Memphis. Good ol' Damon. He was my only hope. I told Damon I didn't know what I wanted anymore. I didn't know if I wanted Natalie or Avril. I didn't know what I wanted to do with my life. I didn't know who I was anymore. I didn't know anything.

I sent the text. I had no idea what time it was in Memphis. I moved to return my phone to the desk. The phone lit up and vibrated. Damon had texted me back.

"Bitch you're in HAWAII."

I didn't bother Damon anymore after that. I stayed awake for a while longer, staring at the darkened ceiling and listening to the howling from the parking lot. Eventually I slept. A few hours later I woke to the sound of a man vomiting outside. He puked loudly, then moaned, then puked again.

ONE HUNDRED NINE

I woke up in the morning and saw lizards. A pair of them crawled along the ceiling above me. The lizards freaked me out. But they weren't big Godzilla-type lizards, so I didn't scream or wet the bed or anything. I lay beside Avril's warm body and watched them. They had wriggly green skin and splayed toes. Geckos. They ran to and fro, and I couldn't tell if they were scouting for food or playing. Maybe for geckos, scouting for food is a kind of play. The geckos made me happy, after a while. Something about them made me feel stupid for always fantasizing about the end of the world. If the world ended, what would happen to the geckos? The geckos would be fucked.

Avril stirred beside me. Kissed me. Her hair brushed against my face. The scent of her hair depressed me, because I no longer deserved her. Avril moved close and kissed me again. She told me she wanted to fuck.

ONE HUNDRED TEN

Later we went out to breakfast at a little bakery downtown. Avril paid, even though she couldn't afford it. Afterward she drove me back to the hotel. We'd already checked out, but I was supposed to wait in the parking lot for Natalie to pick me up. Avril kissed me and told me not to do anything stupid. Then she put the car in gear and drove away.

I texted Natalie. She texted back to say she'd be late. I sighed. I wasn't surprised. I killed time by walking around town. I followed Haili Street downhill toward the bay. All the houses looked alike, with those long roofs made out of sheet metal. I turned down a side street. The houses there looked like the others, only more rundown. Every house on the street looked like a crack house. I walked by a stone wall covered in moss. It was more moss than I'd seen in my life. The moss looked like a field of tiny blades of grass.

The sky was gray. Kamaka had told me Hilo was always like that. He'd said it rained a lot. He'd said the town got about one hundred and forty inches of rain every year, but one year they'd only gotten eighty inches, and everybody freaked out because of the drought. The whole town smelled damp, like wood that had stayed wet for too long and begun to rot.

I turned at an intersection and walked toward the bay, down a steep hill where the sidewalk had cracked and busted apart. *1942 WPA* was stamped on the sidewalk. I tried to imagine the people who had laid the sidewalk. I imagined burly men with big muscles smoking hand-rolled cigarettes.

I crossed Kinoole Street. The city grew denser toward the bayfront. I passed a Hawaiian restaurant. I passed a wine store and a Middle Eastern restaurant and a Chinese restaurant. I walked into an art gallery. Most of the artwork was paintings of turtles. I decided that if I ever moved to Hawaii, I would decorate my home exclusively with turtle paintings. Even if I didn't move to Hawaii, maybe I could still decorate with turtle paintings. It would be great.

I exited the gallery. A light rain began to fall. Tiny, misty drops. I stood on a sidewalk across the street from Casa de Luna. I went inside to drink something and wait out the rain. The hostess was an older lady. She asked if I wanted to sit at the bar. I told her I'd like a table close to the sidewalk. It wasn't noon yet, and the restaurant was mostly empty.

I sat at my table and watched a crowd of people down the street at a farmers market. People walked around with bunches of bananas and sacks of exotic fruits I didn't recognize. I felt hungry for fruit. I wanted to gorge myself on dragon fruit and mangoes. A guy at the market sold coconuts. When someone bought a coconut, he would chop it open with a machete, then stick a straw in it so the customer could drink the juice. This man was my hero. A genius businessman. There was no greater man on Earth.

A waitress came to the table. She looked young and pretty. A lot of waitresses are young and pretty. It must be a big advantage when applying for the job. I told her I wanted a beer and asked what was good. She recommended Mauna Kea Pale Ale.

I took out my phone and read news stories. A factory caught fire in India. The factory produced shoes and bags for school children. More than one hundred workers were sleeping in the factory when the fire broke out, and forty-three people died. Workers on the third floor were trapped inside the building because the windows were covered with iron grills. I read another story. Al-Shabaab militants attacked a hotel in Mogadishu. They detonated car bombs at the entrance, then stormed the compound and began shooting people. They killed fifteen people. I swiped across the screen to read another story. A virus had killed several people in China. The virus was something new, and scientists didn't understand much about it or how it was transmitted. The virus attacked victims' respiratory systems and appeared to be incredibly communicable and deadly.

I performed a little magic trick. I tapped the screen to turn off my phone, then put it back in my pocket. All the bad news in the world disappeared. Poof. Disintegrated. Nothing could hurt me now. Anyway I didn't want to be depressed. I was in Hawaii. Beautiful Hawaii. I had nothing to worry about. I could relax and be happy. And I did very much want happiness. You can't read the news and be happy. The secret to happiness is never reading the news.

I looked down Mamo Street, where the buildings and palm trees framed a small window of ocean. I tried to figure out what direction I faced. I looked in a direction that might have been east, toward the mainland. It was weird to think about the rest of America being so far away. Hawaii provided a comforting sense of disconnection. America seemed smaller somehow. Broken and weird. Maybe there was a time when America really had been the center of the universe, but now it was a sad ghost, one who doesn't know it's dead, so it haunts its family's home, tries to make its parents take notice and listen. *I'm here*, it says. *Can't you see me?* But all they hear are dry branches creaking in the wind.

The waitress returned with the beer. I took a sip and told her it was good, and she smiled and turned to leave. I asked if she was a college student. She said she'd graduated. She'd come from Nebraska to Hilo to attend the university, but even after getting her diploma she couldn't find good work. The best job she'd found was waiting tables.

"All I know is I don't want to go back to Nebraska."

"Nebraska sounds nice," I said. "Corn fields. Wheat fields. The Great Plains."

The waitress let out a short laugh that sounded more like a grunt.

"I'll never go home," she said. "Nebraska is the most boring place on Earth. I'm not sure if I'll stay in Hawaii, either. Maybe. I don't know. Everybody thinks Hawaii is paradise, but it's not. It's just better than where I'm from."

ONE HUNDRED ELEVEN

I took an Uber back to the hotel. A Hawaiian woman picked me up in a Mazda 3. I told her I liked her car. She thanked me and told me she loved it. The driver looked older than me, maybe in her thirties. I looked out the window at palm trees. The rain had stopped, and patches of blue appeared in the sky. The driver asked where I was visiting from. I told her I was from Murfreesboro, Tennessee. She said she'd never heard of it. I told her she wasn't missing much. It was the most boring place on Earth. More boring than Nebraska. I told her I loved Hawaii. I told her I wanted to move to Hilo. She laughed. She'd lived her whole life in Hilo. She said it was boring. A town for old people.

"I guess everybody thinks their hometown is boring," I said.

"Where's a good place to live?" she asked.

"Norway," I said. "I hear good things about Norway."

ONE HUNDRED TWELVE

Natalie picked me up an hour later at the hotel. She drove the Mustang and pulled up with the top down, her blond hair rippling like the surface of the ocean. She wore a new pair of sunglasses that looked as expensive as the car. It had only been a couple days since I'd seen her, but it felt like decades. Even after all our years together, I didn't know her anymore.

"Your hotel looks nice," Natalie said after I sat down in the passenger seat.

"It's terrible."

"I was joking," she said. "Does your hotel have a bathroom? Do they make you use the outhouse?"

"Nobody has an outhouse anymore," I said. "Nobody's had an outhouse for a hundred years."

"Everything in this town is old," she said. "Everything looks like some shack about to topple over. Hilo looks like a third-world country."

"My hotel has a toilet."

"Your hotel looks like a shack about to topple over," she said, backing the car onto Haili Street. "I don't see how you could sleep in a place like that. You should get a tetanus shot. You should wash your hair with lice shampoo."

Natalie drove to the bayfront, where the ocean looked cold and gray. Waves broke against the seawall in the distance. A thin strip of black sand stretched along the highway.

"Why is nobody swimming?" Natalie said. "Perfectly good beach here in town going to waste."

"Sharks," I said. "Kamaka told me all about it. The beach has problems. All the gutters in town empty into the bay, so the water is dirty. Dangerous microorganisms feed on the pollution. Hammerheads like the murk. "

"Jesus," Natalie said. "This town is a horror movie."

She drove with one hand while I held her other. I squeezed it softly before placing it in her lap and letting go.

"We should talk," I said.

"Not yet," she said. "Talk all you want later. I don't want to think about it yet."

She made a hard left onto Banyan Drive. We passed a beachfront park. Kamaka had told me that the county built it to attract tourists. He'd said the locals liked the beach the way it was before the county came in and added the grass lawns and sidewalks. They preferred it in the old days when you could drive your truck onto the sand right up to the water.

"This is where they keep the tourists," I said to Natalie.

"This is the only decent part of town," she said. "I don't feel safe anywhere else. Hilo looks rapey. I bet girls get raped in Hilo all the time."

"Jesus," I said. "It's not like that."

She drove up a ramp to the Hilo Hawaiian Hotel, then down a ramp into an underground parking lot. The hotel was white, many stories high, and built in an arc like a rainbow that had toppled on its side. The building sat beside the ocean. We walked up some steps into a big open lobby. Instead of going directly up to her room after checking in, we took a walk outside. The grass lawn of the hotel ran right up to the water. We followed a sidewalk along the bay to a pedestrian bridge, leading to a small island.

"Kamaka told me about this place," I said as we crossed the bridge. "Coconut Island used to be a place of refuge, like the one at Two Step. Now it's a place where people hang out and have parties. Tsunamis destroyed the bridge a few times, but they always build it back."

"This is actually nice," she said. "I like it here."

"It's great," I said.

"I bet nobody gets raped here," she said.

We walked around the island. Held hands. Usually we would hold hands only out of force of habit, or to send a signal to onlookers that we belonged to each other. But there on the island, I took her hand because I'd missed her and was glad to be with her again.

Kids played ball and threw Frisbees. Their parents ate picnic food at wooden tables beneath park shelters. Women in bikinis sunned themselves on tiny beaches. Coconut trees grew on the island, and some were tagged up high to mark the height of tsunamis that had hit the island in years past.

"I can't even imagine a tsunami," Natalie said.

"You would think a tsunami would destroy everything forever. But it didn't. Not forever. Everything looks nice today."

We walked along an outcropping of lava rock. Local kids jumped off a diving platform. They would yell all the way down and splash in the water, then climb a set of crumbling stairs and do it again. Me and Natalie walked to a miniature beach on the side of the island. White-sailed boats traversed the bay. We walked back across the island and took the bridge again. Halfway across, I spotted something round and gray in the water. Then it disappeared in the murk.

"Did you see that turtle?" I asked.

"No fair," Natalie said. "I want to see a turtle. I came all the way to Hawaii. I deserve a turtle."

"There's a beach with lots of them nearby," I said. "I'll take you. If we meet up with Kamaka and Avril, all of us can go."

"I'd push that slut in the water," Natalie said. "Do turtles eat people? I hope they bite her face off."

We went into the hotel and took the elevator to a room on the fifth floor. We stood beside each other as the elevator rose. I listened to the hum of machinery. I looked at Natalie. I thought about what we were about to do. I thought about Avril.

"Everything is weird now," I said.

"What?" Natalie asked.

"Nothing," I said. "I was thinking about nothing."

The room looked decent but not as nice as the resort in Kona. Everything in the room looked old, like the owners stopped updating the place in the late 1990s. We stood on the balcony. Her room didn't face the ocean. It faced a road, where tourists walked along the sidewalk beneath mammoth green banyan trees.

"The view is shitty," she said. "Not that I'm surprised."

She turned, putting her arms around me and burying her head in the space between my neck and shoulder. She didn't speak. I held her and we swayed, slightly, like dancing. I liked the feel of her body against mine. We'd moved like that a thousand times. The sensations were familiar. A week ago, they would have been tired and boring, but now they were a lost secret we'd rediscovered. She let go and sat down on the bed and looked up at me. Her eyes had never looked so big. Her lips—plump and glistening—parted slightly as she breathed.

I asked myself what Jean-Pierre Léaud would do. Probably he would fall in love with a record store clerk named Sabine. Then, after finalizing his divorce from his wife, he would spot the actress Marie-France Pisier and follow her onto a train. There, they would reminisce about the love affair they had when they were younger, the happiness they'd shared, and how the troubles that had come between them seemed—in hindsight—insignificant. What can I say about Jean-Pierre Léaud? When he's right, he's right.

I kissed Natalie. This was all the encouragement she needed. She kissed back, aggressively with her tongue. She pushed her crotch against mine. She took off her shirt and bra, showed me her tits. They belonged to me. She'd given them to me when we were fourteen. Natalie slipped out of her shorts and panties. She reclined on the bed with her legs spread, arms behind her. I looked at her shaved cunt. I owned that cunt.

"How do you want me?" she said.

I told her to roll over onto her knees. I told her to face away from me. I grabbed her hips and put my cock inside her. She gasped. She told me she loved me. She started crying. She told me she belonged to me and I owned her. I liked owning Natalie. I fucked her and felt that I did, indeed, own her. Or even if I didn't, it made no difference because she so desperately wanted to be owned. Wanted it so badly she overplayed her part, like a first-time actress auditioning for a role. With Natalie, it was always hard to tell. I fucked her for a long time and didn't come until I believed in my heart I owned her.

Afterward we lay together, me on my back and she on her side, her head resting in the crook between my arm and chest. She told me she loved me and wanted me back. She said she felt awful about everything. She wanted to forget all the bad things we'd done to each other. She wanted to start over, wanted us to be new again. She cried. I held her. I remembered all the years we'd been together, things we'd done, all the times we'd told each other we were in love—and how we'd meant it. For a long time, we'd really been in love, and she'd been the best friend I'd ever had. I held her and told her we could start over. My saying so made her happy. I mean as far as I could tell. No one ever really knows what anybody else is thinking or feeling. Still, I'd known Natalie for a long time. I think, that day in the hotel room, I made her happy.

PART
FIVE

HAIL,
ANCIENT
OCEAN

ONE HUNDRED THIRTEEN

NATALIE'S PHONE RANG later while we were in bed. She wrapped a blanket around herself to hide her nakedness before answering it. I overheard Roger's voice through the speaker. Roger was driving to Hilo and spoke loudly to be heard over the wind. Natalie asked me for the name of a good restaurant. I suggested Casa de Luna. It wasn't a good restaurant, but I didn't know any others. She told Roger to meet us there in the evening. She tapped the screen to end the call. She turned to me and explained her plan. We would meet up with Roger and Avril for dinner. We would announce we were together again, and everything in our relationship was fine, and we were sorry about the drama, but now everything was back on track, back to normal, as if nothing bad or weird had happened between us, as if the whole shitshow had been nothing more than a disturbing dream. Above all, she said, we should be honest. Natalie believed everything would be better if we just told everyone straight away. Told the truth.

Natalie's plan sucked. Instead of telling her so, I nodded along agreeably. I looked out the window. Rain fell—lightly again, hardly more than fog—pattering softly against the wide leaves of banyan trees. I tried to determine which direction was north, but I was confused. I decided to stop worrying about it. It didn't matter which way was north. Nothing mattered. I stared at the far horizon and pretended to be looking in the direction of North Korea. I imagined the slim profile of an intercontinental ballistic missile tracing a path through the sky. The missile reached the apex of its arc and curled downward to the island, hurtled over Hilo Bay, detonated in the center of town with a roar like hellfire and metal and hate. Palm trees swayed, bent and burned. Then all the world fell still and silent, a momentary hush followed by a pulse of white, all-consuming light—the final light, the last light to ever shine. For the first time since my arrival in Hawaii, I thought about the end of the world.

ONE HUNDRED FOURTEEN

Natalie snored beside me. She slept delicately on her side, blond hair spread out like a fan. Natalie's beauty tended to compensate for all the snoring. As I watched her sleep, I imagined what my life would be like after I went home. The same old destiny. Graduate from college. Intern at the IRS. Resume the once-monthly sex schedule. Get married. Get a job. A real one—something boring, something horrible, something in finance. Natalie would begin having babies and keep at it for a long time. Maybe by my fortieth birthday I'd have the courage to put a bullet through my head.

Suddenly I imagined Avril's voice. She told me to stop being dramatic. I felt bad about Avril. Bad about how I'd lied to her. Now that I was in bed again with Natalie, all I wanted was Avril. This pattern of mine bored me. Wanting a girl only to get her and immediately want someone else. It's exhausting to remain so confused for so long. I felt weak. Withering away to nothing.

Anyway it didn't matter what I wanted. Soon enough, Avril would find out about me and Natalie, and that would be that. It would be right and good for Avril to hate me. I didn't deserve her. I understood the enormity of my transgression and internalized the shame. In some ways, my thinking felt clearer than ever.

I regretted hurting her. Regretted everything we'd lost. We could have had fun. Could have run away to Japan or Australia or Norway. She could have radicalized me. We could have marched against fascism, shattered windows at Starbucks, hidden out in the mountains and made class war.

I looked at Natalie sleeping beside me.

I looked at my phone.

I considered calling Avril or sending a text.

I got out of bed.

I turned back to be sure Natalie remained asleep.

I picked up my phone and selected *compose new message* from the interface.

I didn't know what to write.

I looked at the blank screen.

The cursor blinked.

Disappeared and reappeared.

I should have written an apology, or a warning, but instead I did exactly what Natalie would have wanted me to do.

I put away the phone and crawled back into bed.

Blinked back tears.

I clung to Natalie and fell into a gray and dreamless sleep, a sleep I remembered well and with which I was quite comfortable.

ONE HUNDRED FIFTEEN

Me and Natalie showed up at the restaurant a few minutes early. We got a table in the back and ordered drinks, which we were sipping when Avril arrived. Natalie had scooted her chair next to mine. She rested her head against my shoulder and wrapped an arm around me to make sure everybody in the restaurant understood I belonged to her. This message was not lost on Avril. She approached the table, saw us, immediately understood. She didn't say a word. She formed her hand in the shape of a gun and pretended to blow her brains out. She walked away. She went to the bar and ordered a drink. I looked at her from across the restaurant. She flipped me off.

"Why is Avril always such a bitch?" Natalie asked, hugging me tighter.

"Everything is fucked," I said.

"Everything is better now," Natalie said. "We're back together. Now she knows it. I don't care if she's angry. She's a bitch. I hope she fucking dies. Bitch."

I finished my first drink quickly and ordered another. Natalie talked about something. She checked her iPhone. Made a move in *Candy Crush*.

I was into my third drink by the time Roger showed up. He walked over to the table and grinned real big when he saw Natalie with her arm around me. He took a seat across from us.

"Jesus goddamned Christ," he said.

A waitress came over, and Roger ordered a Miller High Life.

"On the way here, I thought up an apology," he said. "All the way from Kona to Hilo. It's a long drive. The apology was fairly elaborate, and I wanted to get the words just right. But now there's no need. You and me are square, Nate."

"It's important to be square," I said.

"I fucked your girlfriend," he said. "Now you've fucked mine."

"I'm not your girlfriend," Natalie said.

"The hell you're not," he said.

A middle-aged Hawaiian couple ate dinner at a table across from us. The woman wore a nice dress. The guy had a goatee, and his face looked dark and deeply lined. He had arms like the trunks of a banyan tree. He looked at Roger and opened his mouth to say something but then turned away and made some remark to his woman instead.

Roger glanced at the Hawaiian guy. Roger looked at me and Natalie. He grinned. He shook his head and laughed. He reached across the table and took my beer, wrapped his meaty hand around the glass. He turned up the beer and drank it in a series of tremendous gulps, then wiped his mouth on his sleeve.

"Natalie," he said. "Just be honest. Tell him the truth. As soon as we get back to Murfreesboro, you'll start fucking me again, like always. You won't even wait that long. You'll fuck me tonight."

The Hawaiian guy at the other table turned around again. He glared at Roger. He leaned over and asked if Roger wouldn't mind keeping his voice down. Roger grinned and patted the guy on the shoulder. Roger said "No problem, man." After the Hawaiian guy turned back to his woman, Roger busted out laughing. He said the natives were restless.

The waitress brought Roger a glass of Miller High Life. He thanked her and took a drink from it. Then he pushed it across the table to me.

"There," he said. "Square."

"You're so full of shit," Natalie said.

"Just be fucking honest," Roger said.

"Shut up," Natalie said.

"Do you think Nate will even want you anymore, once he knows how many times I've been up to my balls in you?" Roger turned to me. "Sorry, Nate, but somebody had to tell you. You're a solid guy. The most solid I've ever known. Somebody had to tell you."

"Shut up," Natalie said. "Shut up, shut up, shut up."

"I fucked her real good, Nate," he said.

"Shut up," Natalie said.

"Natalie likes it rough. You know this about her, right? You know all the fucked-up things she's into?"

"Shut up," she said.

"I sure as fuck hope you do," Roger said.

Now everybody in the restaurant looked at us. The big guy at the table turned to Roger again. He told Roger to shut the fuck up. He called Roger a haole. Roger stood. The big Hawaiian guy stood. The Hawaiian guy was impressively tall and muscular. Roger told him to mind his own fucking business. Roger called him a chink. The Hawaiian guy told Roger to sit down. He called Roger a haole again. Roger shoved the Hawaiian guy, but even though Roger is fairly athletic, the guy didn't budge. Roger might as well have shoved a Mack Truck. The Hawaiian guy cussed. He raised his arm, lunged. He swung at Roger and connected hard to his jaw.

That was the moment I chose to stand up and walk away. I didn't want to be part of it. Didn't want any of it. I was tired of sitting by and letting things happen. Tired of being a tourist in my own life. Everybody in the restaurant yelled and screamed.

Natalie screamed loudest. I heard her voice—panicked, screeching—over all others. She yelled *stop it, stop it, please just stop it!* I heard deep thuds, the sound of heavy fists colliding with Roger's body. We'd been sitting at a table by the sidewalk, so it was easy for me to leave. I raised one leg over the railing, then the other. I said *goodbye everybody*, but nobody heard me over the yelling and fighting. I took off walking but didn't know where I was going. Evening gave way to night, and the wind from the ocean blew cold. I looked down at the sidewalk. I let it take me wherever it would go. I hoped it would take me somewhere nice.

ONE HUNDRED SIXTEEN

Sometime later I stood by the ocean. Along the beach, away from streetlights, the night felt suffocatingly dark. The moon and stars illuminated the ocean a little, stippling the black water with silver points of light. Waves rolled in and crashed on the shore. I considered throwing myself into the water. I wanted to drown or for sharks to tear me apart.

"Everything is fucked," I said. I listened to the waves again for a moment before continuing. "Everything is my fault."

I wanted the ocean to hear me. I wanted it to listen to my confession and absolve me. The ocean, I believed, contained enough water to dissolve my sins. I felt something change inside me. I felt differently about myself and my life. I guess I'd believed for a long time that I was a good person because I had good politics. I'd wanted to be a nice socialist. I wanted a better world, a benevolent and egalitarian society. I wanted to ease the suffering of the people. But while I'd been moving through life so proud of my own goodness, I'd been shitty to the people closest to me. I'd failed Natalie and Avril. Failed Damon. Failed Kamaka. I'd even failed Roger, in a way, by enabling him to be the shittiest version of himself.

I yelled to the ocean. Yelled that I was selfish and weak. Passive. I stood by and did nothing while terrible things happened. I fucked everything up. I wanted the ocean to know how badly it hurt to fuck up. I went on yelling for a long time. Afterward I sat in the sand. A feeling of nausea overcame me. I imagined puking out my badness in a stream of black bile, an Amazon River of dark blood draining into the sea. I felt my mind moving in a familiar pattern. I remembered going to church with my parents when I was a kid, and the grandfatherly preacher who told me about God, how he loved and had saved me. I didn't believe in God anymore but still wanted to be saved. I wanted the waves of the ocean to wash over me and cleanse my sins. I wanted the water to carry them away, change me, make me a new person and better. I took a tentative step into the ocean. The water at night felt cool and cleansing. It's not actually true that the ocean can save you. It's just a nice idea. Even if you've lost everything else, you can still have a nice idea.

ONE HUNDRED SEVENTEEN

I wandered through a shitty part of town in my damp sneakers. My head kept jerking around, looking for crackheads or serial murderers with big, evil knives. I didn't care if they killed me so long as they did it quickly and without much fuss. The wind felt cold. I hugged my body with my cold arms. It was dark, and I was tired and didn't have any place to sleep.

I asked myself what Jean-Pierre Léaud would do. Probably he would loudly declare himself a communist and argue with his friends about their bourgeois politics. Circumstances would escalate. He would shout. He would stop speaking to his friends because they were insufficiently communist. He would devote his life and art to bringing the communist dream to life in the real world. But I couldn't do that. I didn't have friends anymore. I'd already betrayed them. Avril was the only communist I'd ever known, and I'd betrayed her. Betrayed her for my blond capitalist girlfriend. Avril had the wrong idea about me. I wasn't the person she'd believed I was. I wasn't some communist hero. No Lenin or Trotsky. No Gramsci or Bookchin. I would never lead a revolution. All I wanted was to exist on the planet and have fun. I didn't want to give up my life for a cause, however noble. I wanted instead to enrich my life. Lavishly and selfishly. I wanted to exist for myself alone. I hungered for experiences. I wanted to see and know more things. I wanted to travel to Norway and Sweden and meet all the happy socialists. I wanted to observe the capitalists sucking smog and authoritarianism in Beijing. I had lived my life in a miserable bubble. Suddenly I wanted to see the world and know it and belong to it.

A pair of headlights lit up the sidewalk, and a vehicle slowed as it approached me from behind. *This is it*, I thought. *The bloody finale*. Thugs would stab me and stomp my face into the curb. They'd dump my bloody corpse by the side of the road. But when I turned to look, I saw Avril in the rental car pulling up beside me. She motioned through the window to get in. I hesitated. Maybe it was a trick. Maybe she would stab me and stomp my face into the curb. I opened the door and got inside.

"You're a real piece of shit," she said.

"I know."

"Don't fucking speak to me. Your voice is grating and whiny. It's the worst voice I've ever heard. If I hear it again, I'll murder you."

I hunched in the seat and crossed my arms over my chest. She turned the car around and headed downtown. She turned on Banyan Drive and pulled into a parking lot near the bridge to Coconut Island. She stopped the car but kept the motor running. She stared straight ahead through the windshield and gripped the steering wheel with both hands.

"Get out," she said. "Walk to a fucking hotel. Fucking sleep there. Stay out of my life for fucking ever."

I opened the door and stepped out. I closed it delicately, careful not to make much noise. I walked a few steps from the car before looking back. I expected her to drive away. I would never see her again. I would be alone. Everything would be terrible forever. She sat in the parking lot for a long time with the engine running. She mouthed the word *fuck* and switched off the ignition. She got out of the car and approached me. She looked like she wanted to hit me or rip out my eyes.

Avril told me to shut up and walk with her. She took off toward the bridge. I followed a few steps behind. The sky had cleared, and the moon looked very large. Its reflection shimmered on the water below. We crossed the bridge and descended to the island, which was deserted. Waves lapped against the shore. A breeze rippled quietly through palm fronds. I reached out—instinctively I guess—to hold her hand, but she jerked away. I wanted to kiss her but knew that if I did, she would shoot me in the face. She'd drive around town for a twenty-four-hour gun store, and she'd buy the biggest, meanest shotgun, and she'd return to Coconut Island and shoot me in the face. I laughed. Avril glared and frowned. She didn't ask about the laughing.

We walked to a small beach. We stood in the sand, a few feet from the gentle waves rolling in. Lights from the city shined across the bay.

"I wish I'd never come to Hawaii," I said.

"I'm fucking glad I did," Avril said. "Now I know how shitty my friends are. My ex-friends. I knew from the beginning, from the first night I met you, that you were shit. You're a coward. You never fucking do anything unless someone tells you, because you're too scared to make a decision on your own. You're afraid of everyone. Afraid of Roger. Afraid of Natalie. Afraid of your parents. Afraid of Natalie's parents. You're a scared fucking baby. You'll never grow up."

I looked down. The sand on the beach appeared grainy and rough, more like gravel than sand. I leaned down and slipped off my shoes. I pulled off my socks and stuffed them inside the shoes. I walked into the ocean and waded up to my ankles.

"Get out of there," Avril said.

"It's cold, but I expected it to be colder."

"Get out," she said. "You can't go into the ocean at night. Think about what's in the water. Weird things. Eels. Wormy things with poison stingers. Bad sharks. Hammerheads. You'll step on a hammerhead shark."

I walked deeper into the water. I looked down and didn't see any sharks. But I couldn't be sure. The water was black like the sky.

"I'll laugh when a shark bites your leg off," Avril said, raising her voice, the pitch increasing with the volume. "You'll bleed out in the water and die, and I'll laugh. The last sound you'll hear is me laughing at your pain."

I stepped out farther. Water lapped against my thighs. Another step. My foot settled on something soft and squishy, sticky like mucus. I froze. When nothing stung me to death, I took another step.

"Hey all you sharks," she yelled, her voice bellowing over the water. "I'll give the first shark who bites off his leg a fucking medal. A gold medal and a million fucking dollars. Just bite his leg off. Eat his whole body. I don't care. You hear me, sharks? If he dies screaming I'll give you a blow job. I fucking swear it. Spray me with shark cum from your shark dick."

I stood waist deep in black water and looked at the lights of the city—orange, red, and blue—twinkling and glowing like stars. I wasn't a strong swimmer, but I thought, suddenly, that if I started swimming I could make it all the way to shore. I could keep going, one stroke after another. I crouched low in the water, preparing to spring forward mightily. I raised my hands above my head like an Olympic diver.

I heard a frantic splash behind me. Avril grabbed my arm.

"Come back you fucking idiot before you die," she said, jerking me back to shore. Once we got out of the water we sat on a small beach and shivered from having been in the ocean. We huddled together, our bodies pressed tightly for warmth.

I didn't speak for a long time. I felt terrible about everything. I found it difficult to form words or even think. The night was dark. I looked at the stars and moon, the colorful lights across the bay, the dull yellow glow of streetlights and the big hotels behind us. I loved Avril, but it didn't matter. Any love we'd shared had died. I killed it. Our love had only been growing in earnest for a few days. I'd killed it before the roots took hold. I told her I was sorry. I felt like I should say more, go on apologizing profusely and cloyingly, but I ran out of words.

Avril reached down and took a sandal off one foot, then used her fingers to smooth away the sand embedded in her heel.

"We could have had so much fun," she said.

We sat a while longer. Eventually I got tired of sitting. I stood up and took Avril's hand—this time she didn't pull away—and led her to where the surf lapped calmly against the shore. I tried to kiss her, once, as a wave rolled in, but she brushed me off. She walked away and sat in the sand. I followed, and when I sat beside her I made sure not to get too close.

"Roger was amazing tonight," Avril said. "Best performance of his life."

"Fuck Roger," I said.

"Some thoughtful person called an ambulance."

I hoped I'd never see Roger again. Or anyone else, never go back to Murfreesboro. I thought about my entire life. Growing up in my parents' house. A perfectly nice two-story brick home in the suburbs. I hoped I would never see it again.

"Fuck Natalie," Avril said.

"Fuck Murfreesboro," I said.

"Fuck everything," she said.

"I don't want to be a person anymore," I said. "I want to be something else. A turtle."

"Turtles have it made," Avril said. "When life gets weird, they disappear into the ocean."

She leaned back, reclining in the sand and stretching her arms. I looked at the sky. I tried to recognize constellations but didn't know any. Light from the city and the hotels and the moon reflected off Avril's face. I leaned down to kiss her, and this time she kissed me back, and fiercely and for a long time.

"Run away with me," I said.

Avril laughed. She threw sand in my face.

"Come home," she said.

"We could leave the country," I said.

Avril cleared stray locks away from her eyes.

"Where?"

"Everywhere," I said. "Taiwan and the Philippines. Singapore. We'll go to Thailand. Bhutan. To India and Nepal. Turkey. Then Europe. We'll see Rome and Venice. We'll hike the Alps. We'll take a walk in Paris at night. We'll find some nice social democratic country and settle down. Norway, probably. We'll live in a cabin by a lake."

"How will we pay for this lavish excursion?" she asked.

"We'll just go," I said. "We'll panhandle. We'll beg and steal."

Avril smiled with one corner of her mouth.

"I'm going home to America to make class war," she said.

"It's better just to leave," I said. "Run away and become a better person. That's what I want. To be better."

"I know a guy in Oregon," she said. "He used to spike trees for Earth First. Now he does something else. Come with me to Oregon."

"I don't want to go to Oregon," I said. "I want to disappear."

"It's time to get serious, Nate. Do or die. You know what's coming. Global warming. Overpopulation. Overconsumption. Resource depletion. Peak oil. The Crash. Famine. Fascism. World War III. Chaos. A whole new fucking Dark Ages."

"Not my problem," I said.

"You and I could do some good. We don't have to be robots like everybody else. Let's do something big. Change things." Avril squeezed my hand. "Please consider taking that chance with me."

We slept in the car that night, sharing the back seat. We didn't fuck, but we held tightly to each other, nestling like a pair of newborn kittens. Periodically I'd wake up and sense her comforting weight against my chest. I awoke for good sometime after dawn. I don't know what time exactly, but the sun hung low over the horizon. I kissed Avril, then slipped away. She looked up and smiled before laying her head back down on the seat cushion. I left the car and followed the pedestrian bridge back to the island, where I walked around the perimeter. Enormous green palm fronds rustled in the breeze and cast long shadows on the ground. The island was very small, and soon I arrived at its farthest point. I stood on a ledge of black volcanic rock jutting into the bay and watched kayakers and paddle boarders ply their way over the surface, stroke after laborious stroke.

I looked east in the direction of the mainland, my old life. Suddenly I felt homesick for Murfreesboro. It was a nice town full of decent people, and I had been unfair to it. I missed my family. I even missed Natalie and Roger. Already I was leaving them. The images of their faces grew fuzzy in my memory. Someday I wouldn't remember them at all. I looked toward the interior of the island. If I kept going in a straight line for a few thousand miles I'd arrive on the continent of Asia. I wanted to go everywhere, see everything. I'd wasted so much time in hopeless passivity. Now I would take action. Travel the world. I felt a rush of energy. Elation. It felt good to have a goal. A purpose. One I had chosen for myself. It hardly mattered to me if travel was a *good* decision or a *bad* one. All that mattered was that I'd made it of my own free will.

I heard a noise behind me. Avril.

"Good morning," she said. "Are you ready to go home?"

"Funny you should ask."

"I can't tell if you're serious or joking," she said. "Come home with me. It's almost Christmas. Come home."

"I'm sorry."

"We've been stupid. All of us. But that's over. It's time to go."

"I mean it. I really am sorry."

"You and me, Nate," she said. "Us against the world. We can be weird. We can be different. I love you and don't want to lose you. Come home with me. We'll live in a tree house. Join a brotherhood of eco warriors and unreconstructed Marxists. We'll save the whales and build toward the general strike. While there's a lower class, we'll be in it. While there's a criminal element, we'll be of it."

To love Avril was to love her words. I knew I would go home with her. I had all these fantasies of travel and adventure, but—as much as it ripped at me to admit it—they were only dreams. I was always better at imagining things than doing them. I closed my eyes. I saw myself in Japan, riding a bullet train from Tokyo to Kyoto. Walking in autumn up a mountain, passing through the torii gates to the shrine of Fushimi Inari. I imagined Mt. Fuji wreathed in white snow. Imagined the atolls and turquoise water of the Maldives. Imagined Beijing and the Great Wall of China. Seoul and the Demilitarized Zone. The Eurasian Steppe. Tibet. New Delhi. Bangalore. Imagined a journey to the Congo, silverback gorillas in the hills. Algiers. Tunis. The Sahara. Malta. Istanbul. Budapest. Barcelona. Athens. Florence. Oslo. Berlin.

I sobbed. I kept my eyes shut tight, but tears spilled out the corners. My chest heaved from sobbing. Avril put her arm around me. She was confused. She didn't know why I was crying. She didn't know I was crying for all of the beautiful places I would never see.

I would go home with Avril. And we would have a good life. Maybe not the life she dreamed of. Avril was the only person I knew who was worse about imagining things than me. I guess that's why I loved her. We wouldn't be communists or anarchists or eco warriors. We wouldn't change the world. Those are just the facts. We'd go home, and at first we'd talk a good game. Read some books. Subscribe to *Jacobin*. Eat vegan. Maybe we'd go to a protest and shout some slogans, throw a water bottle at a cop. But we weren't going to change the world. It wasn't in the books for us. Just wasn't. We'd go home and pretend to be radicals for a while. Then we'd fall into the routine. We'd both get shitty jobs—radicals have to eat, right?— and come home in the evening, tired from the daily grind. We'd heat up some frozen food and watch Netflix together on the couch. Buy stuff on Amazon—a Fitbit, the new

PlayStation. We would brag about voting for Bernie Sanders, but when push came to shove, maybe we'd pull the lever for Joe Biden. We'd get saddled with a mortgage, make car payments. Have a few kids. Start looking for a bigger house in a better school zone. Who has time for revolution when you have to finish laundry and potty train the baby? Me and Avril meant well. We absolutely did. But the real world is a hell of a thing. After a few years of monogamy and domesticity, we'd be just like everybody else.

"Let's go home," I said.

Not that I knew where home was anymore. Still, I liked the idea of going there with Avril. I imagined our boring life together and laughed. And maybe I had it all wrong. Maybe we'd be class war superstars. The future is slippery, especially if you don't know yourself—and I didn't. All I knew for sure was that the sadness that had lived within me for so long had been displaced by new hunger.

Avril stood with me on the lava rock, already warm from the morning sun. Seemed like I'd been standing there my whole life. It felt good to be with Avril. I held her and looked over the water. A seabird coasted above the surface, scouting for a meal. It pumped its wings and flew off, empty-handed, into the sky. I imagined I was the bird. Soaring the heavens, piercing the clouds, aiming for the sun. Higher. Faster. Over the mountains. Gone.

"I'm so tired," Avril said. "It will be nice to go home."

The waves of the ocean rose and fell in an ancient pattern.

Gleaming in the sun.

Roaring.

Bursting against the shore.

Carrying us away.

A L E X   M I L L E R is the author of two other books of fiction—the story collection *How to Write an Emotionally Resonant Werewolf Novel* and the novella *Osama bin Laden is Dead*. His stories have been published in dozens of literary magazines including *Pidgeonholes*, *Back Patio*, *WhiskeyPaper*, *Maudlin House*, *MoonPark Review*, and *Fifth Wednesday Journal*. His career as a newspaper designer has allowed him to live and work in Hilo, Hawaii; Daytona Beach, Florida; Chattanooga, Tennessee; Pittsburgh, Pennsylvania, and Denver, Colorado, where he currently resides. A Florida native, he grew up in Spring Hill and Columbia, Tennessee.

AVAILABLE FROM MALARKEY BOOKS

**The Life of the Party
Is Harder to Find Until
You're the Last One Around**
by Adrian Sobol

Forest of Borders
by Nicholas Grider

Teacher Voice
edited by Alan Good
and DeMisty D. Bellinger

King Ludd's Rag
a zine series featuring long
short stories

Faith
by Itoro Bassey

Music Is Over!
by Ben Arzate

Toadstones
by Eric Williams

It Came from the Swamp
edited by Joey R. Poole

Deliver Thy Pigs
by Joey Hedger

Guess What's Different
by Susan Triemert

Your Favorite Poet
by Leigh Chadwick

Man in a Cage
by Patrick Nevins

Pontoon: Volume 1
edited by Alan Good

**Don Bronco's
(Working Title) Shell**
by Donald Ryan

Fearless
by Benjamin Warner

**Thunder from
a Clear Blue Sky**
by Justin Bryant

Un-ruined
by Roger Vaillaincourt

MALARKEYBOOKS.COM